THE (OTHER) YOU

STORY COLLECTIONS BY JOYCE CAROL OATES

By the North Gate (1963)

Upon the Sweeping Flood and Other Stories (1966)

The Wheel of Love and Other Stories (1970)

Marriages and Infidelities (1972)

The Goddess and Other Women (1974)

The Hungry Ghosts: Seven Allusive Comedies (1974)

*Where Are You Going, Where Have You Been?:
Stories of Young America* (1974)

The Poisoned Kiss and Other Stories from the Portuguese (1975)

The Seduction and Other Stories (1975)

Crossing the Border (1976)

Night-Side (1977)

All the Good People I've Left Behind (1979)

A Sentimental Education (1980)

Last Days: Stories (1984)

Wild Saturday (1984)

Raven's Wing (1986)

The Assignation (1988)

Oates in Exile (1990)

Heat & Other Stories (1991)

Where Is Here? (1992)

THE (OTHER) YOU

stories

JOYCE CAROL OATES

ecco

An Imprint of HarperCollinsPublishers

HarperCollins books may be purchased for educational, business, or sales promotional use. For information, please email the Special Markets Department at SPsales@harpercollins.com.

Ecco® and HarperCollins® are trademarks of HarperCollins Publishers.

A hardcover edition of this book was published in 2021 by Ecco, an imprint of HarperCollins Publishers.

FIRST ECCO PAPERBACK EDITION PUBLISHED 2022

Designed by Michelle Crowe

Library of Congress Cataloging-in-Publication Data has been applied for.

ISBN 978-0-06-303522-5 (pbk.)

22 23 24 25 26   LSC   10 9 8 7 6 5 4 3 2 1

FOR BOBBY FRIEDMAN

CONTENTS

1.

2.

1.

THE (OTHER) YOU

Bought a bookstore. Mostly secondhand books.

Never left your hometown on the Erie Barge Canal, upstate New York.

Never wanted to leave because why?—you have family here, relatives. High school friends. Found a house just three blocks from the house you'd grown up in.

Fact is, you failed to get the scholarship you'd needed to escape.

So, after you graduated from the local community college you got married. First man you believed you loved, and certainly the first who claimed to love you. And you and your husband bought South Main Books where you'd spent so many enthralled hours as a schoolgirl.

By the time the elderly proprietor died the stock had become primarily secondhand. Waterlogged, stained. Fire-scorched. Heaps of books assembled onto metal bookcases with hand-printed labels—Mystery & Detective, Sci-Fi, Fantasy. Popular Fiction, Classics. History, Military History, How-To. Children's Books.

Teetering stalagmites of books rising from the floor waiting to be sorted, shelved. And in the cavernous basement a vast graveyard of moldering paperbacks in bins.

Yet, there was romance in such a place. A universe of books. A universe of souls. Except unlike souls, books endured. You could hold a book in your hand, as you could not hold a soul in your hand. You could turn the pages of a book—you could *read*.

In the act of *reading* you could enter another time, the time of the book. It had to be a past time—a parallel time. Such an act felt subversive, secret—like dreaming, except the dream belonged to another, not you. You could become one with sentences as they flowed like a thin stream of water over rock—rippling, transparent. You could become one with the stranger who had written the book, who was not *you*.

You stared in wonder, mesmerized. How on the spines of books, including even the cheapest paperbacks, there was the imprint of a singular name.

A book is something to be held in the hand. What a book *is*, is not so easy to summarize.

Everybody predicted you'd go bankrupt in the first year. Then, they extended the time to two years. Three years? Five? Just wait.

Unlocking the rear door of South Main Books each morning you see that wraith of a girl in the shadows, turning the pages of a book—staring at you with startled eyes, in the very act of vanishing.

Yes. I love books. To read, not to write. I never wanted to be a writer, I will leave that to others more courageous and more reckless.

Fact is, as long as you could remember you'd wanted to be a writer. You'd wanted to be a poet. You'd wanted to tell stories. You'd wanted to see your name on the spine of a book.

You'd wanted to hold that book in your hand. You'd wanted to open that book, turn to the first pages . . . *Only I could have written this. Here is my truest self!*

You'd begun before you could read. You'd begun with Crayolas, coloring books. Your favorite crayon colors were burnt umber, scarlet, purple. You'd begun by copying comics out of the newspaper by hand, on tracing paper. In grade school you illustrated your own fairy tales.

Talking-animal stories. Space travel stories. Werewolf, vampire stories. Weird tales in the lineage of Edgar Allan Poe, H. P. Lovecraft. In middle school, elaborate mysteries in the lineage of Ellery Queen.

You published poetry and fiction in school magazines. In the local newspaper where there was a weekly poetry column on Sunday. Young, you'd gazed into that seductive abyss, the abyss gazed back into you. Deeply.

Never failed to trip your heart, the sight of the front window shimmering with reflected light, and displays of books inside. SOUTH MAIN BOOKS NEW & SECONDHAND. BROWSERS WELCOME.

After you bought the bookstore you never wrote again. Not enough time!—you said. Not enough hours in the day.

Maybe it had been a mistake, you conceded. Buying a (failing) bookstore. In a (failing) economy. Like having kids which you'd done (also). Like getting married (also). Maybe it's a mistake but you want to try it, see how it feels, when you're young you think you have plenty of time to change your mind. You think.

Not even a line of poetry, you wrote. Not for years.

Well—in fact poetry sprang from you like wildflowers pushing through the (empty) eye sockets of a skull in the woods. Lines of poems, radiant as raindrops. Melting icicles. A bird's high trill. Like love, a mystery. Like the very word *mystery*—how close to *misery*.

Falling in love, falling out of love. And again, falling in love. All with the same man who'd had to work at a radiator factory in Niagara Falls, to help support the God-damned bookstore (as he called it, with exasperated affection) that was your first love.

Shoveling books, there were so many. Needed a bulldozer to organize the basement. Needed to wear a gas mask, so many mold spores. So Gerard joked.

(Except: Are there jokes? What is the secret meaning of laughter?)

One autumn you repainted the interior: robin's-egg blue. Cream-colored ceiling, trim. Iridescent suns, moons, stars on the (twelve-foot, hammered tin) ceiling. Likenesses of classic writers and poets on the walls—Virginia Woolf, James Joyce, Franz Kafka, Ernest Hemingway, Robert Frost, Emily Dickinson, Walt Whitman. The old gods, gazing down upon you bemused, benign. You invited local artists to display their work on your walls. Sculpture in the front window.

Any time of day until 6 P.M. you were in the store. After Gerard died you extended the hours on Thursdays and Fridays for there was no reason to hurry home. You initiated poetry readings at the store, high school students, community college.

You provided coffee. Cookies, brownies baked in the night when you couldn't sleep anyway, empty house, no husband, no kids, hours before it made sense to open the God-damned bookstore and even then, when you arrived, you'd be the first merchant on Main Street to open.

In wintry months, switching on lights. Sudden warmth of lights in the gloom. That wraith-girl, surprised in the act of turning away, clutching a book in her hand which no adult would have allowed her to see if they'd known . . .

At last, aged forty-four you dared to read your own poems. At the conclusion of an evening celebrating women's poetry. A published woman poet from the community college, several other local poets, then you rising hesitantly daring to read from a sheaf of typed poems in a low, hurried voice. Applause startled you, your eyes glanced up widened and affrighted.

Were you naked, on display? How, why had you done such a thing?

Your customers, your friends. Neighbors. Astonished that you'd written poetry. Astonished that you'd been camouflaged among them for all of your adult life. Applauding you, love for you shining in their eyes. (Re)creating South Main Books, this center for a community of loosely affiliated women and men in the very heart of the dying-out downtown of Yewville, perhaps it isn't surprising that you who have urged books of poetry upon customers for years turn out to be a poet too.

The women hug you, weep over you. How brave you've been, since Gerard died! Keeping the store open, alone. So much effort you've expended, alone. They make too much of you, you think uneasily. As friends will do.

But it is safe now. Your parents are no longer living. Your husband has died. Your children who haven't moved away from Yewville rarely come to the store to be embarrassed by their silvery-gray-ponytailed mother in overalls and T-shirt emblazoned with a subtly demonic likeness of Emily Dickinson.

Too late for poetry, for the sustained effort of poetry, the bookstore has become your life. What remains of your life. No intention of retiring—ever.

Hell, no. First thing they'd do, a new owner of this property would dump our inventory into the trash, tear the place down and remake it into anything other than a bookstore. Never going to happen, I promise.

✦ ✦ ✦

But really, what you did was—you had children. Babies sprang from your astonished body. Blood gleamed on their perfect skin, their cobalt-blue eyes opened in amazement. *Who are you? What is this? Where have I come? What will happen to us?*

I am not like her, that childless woman.

You'd grown up believing: children are a blessing. Children give meaning to life. If life has no intrinsic meaning nonetheless children provide meaning. Families provide meaning. Existence itself is the meaning. You give life, you sustain life. You feed, and you feed, and you feed this life. You dare not stop, for your own life would stop. You never question.

You pity those who have not had children. That other self, the woman you are relieved you'd never become, is to be pitied—*childless.* Somehow you know that was part of her scheme, in escaping Yewville—to remain, to be, *childless.* She might have written books, established a career for herself but what is this set beside your accomplishments?—children, husband, bookstore beloved in a community.

Yet more strongly, you resent those who did not have children for they have escaped the fearfulness of life.

As soon as the first baby was born already in the hospital you understood—*Oh God. This gift I have been given, I must keep alive.*

Your (young) husband, gripping your hand in the hospital. Beside your hospital bed. Wiping at his eyes wet with tears and with the panic of realization—*We are responsible*—"Parents."

Jointly you knew: so long as the child draws breath, you live in terror that that breath will cease. You pray to die first. In secret, you pray to die first. Cannot bear even to contemplate outliving your child.

For your lifetime, this is the sentence. A life-sentence.

The girl who'd wanted so badly to escape Yewville, and to

become—somewhere, somehow—a writer: she has never experienced this clutching of the heart when the phone rings, late. She has never experienced absurd scenarios of accidents, premature deaths in the family. You pity *her*. You do not envy *her*.

How you parted ways. In total innocence, ignorance.

Anxiously preparing for the state regents exam at the age of eighteen. Determined to perform well. To excel. To fling yourself away from home as you might toss dice exuberantly onto a tabletop.

But the snowy-bright morning of the exam you'd been distracted, exhausted. You had not slept more than an hour or two the night before. Your father had returned home late, his footstep heavy on the stairs. Your mother had spoken sharply to him and he had spoken sharply to her. There'd been a shutting of doors. Muffled voices within. Confused with the beating of your heart. Confused with your anxiety over the future. *Dear God, help me. I will be a good person forevermore if...*

Since elementary school your grades had been high. Particularly in English, history, biology. You were not so strong in math. You gave up too quickly in math, you felt your eyelids flutter staring at problems, a kind of willful blindness. For it was predicted, girls do not do well in math. Girls should not feel anxiety, if they are not quite so gifted as boys in math. Or in science. *For a girl, this is good work. No need to push yourself so hard.*

Light-headed, with a sore throat. Spasmodic coughing. Your balance seemed off, as if you were making your way across the pitching deck of a ship. Uncomprehending you stared at some of the exam questions. Words swirled, tangled like knots. The remainder of your life depending upon this performance: two hours on a January morning when you were a senior at Yewville High, eighteen years old.

You panicked, you were perspiring, trembling. You would blame your quarreling parents. You would blame your teachers who had always seemed to like you but (perhaps) did not take you seriously. Your poetry and short stories they praised, but in the way that adults praise young children. Without quite reading you, perhaps. Surely, without knowing who you were.

Eventually, you would blame yourself. For who else was there to blame?

It was your usual practice to answer exam questions swiftly. To answer the questions you knew, and knew that you knew, in order to give yourself time to spend on other, more difficult questions. But this time you ran out of time. Fumbling, faltering, you lost confidence in yourself. The final questions were rushed. Your head rang with pain. Within a few days you would be diagnosed with bronchitis which you would have, with varying degrees of intensity, for six weeks. You'd left the exam room dispirited, defeated. Next day and for days following you'd tormented yourself with thoughts of suicide. Hating yourself, in disgust with yourself. Expecting the worst. Finally talking yourself into accepting failure—defeat. Probably you hadn't scored as highly on the exam as you'd hoped, that was only reasonable to expect.

And it was true: your score was above average, but not exceptional. Others in your class scored higher, who were certainly not superior to you. It was a matter of shame to you, an outrage, unfair and unjust, yet irrevocable. You'd had your chance—that morning. And now that morning was past.

One of your closest friends would attend Cornell on a regents scholarship while you remained in Yewville. Your friend had never had higher grades than you did but—somehow—she'd performed well on the exam. You congratulated her, you were happy for her. (Not for yourself. You were not happy for yourself. But for Sandra, you were happy.)

Eventually, you would take courses at the community college. You believed yourself superior to your instructors at the college but you had no choice but to please them. To receive good grades, you had to please them. Flatter them. You hoped to transfer to a four-year college or university but that did not happen. Much you'd hoped for did not happen. Even if you'd received a scholarship to a university you might have had to remain in Yewville to help support your mother after the collapse of your parents' marriage; in time, you had to look after your mother when she was ill with cancer, you'd had to take on some of the household duties of an adult. No fault of your own, you'd become one of the adults of the world by the age of twenty and the world was no longer open to you as it had seemed when you were eighteen.

You remained in Yewville. Gnawing at your embittered heart.

But no: not at all. You were not embittered, you were grateful to be needed. To love and to be loved. Eventually you would marry, as your girl cousins and friends married, in the years following high school. And you and your husband would make a down payment on South Main Books, you would secure a mortgage and put your life in hock for the next thirty years, as Gerard said.

But that exam!—the morning of that exam! Waking in the night you recall. In the grocery store, pushing a cart—you recall. Shelving books, ringing up a sale. Leafing through a newly published book of poetry, you recall. Your fevered skin, sensitive to the touch. Swallowing with pain, unease. Others in the examination room, row after row of your classmates, strangers to you now, deadly competitors. Frowning, earnest, determined. For only those students who had some reasonable expectation of doing well on this lengthy exam troubled to take it. You'd always been one of the highest achieving girls in your class and yet—things did not turn out well for you after all.

The other girl, the one you'd been meant to be, had scored very high on the exam. Upper one percentile of high school seniors who'd taken the exam that day in the State of New York. That girl had gone on to attend a first-rate university. She'd studied exactly the subjects you'd hoped to study: literature, philosophy, psychology. She'd been praised for her excellent critical writing and for her poetry and fiction. Her professors had encouraged her. No one had discouraged her. Her parents had not quarreled, her father had not been an alcoholic who'd walked away from his family when his wife was first diagnosed with stage three breast cancer. That girl was free of family responsibilities. That girl knew nothing of the dread of waiting for her mother to be discharged from the infusion room at the hospital, helping her walk down the hospital steps, trying not to be nauseated by the smell of chemicals on her skin, in her hair. That girl knew nothing of the fear of being pregnant when it was not a good time to be pregnant. That girl did not weep in a man's arms that she might persuade him to marry her though (she guessed) he did not really love her, as she did not really love him. Unfettered as a child in a place other than Yewville where she would have been held captive as surely as an insect in an elaborate spiderweb that girl began to write seriously as an undergraduate: poetry, short fiction, novel. She began to be taken seriously by supportive adults. She had not even known how ambitious she seemed to others, and how fortunate. She'd believed herself to be no more exceptional than certain of her friends, particularly you; indeed she is *you*.

You never think of her. Not in years.

In Yewville, in the life you do not think of as *left-behind*, you have been happy. For happiness is measured differently here, in a quieter inlet opening onto a rushing river; life is slower here than on the great, rushing river, but perhaps it is deeper. (You want to think.)

And now, at age forty-four, you have returned to writing, on a modest scale. The other girl, grown now into a woman, a "known" person, has certainly not been modest—she has published many books, she has been the recipient of awards. She has been translated into languages of which you have never heard. You don't envy her, however. You don't think of her at all. Would you trade your life for hers?—would you trade yourself for her?—certainly not.

You would not have wished to marry a man other than Gerard. But Gerard was available to you only in Yewville, where you were both born. And from Gerard, your children. Without Gerard in your life, your children would not be in your life. Your children would not exist.

In any case you are a widow now. You are something of a hero—a heroine—to local women, your own age and younger. You are famously generous with time, if not money. (You have not an excess of money.)

You have helped establish a local literary magazine. You have encouraged younger readers who come into the bookstore. Your body has softened, slackened. Once you were lean and hard-muscled as a racehorse, your nerves strung tight as wire, now you are a cushiony sort of person, prone to hugging and being hugged. You wear loose sweaters, jeans. You wear caftans, denim jackets, sandals. Your adult children roll their eyes, seeing you, your hair skinned back from your face, your silvery-gray hair in a swinging ponytail. Your skin is ruddy, flushed. Often you feel feverish. It is an excitement for life, you think. For the surprise, the unexpected *livingness* of life. You are no beauty, you look your age. Fine lines crisscross your face. Between your eyes, a vertical line. Bracketing your mouth, smile-lines. Thank God you have never been concerned about money. Ignominious and embarrassing, to care about money. Your relatives shake their heads, behind your back they are still predicting the bankruptcy of South

Main Books. Not surprising that, in middle age, you don't have adequate medical coverage.

Out of pride, as well as satisfaction for the life that you have, you never think of that other life beyond Yewville. The girl who'd taken up her pen, attacked the regents exam with confidence, intelligence. The girl who'd managed to remain calm. Whose parents hadn't quarreled and kept her awake on the eve of the most important morning of her life. The girl without a sore throat, a racking cough.

Shake your head irritably, in fact happily, don't ask me, what a silly question. *Of course I am happy. I have everything I want. What is missing from my life?—not a thing.*

THE WOMEN FRIENDS

The women friends met for lunch at the Purple Onion Café as they'd done frequently for nearly twenty years. As usual Francine, the elder by seven months, arrived first, and secured their preferred table, outdoors on the terrace, in a corner farthest from the street. There, she could see Sylvie approach before Sylvie was likely to see her.

It was just noon. By quick degrees the popular vegetarian restaurant, recently reopened after an extensive renovation, would fill up with customers on this balmy September day.

Not because each was the other's closest friend, though it was true, they'd met as four-year-olds in the Montessori preschool, but because each was, to the other, crucial: this fact, if it was a fact, bound the women together. Closer than sisters!—because chosen, as sisters are not. Closer than husbands, for of course husbands could not be trusted. And closer than children, that goes without saying, for children, regardless of their ages, must be protected (by their mothers) from the most fundamental truths of existence.

Today was the first day Francine had driven anywhere alone following her surgery the previous week. It had been minor surgery (she was quick to explain) performed at the outpatient Women's Clinic, from which she was recovering steadily—she'd experienced some pain and nausea, insomnia, and a curious mild dislocation regarding time: minutes passed with excruciating slowness, like a column of poisoned ants, while entire days rushed past like empty freight cars rattling in an interminable train.

Francine smiled, thinking how she would make this droll observation to Sylvie, the only person she knew who could understand and appreciate her mordant humor. Francine's husband would usually frown at her perplexed, if indeed he heard her at all, while her children rolled their eyes rudely—Oh Mom! Please. Anything uttered by Francine that called attention to her as a distinct, idiosyncratic person was mortifying to her family as if she'd suddenly torn off her clothes and cried, Look at me!

But with Sylvie, everything was altered. What was important, if unvoiced, to Francine, was important to her friend, too. If in the night Francine lay awake pondering her life as mysterious to her as graffiti scrawled on a wall she could measure herself against Sylvie, and feel immediate relief. For, if she could speak of it to her dear friend, it could not be so bad. Nothing fully happened to Francine until she transformed it into an entertaining little story for Sylvie who was likely to exclaim, Oh I've felt exactly that way, too.

But where was Sylvie?—Francine saw that her friend was eight minutes late.

Nadia, the locally famous owner of the Purple Onion, brought two menus to Francine's table. Recommended specialties du jour, peach-watermelon gazpacho, kale and cranberry salad, grilled tofu with Balinese sambal, Portobello and Brie, non-gluten nut bread, mango juice, iced Bengal tea . . . Francine was surprised to see that the presumably new Purple Onion menus did not differ much from the old, as she remembered them, nor did the specialties du jour seem very different; Nadia herself, though said to have been injured in the explosion, and traumatized by the stress and expense of renovating the Café, did not look much different than Francine recalled: she was a plain, pleasant-faced woman of middle age with long loose-flowing gray hair, a smile that bared her gums, a manner both diffident and bossy that had endeared her to customers over the years. "Is your friend joining you today?" Nadia inquired, and Francine said, "Of course." Wanting to add, for the question annoyed her, "Why would I be here, otherwise?"

Francine would never eat lunch alone in a public place, if she could avoid it. Even with an absorbing book to read, the prospect would be too lonely.

Boldly, bravely the Purple Onion had reconstituted itself after a homemade explosive device had been detonated on this very terrace the previous fall, by a nineteen-year-old area youth subsequently described in the media as "troubled." A graduate of the local high school, unemployed and living with his divorced mother, the boy was said to have constructed the crude bomb from instructions he'd discovered on the Internet—"How to build your own bomb for less than thirty dollars." Fortunately the device had misfired, inflicting less damage than the suicide bomber had intended: three persons killed, in addition to the bomber, and nine persons injured, including the owner of the Café; the destruction of part of the interior of the Purple Onion, and approximately half the terrace, since the bomb had exploded in only one direction. As many as twenty-five people might have been killed if the bomb had fully exploded, authorities had estimated . . . With relief Francine saw that a row of flowering crab apple trees bordering the parking lot had not been damaged. Her eyes filled with tears as she recalled how beautiful these trees were, blossoming in the spring!

A terrible act, senseless, vile. Brainless. The boy's name was Lasky— Howard, or Harold. Francine's daughter who was a junior at the high school thought she knew who he was, or had been—a "nonentity"—a "loser." Lasky had worn a black nylon hoodie to the Purple Onion, and dark glasses; he'd allegedly seated himself at one of the outdoor terrace tables, carrying the homemade bomb in a Whole Foods tote bag belonging to his mother. On his laptop computer it would be revealed that he'd researched the websites of Islamist terrorist sui- cide bombers. He'd left only a terse note behind in his room.

I am not politicle, I did this for mysef

Commentary on social media had been swift and merciless. "Poli- ticle! Mysef!" Who had Lasky's teachers been? How had anyone so illiterate managed to graduate from the local high school, that prided itself on sending so many graduates to college?

In the event of a bomb, Francine thought, this part of the terrace might be spared again, in the corner farthest from the street . . .

"Franny, h'lo! Sorry I'm late."

Sylvie advanced upon Francine who'd been dreaming with her eyes open, stooping to brush her lips against Francine's cheek in greet- ing, the very lightest touch, a most hurried and perfunctory greeting, and then Sylvie was seated across from Francine at the small round table frowning at the oversized menu in a purplish hemp binding as if nothing so merited her undivided attention as the menu. Two remarks Sylvie made in her throaty theatrical voice, almost simul- taneously: "The gazpacho looks good, or was this what I'd had last time, and hated?" and, "Have you ordered yet?"

Had she ordered yet? Francine was annoyed, insulted. "Of course I haven't ordered yet, I've been waiting for you, Sylvie."

"Sorry! I've been unavoidably delayed."

"Unavoidably delayed." This too was a perfunctory excuse, and not original.

Sylvie's canny green eyes scanned the menu, which must have been as familiar to her by now as her own face. Kale, non-gluten, Portobello, grilled tofu, local-grown, twelve-grain, lemongrass, brown rice and yogurt . . . Neither of the women friends was actually vegetarian but vegetarian seemed a worthy principle and vaguely of the future, of an era of youthful idealism that would outlive them.

But Francine was feeling hurt. Her closest friend had scarcely glanced at her since her breezy arrival, and had not inquired how she was feeling; had not assured Francine, as Francine would have assured Sylvie by now, that she was looking good—remarkably good, considering that she'd had surgery less than a week before. (Though it had been minor surgery as Francine had taken care to point out, explaining to Sylvie over the phone, and she hadn't been fully anesthetized, just partially—"You know, what they call twilight sleep.")

And here too was something strange—in the weeks since Francine had last seen her Sylvie had let her beautiful dark-rinsed hair relapse to its previous color, a dull brown threaded with gray; for months Sylvie had fretted over the decision to have the color restored to the rich glossy dark mahogany it had been when they were girls. Only now, for some reason, and without even mentioning it to Francine, she'd let the rinse grow out, and was looking far less attractive than Francine had ever seen her, with something puffy about her eyes and mouth, as if she hadn't been sleeping well. Sylvie's usually flawless makeup had been hurriedly applied, her skin was pale as curdled milk. (With a thrill of dread Francine wondered: Was there trouble with Sylvie's marriage? With one of the children, or with all of the children? Only rarely had Sylvie confided in Francine, that things were not so perfect in her family, that Francine had always envied; the women had married within a year of each other, in their early twenties, and had had their first babies around the same time, like mirror reflections.) It was frightening to Francine, though in a way satisfying, that her friend, always so much more glamorous than Francine, and self-assured, was now not looking quite so chic, or so young.

When at last she had Sylvie's full attention Francine murmured, "Your hair!" with a quizzical smile, as if to ask why, and Sylvie grimaced and said, "Oh I know, I didn't have time to do anything with my hair this morning, the ends are all split, I hate the way I look."

"But why'd you let it get gray again?"

"Gray again? You mean, still."

But Sylvie, intent upon capturing a waitress's attention, wasn't really listening. She'd decided upon her lunch, and wanted to give her order, for she was pressed for time that afternoon, it was one of those days, one of those weeks. Complaining of her children's demands upon her time, and her husband's demands, and still not looking at Francine but only in Francine's direction and not at Francine's face so that Francine was thinking in exasperation that maybe twenty years was long enough, the friendship had worn out, worn thin, like an overused roller towel; it was time for Francine to cultivate another close woman friend. Too often had Francine lain awake at night pondering her life, and what her life might mean, if indeed it meant anything at all, and thinking eagerly of Sylvie as if Sylvie might supply the meaning of her life, or was in some way the meaning herself; for Francine had always felt that Sylvie was not only her closest friend but in a way represented friendship itself—its essential mystery. It was even the case that Francine had often measured her husband against Sylvie's husband, and her children against Sylvie's.

Though she had never told anyone, and had only hinted to Sylvie, she'd had a third child in emulation of Sylvie who'd had a third child at thirty-five; Francine would not have had Donnie otherwise, at the age of thirty-six and a half. So belated a pregnancy had seemed to Francine defiant and courageous in Sylvie, and reckless and (possibly) misguided, in herself.

They gave their lunch orders to a waitress in Purple Onion T-shirt, jeans, and sandals, young enough to be a daughter, who called them "ma'am." Kale and cranberry salad for Sylvie, Portobello and Brie for Francine, unless it was Portobello and Brie for Sylvie, and kale and cranberry salad for Francine. At last Sylvie asked how things were? How was Francine feeling?—though in such a way, with a forced smile, you could see that she really didn't want to know. Francine laughed a little too loudly saying, "Well. I'm still here."

Still alive, she might have said. But why was that funny?

Though Sylvie didn't press her for details Francine heard herself say that since the surgery she was feeling just a little "strange"—"Disoriented"—as if time was passing very, very slowly—"Like poisoned ants in a column"—and yet, entire days were rushing by—"Like empty freight cars"; yet Sylvie did not seem impressed by this remark, or had not even heard it, for she failed to say with a pained smile, "Oh, I know exactly how you feel!" Though not much encouraged Francine went on to say that she'd never had such a sensation of "dissolution"—"Disintegration"—in her life, at the time of the anesthesia; it was as if every neuron in her brain was breaking off from the others, like grains of rice falling through her fingers onto the floor. The anesthesiologist had spoken to her in a playful, teasing manner, instructing her to count backward from one hundred, as if daring her to keep awake; indeed, he'd taunted her by challenging her to get to ninety before she fell asleep, and Francine had feared the man, and hated him. But Sylvie did not exclaim,

"What a bastard, you should report him," as Francine might have predicted, but rather, in a bemused voice said, "Franky, come on! I'm sure that never happened."

Never happened? How could Sylvie say such a thing?

The waitress brought them iced tea, which Francine did not recall having ordered. She was shaky, tremulous. How could her closest friend so abandon her, emotionally!

Because you are not alive, Francine thought suddenly. Sylvie is embarrassed for you, she doesn't know how to speak to you any longer.

This would explain so much, that was otherwise inexplicable.

Francine remembered how in dreams of her beloved grandmother, who'd died when Francine was eleven, her grandmother had not seemed to realize that something had happened to her, to set her irrevocably apart from others; she was silent in Francine's dreams, smiling at Francine with a melancholy, inscrutable expression unlike any expression Francine had ever seen in her, in life. And Francine had known instinctively that, in the dream, she must not acknowledge her grandmother's altered state—only that something profound and terrible had happened to her grandmother, to make her different from others.

That was how Francine saw herself as an adult: she must shield others from the most obvious truths about themselves.

The waitress brought their food. Very attractively positioned on brightly colored platters, garnished with sprigs of fresh parsley and nasturtium petals. Francine lifted a fork but could not bring herself to eat, just yet. Though Sylvie was behaving strangely, peering at the kale and cranberry salad with her fork poised above it, as if trying to summon the appetite to eat, Francine couldn't keep from confessing to her friend that she was very afraid of something she couldn't define—didn't know how to name.

"As if—I don't know why—I think that I will look up suddenly, or look around—and everyone—everyone I know, and care for—will be gone." Francine paused, wiping at her eyes. Her voice faltered, the moment was lost. "Just—vanished . . ."

To this, stiff-faced Sylvie had no reply.

As if Francine were reminding her of something she'd nearly forgotten Sylvie stood suddenly, and murmured an apology—she had to make a phone call, to rearrange an appointment; and she had to use the restroom, which was inside the restaurant.

"Of course. Of course, take your time, Sylvie," Francine said, almost gaily. "I'm not going anywhere."

Francine smiled after her friend as Sylvie hurried away without a backward glance.

From Sylvie's plate Francine took a forkful of kale salad, for Sylvie had left most of her lunch. It was a habit between the friends, an old custom—to share food. Just a taste.

But the kale was bitter, and nearly impossible to chew. You'd need the grinding teeth of a goat, Francine thought. (A remark she would make to Sylvie when Sylvie returned, to make Sylvie laugh.)

It was then that Francine happened to see, seated at a table a short distance away, an outlandish dark-clad figure—a young man, or a boy, boldly dressed to resemble the suicide bomber Lasky. He wore a dark hoodie, dark-tinted glasses crooked on his nose, rumpled dark pants.

Francine stared at this person, shocked and disapproving. Was this a joke? Some stupid prank cooked up by teenaged boys? (There was sure to be an accomplice somewhere in the vicinity.) If so, it was not funny. Innocent persons had died in the bombing of a year ago, in this very place. Many more had been injured, and traumatized for life.

But there sat a brazen replica of the suicide bomber, with a tote

bag close beside him at his feet. Whole Foods! Francine had an identical bag in the trunk of her car. You were supposed to think that
there was a ticking bomb inside the bag—was that it? Behind the
dark lenses askew on the bridge of his nose, the boy's eyes were hidden. His face was pasty-pale, blemished. He appeared nervous, visibly
perspiring; there was a twitch in his left cheek. He was tall, lanky,
underweight—it would be said of him. He'd shaved his head, inex-
pertly; the hood hid it. Other customers on the terrace glanced at
him quizzically but seemed more amused than offended or upset.
Nadia must have seated him, as if nothing were amiss, for there was
a purple-hemp menu on his table, facedown, unopened.

Then, Francine realized—the explosion had not happened yet.

That was the explanation. Somehow, there'd been a pleat in time.
Or, Francine had wakened (from the anesthesia?) at the wrong
time.

Francine sat transfixed. A sensation of horror washed over her.
There was the suicide bomber at a nearby table—presumably, in the
seconds just preceding the explosion. No wonder Howard Lasky
was looking so agitated, a twitch in his cheek. And Sylvie had disappeared into the restaurant, and was in danger of her life, for the
bomb had leveled much of the interior of the restaurant at the
time of the explosion, and at least one victim, a woman, had died
in the fiery and collapsing debris in the women's restroom.

Francine's heart was pounding rapidly. What to do? What to
do? Did no one else notice the dark-clad bomber, and fear him?
Even if no one had—yet—heard of Howard Lasky, why had Nadia
seated so suspicious an individual, a bizarrely attired adolescent,
alone, at a table on the terrace of her restaurant? Did Francine have
time to run after Sylvie, to lead her to safety? Or had Sylvie, knowing something that Francine didn't know, already fled to safety,
and left Francine behind?

But she could not get to Sylvie in time—not now. She could not bring herself to pass by the suicide bomber's table—so close to the blast! Nor could she run away in panic, drawing the astonished attention of other customers who would think her insane—plunging through a row of low-lying evergreen shrubs and into the parking lot stumbling and sobbing. . . . The deafening sound of the explosion, screams of terror and agony, would devastate her.

And so, Francine would do nothing. Whatever would happen, it was already too late: even this melancholy thought, *it was already too late*, was not occurring to Francine for the first time but was familiar to her as the look and feel of the Purple Onion menu and the list of specials. With her fork she picked again at Sylvie's salad, in a sisterly-intimate gesture that would make Sylvie smile, should Sylvie happen to be headed back to the table now, and see what Francine was doing.

THE BLOODY HEAD

In the secluded inner courtyard of the Hôtel de l'Abbaye on the rue Cassette, Paris, the American woman sat alone at a small wrought-iron table, at breakfast. She was skimming the European edition of the *New York Times* which was scarcely recognizable here, thinned of lavish full-page advertisements; she was making out postcards for family and friends back home though she understood that postcards had become passé, quaint gestures from a pre-digital age at which her young grandchildren, enthralled by *texting*, would only glance quizzically.

It was early, not yet 7:15 A.M. Fewer than half the tables in the courtyard were occupied. A fountain at the center of the courtyard made comforting sounds as of a slow-pumping heart: soothing and restful and (yet) suggesting promise. The American woman was the only individual in the courtyard at this time without a companion which gave her a sense of expansion, exhilaration.

That morning she intended to visit the Musée d'Orsay; she would not be hurried through the elegant high-ceilinged rooms, and would not press herself to see every work of art on display. She might return the next day to the d'Orsay, or she might go to another, smaller museum—there were numerous small museums listed in the guidebook, including the Musée Picasso, of much interest. Later she would stroll along the Seine with no particular destination, rejoicing in her freedom amid the languid beauty of Paris in autumn, and here too she would feel no pressure to hurry; that evening she would have a leisurely dinner at a new, one-star Michelin restaurant near the Hôtel de l'Abbaye, which had been recommended by friends for its highly regarded female chef from the south of France.

She was an attractive woman of late middle age with faded, fair hair and a smile that came easily, in formal settings like this; she was unfailingly gracious with service people—indeed, with everyone she encountered. She wore a white linen jacket and perfectly creased white linen trousers, with ropes of white pearls; on her head, a fashionably wide-brimmed straw hat. On her feet, her most comfortable low-heeled shoes.

The American woman's name was not "Isabel Archer" but closely enough resembled that classic name that the woman had come to think of herself in secret as a descendant of Henry James's naively noble-minded heroine, one who'd avoided the tragedy of Isabel Archer's constricted life.

Sheer chance, it was. For most women. An accident of time, generations. If they lived freely, or not. Isabel Archer whom Henry James had adored had been a *lady*, inescapably. But no woman was required to be a *lady* in the twenty-first century.

The American woman was making annotations in her Paris guidebook when she became aware of guests at other tables glancing upward at a third-floor window of the hotel, and then shifting their eyes away; she heard a chilling, strangulated cry, and turned in astonishment to see how, in an opened window, a man was calling

Help! Help me!—unmistakably, in English. The man appeared to be only partly clothed; at least, what the American woman could glimpse of his chest and part of his belly appeared to be bare. Clumsily, the man had wound himself in something white—a sheet, a towel. But there was also something white wound around his head. *Help! Help me . . .* Oh, what was wrong with the poor man? Why did no one seem to care? The American woman tried to signal the elegantly black-clad hostess who'd been hovering at the periphery of the courtyard but the hostess was now nowhere in sight; a waiter who'd been pouring coffee for guests had vanished as well.

The American woman did not want to become involved, desperately she did not want to become involved, the fleeting thought came to her—*I cannot give up the promise of my beautiful morning: I will not.* If only she'd slipped away from the courtyard a few minutes before . . .

But still the man in the third-floor window was calling for help, desperately. Indeed he seemed to be calling now to *her*, since the others were looking stonily away. Why was it always thus, *she was responsible!* She could not ignore the man as others were doing: he spoke English, no doubt he was an American like herself, and must have had no one to take care of him.

Instinctively the American woman reached for her handbag, which contained her passport, credit cards, currency, and enough tissues for an entire day, and hurried from the courtyard, which was bounded on three sides by hotel walls and on the fourth side opened into the little lobby. At the front desk there was no one— though she rang the brass bell several times no one appeared from the inner office. Oh, where were they all hiding? Why would no one help? Though she knew that the quaintly small lift, that could hold no more than three adults at a time, would be slow to arrive, yet she wasted precious seconds waiting for it, then gave up and ran up the carpeted steps, to the second floor, and to the third; now breathless, and crying softly to herself—*My morning! My beautiful morning.*

In the third-floor corridor the American woman tried to calculate where the man's room was, obviously had to be overlooking the courtyard at the center of the hotel, not an outer room, and so made her blundering way in what she believed to be that direction, seeing at the far end of the corridor a door that was ajar, though a sign was looped over the doorknob—NE PAS DÉRANGER.

The stricken man had had enough sense to leave the door open, at least! If he wanted someone to come help him.

The American woman entered the room hesitantly, with an anticipation of something terrible, and was astonished to see a naked man of late middle age, somewhat heavy, his chest and belly covered in glinting silver hairs, seated slouched on the bed, badly bleeding, stunned. He had wound a white towel around his head but blood was seeping through the towel, streaming down his neck, onto his fleshy shoulders and back, and into the glittering chest hairs. His face was a lurid mask of red through which his widened eyes, glassy-white with alarm, shone. *Thank God!—help me—see if you can stop this bleeding.* The voice was both desperate and reproachful as if he had been waiting an unconscionably long time for the American woman to ascend to him, and was reaching the end of his patience.

No choice, I have no choice, the American woman thought, despite the white linen jacket, and the white linen trousers, she had no choice but to come to the assistance of the stricken man, who seemed to have no one else to help him and was trying to explain to her, in a rush of words like a vehicle careening downhill, he'd had an accident, in the bathroom, slipped on the tile floor, fell hard and struck his head against the porcelain toilet and could hardly move for some minutes, possibly he'd lost consciousness, it had happened too quickly for him to comprehend, then with much difficulty he'd managed to get to his feet, maneuvered himself to his feet by first turning over, and kneeling, and then grabbing hold of the sink and lifting himself grunting, in a delirium of shock and pain, and he'd seen himself in the mirror, bleeding from a cut in his head, at the crown of his head, and grabbed a towel, and had hoped to stop the bleeding but the bleeding hadn't stopped, or anyway he wasn't sure if the bleeding had stopped, couldn't see the actual wound so maybe—she could look? She could help?—determine if the bleeding had stopped?

Of course, the American woman came to the pleading man as he bade her. Gingerly she removed the blood-soaked towel from his head and saw, with a sensation of faintness, what appeared to be a deep wound in his scalp, or in any case a wound that was badly bleeding, that had turned his silvery hair a savage hue of red, and was even now bleeding onto his shoulders. *Here! Use this*— thrusting into her hands the thick white bath towel he'd wound clumsily about his body, that was only partly soaked with blood.

But this towel was really too big, brisk as a nurse the American woman fetched from the bathroom another, smaller towel, to be wound like a turban around the bloody head, with care, for the towel must not work loose and fall off, and this she managed, though without much help from the agitated man who continued to describe, in a voice of incredulity, how the accident had happened—how it had happened to *him*; and nothing like this had ever happened to him before, it was the damned bathroom, the slippery tub, the too-small bath mat, how quickly it had happened, he'd found himself on the floor and his head was oozing blood, and there was no one to call to, no one to help, he'd been left alone in the damned room, and when he staggered into the bedroom to call the front desk the damn phone did not work, or he had no idea how to operate it, and so he'd had no choice but to stagger to the damned window, and call down into the courtyard, making a spectacle of himself . . . And no one had come for the longest time though he'd seen *her* looking at him—obviously, she'd heard him, but had not seemed to react at once, as he'd have expected. But—*Thank God you're here!*

The American woman was still upset, her heart was racing dangerously, for the sight of the badly bleeding naked man slouched on the bed had been, in the first instant, terrifying. But it did seem that the stricken man might not be in great danger, so far as the woman could determine the bleeding was beginning to slow, his skull had (surely) not been fractured; the scalp wound was probably less severe than it appeared, for excessive bleeding was common from even shallow scalp wounds, as the stricken man was assuring her, for he seemed to know about such matters, using the term *vascularized*, there being many more small veins in the scalp than elsewhere in the body, and all close to the surface of the skin. Which was why, the man said, he wouldn't need to see a doctor, no need to go to a hospital, in a few minutes he would be all right, he was sure.

All this while as the man spoke the American woman was trying to breathe calmly and deeply and not to be caught up in the man's rushed words and his hint of reproach; for there was something about the man's forceful head-on manner, like that of a vehicle careening downhill, that might draw another in its wake, like a scrap of paper in an updraft; when she could interrupt the flow of his speech she managed to tell him that she'd come as quickly as she could, it was true that she'd lost precious time waiting for the elevator, before deciding to run up the steps; and the man cursed the elevator—*Why do they make elevators so small in Europe, did everyone used to be dwarfs?* And, with an air of reproach tinged with some humor, for this was an exaggeration surely—*If you'd waited for the damned thing I'd be dead by now.*

By degrees the American woman was feeling less faint. She was not by nature an excitable person and the proximity of others who were excitable or overwrought had a disorienting effect upon her; at a distance, she imagined that she could control such persons, or at least guide them purposefully, but closer to them, within their gravitational orbit, she soon lost the thread of her own concentration, and succumbed to theirs. But it seemed clear that the stricken man was calmer too, less agitated, since his bloody head had been wound by the woman tightly, comfortingly, in a proper-sized towel, like a tourniquet; he was aggrieved yet managed to speak fairly cogently and not incoherently, like a man who has gained control of an emergency situation, and could begin to assess it, with an expression of incredulity, disbelief, annoyance, but amusement too; a man accustomed to giving orders, and to being obeyed; but also a man who is unaccustomed to being so incapacitated, so bereft of control, at the mercy of another, in such a dramatic visual display of masculine helplessness. By this time the American woman had determined that he was (probably) all right, she could leave him for a minute sitting on the bed, and went to fetch from the bathroom washcloths soaked in hot water, more towels, she would wash the blood from his neck, which was a thick, muscular neck, alarmingly crimson in the morning sunlight slanting through the window; she would wash the blood from his back, his chest, his upper arms, for she did not trust the man, in his condition, to return to the shower, as with a halfhearted sort of bravado he was suggesting.

He would need to see a doctor, she told him. She would arrange for an ambulance to take them to a hospital.

But—*No. No doctor. No hospital.* The man insisted, he would be all right in ten minutes, he had no intention of going to a hospital in Paris. *Non.*

The woman objected: of course he must go. The wound in his scalp required stitches . . .

No. Absolutely not. No hospital here, they'd all be speaking French.

He was being ridiculous, the woman cried. He'd seriously hurt himself! He might have died. She would notify the front desk that he needed medical treatment, they could call an ambulance, or at least a taxi, at the nearest emergency room he could be examined, an X-ray taken of his skull, for what if there had been a fracture, and the wound must be cleaned more thoroughly, disinfectant was needed to prevent infection. The wound would have to be stitched up properly so that it would heal and not continue to ooze blood . . .

Still, the man objected. There was not a chance he would go to a hospital here in Paris. It was the *shock* of it—the accident. A little blood wouldn't hurt him, he'd had worse head wounds as a kid, it's well known that head wounds bleed like hell but heal quickly, so *vascularized*. What he needed urgently was to get dressed, to get out of this hellhole, all this mess, look at the bedclothes, look at the towels, he needed to go downstairs to the courtyard, that great place with the fountain, and have breakfast—croissants, jam. Why he'd slipped was partly he was damned *hungry*.

The woman could not bring herself to argue with the man, since it only excited him, and it was not likely that his wishes could be overcome, regarding a doctor, hospital, stitches; he would never consent to go, now that he'd begun to feel stronger, and the shock of the fall was fading. So the woman pleaded with the man at least come into the bathroom so that she could wash him more thoroughly, he couldn't get dressed otherwise, he would get his clean clothes bloodstained. And there was blood in his hair that would have to be rinsed out before it dried and they would never be able to get it out.

With a nervous sort of exasperation the woman spoke. Yet vast relief as well. Her heart was pounding so rapidly, she feared that she might faint after all.

She was looking white-faced, the man said, with sudden concern. Maybe she'd better sit down . . .

But no, she would sit down later. She would finish her breakfast, with him. Now, she needed to wash away the rest of the blood so that no one would see it.

A shocking amount of blood in the bedclothes, the woman saw, appalled. The front desk would have to be alerted. If a housemaid entered the room unaware the poor woman would be horrified, thinking that someone had been murdered.

The man was concentrating on heaving himself to his feet, which took some effort. It was clear that this was a man who'd once been stronger, more certain of his body, better coordinated, difficult for him now to realize that he no longer inhabited that body, though he was (was he?) the exact same person. Indeed, he could probably not have managed to stand without the woman slipping an arm around his fleshy waist, and gripping him tight. He was panting, though also laughing, or making a sound of a certain sort of incredulous laughter, a laughter that signaled *How could this happen, how to me, nothing like this has ever happened before in my life but it's nothing really, ridiculous to make such a fuss.* In the bathroom the woman ran hot water into the sink, used the excellent fragrant soap to wash the man's neck as he stood submissively before her, with an air of patience; from time to time he stole sidelong glances at himself in the mirror, smiling ruefully, wincing, allowing the woman to wash him as if humoring her, acquiescing to another's overzealous solicitude, out of consideration for the woman. Though he stooped to help her, when required, and took his hairbrush from her hands to make swipes at the silvery-white hair that was disheveled and wild, and marveled at what he could glimpse of the wound in the mirror, whistling thinly as if the wound were quite an achievement.

Though wincing when the woman daubed gently at the wound. Warning her not to start the damned bleeding again—*Please!*

The woman saw that the interior of the bathroom looked like— what was the French word?—an *abattoir*. Smeared blood on the impracticably white tile floor but also on the edge of the bathtub, which was made of old, yellowed marble, and on the shower curtain, which was a double curtain with a practical plastic inside and an outside of an impractical white lacy fabric, and onto the sink and counter, for in his flailing about the stricken man had gotten blood everywhere; the woman could not bear leaving the bathroom quite so shocking, for a poor chambermaid to clean, and swiped at the bloodstains with tissues and toilet paper while the stricken man continued to peer at himself in the mirror, tried to see the wound at the crown of his head, with a kind of pride now, and finished brushing his wavy, silvery-white hair that was thin at the crown of his head but thicker elsewhere.

He was a sturdy-bodied man of something beyond late middle age, in fact. A former athlete perhaps, or at any rate a man who'd kept himself fit longer than most out of determination, and vanity; the woman found herself admiring the man's body, so much more solid than her own, so much more stolid, that resembled the Greek warrior statues she'd been seeing in the museums, broad-shouldered men with curly beards, broad chests covered in a sort of pelt, muscular arms, shoulders, legs wrought in the most exquisite antique marble. What gratitude the woman felt, what a flood of relief, that the man she'd discovered in the hotel room had not been seriously hurt!—had not been mortally injured. *Never forget this moment, when things might have gone so differently.*

Feeling better now, decidedly stronger, the man scarcely took note of the woman's mood. Naked and confident he returned to the bedroom, to seek out underwear in a bureau drawer, step into shorts, needing the woman to steady him as he balanced on one leg; navy-blue spandex shorts that fitted his drum-like belly almost too tightly. On his torso a much-laundered undershirt through which short crinkly chest hairs poked like the quills of a small beast.

Will you pick out a shirt for me, dear?—the man asked, with a curious sort of submissiveness. *Please.*

As if after the debacle of the accident, a man so foolish could not dare to select a shirt for himself.

The woman peered into the closet, and selected a long-sleeved cotton shirt with a small geometric pattern, dark blue on white, not the sort of shirt an American tourist might wear on a balmy September day in Paris but a shirt that suggested a measure of dignity, and authority. A shirt that might have been worn by a professional man, a Parisian—attorney, physician. Professor. The selection of this particular shirt the man appreciated, for the shirt was one of his favorites, and fitted his image of himself as essentially dignified, and possessing authority, as well as a certain degree of achievement, reputation, affluence though (in fact) he was the very man who'd slipped ignominiously on a bathroom floor less than an hour ago, struck his head on a porcelain toilet, stunned himself, and might easily have died, in which case he would be dead at this very moment and not buttoning up his favorite shirt; and the American woman downstairs in the courtyard making annotations in the Paris guidebook would not (yet) have known what awaited upstairs in room 341 of the Hôtel de l'Abbaye.

As he dressed, and tied his shoelaces, the man could not resist recounting to the woman another time what had happened to him, for it was quite a remarkable episode—an accident; a freak accident; nothing that had ever happened to him before, or would ever happen again. His voice was expansive, bemused; the woman understood that soon the incident that had occurred in the bathroom of the French hotel would become an anecdote, one of the man's travel anecdotes, to impress others, to startle others, to entertain others, to make them feel concern for the man even as his affable manner deflected concern, and to make them smile, for there had been no tragedy, no cracked skull, no abrupt and irremediable death, only a comical sort of accident involving a slippery floor, a mere *pratfall* the man would call it.

So relieved was the woman to see the man in good spirits, so relatively quickly after the accident, she came to him, to kiss him; and to give him a hug, as a mother might give a difficult child a hug, of reassurance, yet chidingly, with a sort of warning in the gesture, that the child might or might not acknowledge; and the man thanked her again for saving his life, as he said, extravagantly, helping him when he was helpless, abandoning her breakfast to come to his aid; and he kissed her in return, though distractedly, for there were other things on his mind, and he was very hungry by now, and was looking forward to the *New York Times* downstairs in the courtyard, and a basket of croissants, and those jams in miniature jars.

By the time the man was ready to leave the hotel room the woman had discovered belatedly that she was looking disheveled herself, and would have to comb her hair again; to her horror she saw that there were blood-smears on both the white linen jacket and the perfectly creased trousers, and so she would have to change her clothes; the man was leafing through the guidebook which the woman had brought to the room, telling her what he wanted to see that morning which wasn't the *Musée d'Orsay* but the *Musée Picasso*.

He'd never seen the Picasso museum, he said. Every time he'd come to Paris he had wanted to see it and he never had.

The woman objected, she'd thought they had agreed on the d'Orsay and the man said no, they'd agreed on the Picasso. Looking at the guidebook the previous day, that was what they'd decided.

The woman protested faintly but it was no use—it was never any use. Even if she were correct, and she could not now absolutely recall if she were correct, as the man adamantly recalled that *he* was correct, if he were obliged to give in to her he would be sulky and sullen and not enjoy the museum despite its great art and its extraordinary setting; better if they visited the Picasso museum, which was much smaller, and would not tax the man's strength so much as the mobbed Orsay. And no doubt the Picasso museum would be excellent, too. The woman would purchase postcards in the gift shop to send back home, and no doubt these would be perfectly adequate, it really didn't matter what the postcards pictured at which the young grandchildren would do no more than glance, and perhaps not even glance.

At last making their way along the dimly lighted corridor to the carpeted steps the woman slipped her arm through the man's arm, not to steady him or even to guide him, or rather not obviously to perform these functions, but out of great relief, a vast swell of relief, which would return to her through the day in waves, long after the man had (more or less) forgotten what the reason for such relief might have been, in the Hôtel de l'Abbaye on the rue Cassette, Paris.

WHERE ARE YOU?

The husband had gotten into the habit of calling the wife from somewhere in the house; if she were upstairs he was downstairs, if she were downstairs he was upstairs, and when she answered "Yes? What?" he would continue to call her, as if he hadn't heard, and with an air of strained patience—"Hello? Hello? Where are you?" And so she had no choice but to hurry to him, wherever he was, elsewhere in the house, downstairs, upstairs, in the basement or outside on the deck, in the backyard or in the driveway. "Yes?" she called, trying to remain calm, "What is it?" and he would cup his hand to his ear and tell her—a complaint, a remark, an observation, a reminder, a query; and then, later, she would hear him calling again with a new urgency, "Hello? Hello? Where are you?" and she would call back, "Yes? What is it?"—trying to determine where he was. And he would continue to call her, not hearing her, for he disliked wearing his hearing aid around the house, with only the wife to be heard, he'd complained that one of the little plastic devices in the shape of a snail hurt his ear, the tender inner ear was reddened, and had even bled, and so he would call, pettishly, "Hello? Where are you?" for the woman was always going off somewhere out of the range of his hearing, he never knew where the hell she was or what she was doing, at times her very being exasperated him; until finally she gave in and ran breathless to search for him, and when he saw her he said reproachfully, "Where were you? I worry about you when you don't answer." And she said, laughing, trying to laugh, though none of this was funny, "But I was here all along!" and he retorted, "No, you were not. You were not. I was *here* and you were *not here*." And later that day after his lunch and before his nap, unless it was before his nap and after his lunch, the wife heard the husband calling to her, "Hello? Hello? Where are you?" and the thought came to her—*No. I will hide from him.* But she would not do such a childish thing. Instead she stood on the stairs and cupped her hands to her mouth and called to him, "I'm here. I'm always here. Where else would I be?" but the husband couldn't hear her and continued to call, "Hello? Hello? Where are you?" and at last she screamed, "What do you want?—I've told you, I'm *here*." But the husband couldn't hear and continued to call, "Hello? Hello? Where are you?—hello!" until finally the wife had no choice but to give in, for the husband was sounding vexed, and angry, and anxious, but descending the stairs she tripped, and fell, fell hard, and her neck was broken in an instant and she died at once at the foot of the stairs as in one of the downstairs rooms, or perhaps in the cellar, or on the deck at the rear of the house the husband continued to call, with mounting urgency and exasperation, "Hello? Hello? Where are you?"

THE CRACK

M__ was a conscientious girl to whom disaster was certain to happen and so she began at a young age to forestall it.

At first she took care never to step on cracks in the pavement on the way to school, until an older girl cautioned her that stepping on cracks was the very thing you must do, to forestall bad luck, and so the girl took care from then on to step on as many cracks as possible; but one day returning home from school she turned her ankle in an especially deep crack in the sidewalk, and fell, and was unable to walk without pain, and had to be driven back home by the mother of a classmate who claimed to be a friend of the girl's mother. This sympathetic woman had seemed to know where the girl lived but was confounded by one-way streets and security barricades since an attempted bombing in the residential neighborhood the previous year and so wound up bringing the girl to the rear, not the front, of the building—"I'd help you upstairs, dear, but there's nowhere for me to park. Can you make it on your own?"

Of course, the girl said *yes*. She was ten years old, not five years

old, and knew very well how to enter the apartment building by the
rear, through the underground parking lot. Security guards checked
vehicles but waved schoolchildren without a second glance. Though
her ankle was throbbing with pain it was not (yet) unbearable pain.

This, M__ would realize in retrospect, was not the first of the
day's missteps but would be its most crucial: entering the building
by the rear.

The girl descended limping into the parking garage, which was
much larger than she recalled. When her parents parked their car
they parked in a designated place (11E) near the elevators; only
vaguely had the girl a sense of the vastness of the underground
space, which was but partially filled with vehicles. An odor of damp
concrete made her nostrils pinch for it was distressing to her, to realize (as she'd never realized before, in the company of adults) that in
the parking garage she was *underground*.

She could not locate the parking space for 11E but managed despite her now-swollen ankle to limp to a flight of concrete steps, that
led in one direction to the laundry machines and in the other direction to the elevators; unfortunately the elevator her parents usually
used was shut down, and a sign affixed to its door—UNDER REPAIR.
So the girl had no choice but to take the freight elevator instead.

Never in her life had M__ stepped into the freight elevator before! Neither with Momma nor with Daddy, she was sure.

In the freight elevator were several other passengers who looked
vaguely familiar to M__ though she did not know their names. A
plump girl of about fifteen with shiny chestnut bangs that fell to her
eyebrows noted the girl's swollen ankle with sympathy. She asked
the girl which floor did she want?—she would press the button for
her. M__ told her *eleven, thank you*.

Others in the elevator were headed for floors three, seven, twelve,
fifteen.

Fleetingly it crossed the girl's mind that to exit the elevator onto any one of these floors, or onto any other floor in the building, would be to enter a new and unknown *life*. But she was too young, and too fearful, to pursue such a thought to the next logical level.

The freight elevator was at least twice the size of the usual elevator and its floor was scuffed and stained. One of the walls was covered in an oil-stained tarpaulin. There was a disagreeable odor here of bodies crammed together, stale air and grime. One of the passengers was a tall lanky boy with a blemished face who stood apart from the others, with a bicycle gripped in his big-knuckled hands. Another was a prune-faced middle-aged woman who frowned at M__ as if she disapproved of unaccompanied children in public places. The plump girl with the shiny bangs was oppressively friendly, however: she asked if M__ was "Molly"—(in fact M__ was not "Molly" but her name resembled "Molly" near enough, she did not think that a correction was necessary)—and she asked how M__'s mother was, after her surgery? Was she making a steady recovery?

In dismay M__ stared and blinked at the smiling plump girl. She had no idea how to reply to these questions. Had her mother had surgery, and she hadn't been told? Or was the plump girl confusing her with another girl who lived on the eleventh floor? Seeing her confusion the plump girl said, "That's the good thing about being little, upsetting things are kept from you to protect you. When I was a little girl our dog Lulu disappeared and for a long time when I called for her or went to look for her my family would say that Lulu was 'sleeping' in some quiet place and did not want to be wakened, or that Lulu was 'visiting' Grandma, until finally when I was older one day I said to them, 'Lulu is dead, isn't she?'—and they laughed at me saying they wondered how long it would take me to realize it. For Lulu had been hit by a truck in the street and killed, and they'd kept it a secret from me for three years." The plump girl laughed bitterly in a way that chilled M__'s heart for she had wanted Lulu to be alive somewhere after all.

The plump girl persisted: "If your mother had surgery, they wouldn't tell you probably. And if she died they would tell you 'Your mommy went away'—somewhere. Wait and see, Molly."

M__ was shocked to hear these terrible things, so matter-of-factly uttered. Even the name *Molly* sounded now like mockery in the plump girl's mouth. The girl with the shiny bangs was not her friend after all but one of those whom M__'s mother had cautioned her to avoid.

M__'s mother had often warned her not to speak to strangers on her way to school, and on her way home from school; not to get into the elevator if there were "suspicious" people in it, and particularly if there was just one person, and that person a "man or a boy." Usually this was not a problem for when M__ went to school she was in the company of other schoolchildren from the building, of various grades and ages; but today, returning alone at an odd time, with her reddened, swollen ankle, and entering not through the front entrance but through the parking garage, she had not glimpsed anyone else from school. She'd had no choice but to get into the freight elevator unaccompanied. All this she would explain to her mother with the hope not to be scolded.

Fortunately, by the eleventh floor most of the other passengers had left the elevator. Here, the plump girl helped M__ out though she herself was headed for a higher floor. "You're sure that you can get to your apartment, Molly?" the girl asked, and M__ insisted, *yes*. She was sure.

What a relief, the elevator door shut and the plump smiling girl with the shiny bangs was spirited away.

And yet, the door to apartment 11E was not where M__ recalled. Usually it was within sight of the elevator as soon as she stepped out.

In her confused state M___ was failing to realize that she'd taken the *freight elevator* and not the usual elevator to the eleventh floor and so she was in an unfamiliar place.

Here the interior lighting seemed dimmer, less certain. The gunmetal-gray carpet was gritty underfoot as if dirt or sand had been tracked inside. And was the building *trembling*? In windstorms sometimes you could feel the building actually shudder and sway; the girl's father had said that the building had been "modernized" to accommodate an earthquake, if the earthquake wasn't too powerful.

What was *too powerful*?—the girl had asked timidly.

That's what we will find out, the girl's father said cheerfully.

Past doors 11J and 11G the girl limped along on her swollen ankle which pulsed with pain like a rebuke. *How silly, how silly—* stumbling into a crack in the sidewalk! She hoped that her mother would not scold her for being *silly*, as she sometimes did.

But no: Momma would feel sorry for her. Seeing how she'd hurt herself, how red and swollen her (left) ankle was, while her (right) ankle was a normal size. M___'s eyes stung with tears at the thought of her mother seeing how she'd injured herself, how she'd endured pain stoically making her way home. *Let Momma kiss where it hurts and make it well. Poor baby!*

At last, M____ was approaching 11E. One of their neighbors appeared to be having a party, a portable coatrack was in the corridor, packed with coats and jackets; a door was open, voices could be heard from inside. On the walls were framed MoMA posters of well-known works of art by Picasso, Braque, Klee, Kandinsky, Munch but the reproductions were exaggerated and mawkish, not at all beautiful, like scribbles in art class which the girl herself had been encouraged to try with Crayolas and colored chalks.

Here was a surprise—the door to 11E was ajar. The party was at *her apartment . . .*

Her parents must have planned a party without telling her. Often at Christmas they gave what was called an *open house*. Though it might as easily have been on New Year's Day, Thanksgiving, Easter. (Was today the girl's birthday? Could this be a surprise party for her eleventh birthday? She was certain, today *was not* her birthday.)

Jammed onto the portable coatrack were cloth coats of various colors, nylon jackets, a single fox-colored fur coat, suede jackets, leather. A scattering of children's clothing. Surprising, and disconcerting, the clothes resembled creatures without heads—*decapitated*.

De-cap-i-tated was a new word the girl had recently discovered. It was not a nice word but it was an impressive word to be whispered aloud at such mysterious times: *de-cap-i-tated*.

In the interior of the apartment voices were solemn and murmurous as a waterfall. You could not distinguish words only just sounds. A baby cried and fretted. Someone hushed it. There was a thin sort of music playing—piano music: M__ was startled to recognize her own tentative playing, which must have been recorded without her knowledge. That airy little rondo by the child Mozart which M__ had tried to play, an assignment in her lesson book repeated for weeks by her teacher Mrs. F__ who'd told her *good, very good, keep practicing*. In the kitchen M__ stood apprehensively awaiting the familiar D-sharp which she usually mis-struck as D-natural, and indeed to her chagrin the mistaken note was struck for all to hear, hovering in the air like a drunken moth.

Oh but why had her parents recorded such a thing? The Mozart rondo? M__ had many months of practice ahead before the piece would sound anything like the charming composition the child Mozart had dashed off at the age of ten.

There did seem to be a sizable audience gathered in the apartment. Some persons were sitting, most were standing. On the floor, a number of children sat Indian-style. (Classmates from M__'s fifth-grade homeroom? Her teacher Ms. T__ whom she adored?) From the kitchen doorway she could see a few familiar adult faces—relatives, neighbors. The faces were averted, M__ could not see them clearly.

How strange! On the living room walls were Crayola drawings and paintings M__ had done in fourth and fifth grades and had brought back home proudly to show her parents. At least twenty of these childish efforts, neatly affixed to the wall with transparent tape, like a serious art exhibit. *Embarrassing.*

On the kitchen counters were empty Styrofoam food containers, empty bottles of Coke, sparkling water, wine, hard liquor. A smell of scorched cheese as if something had been hastily heated in the oven and in the sink, black ashes of scorch that would dissolve when the faucets were turned on. Caps of beer bottles, crumpled napkins on the tile floor.

M__ drew nearer the doorway to the living room, to hear more clearly. The halting Mozart rondo had ended—thank God! There was an awkward silence. Then a woman spoke, and M__ recognized her mother's clear bell-like voice, a beautiful voice except when impatient or exasperated: "Thank you for coming to us! Thank you so much. Our dear, kind, generous friends—in this tragic hour—your presence is so comforting, we are very grateful. As you can see we are barely managing our grief—but we are *managing it*—for that is all that we can do, God has not made us any stronger than we are. To all of you who knew our dear, sweet, beautiful daughter—thank you for your sympathy, and for joining us today in this heartbroken household. Thank you for *being here for us*. And for bringing such fantastic, delicious food. Imagine, so unexpectedly—a *wake!* We loved our little girl very much but as you've just heard demonstrated, and can judge for yourselves seeing her 'artwork' displayed on the walls, M__ was not a particularly gifted child. She was not even 'beautiful'—except to her parents. She was not 'angelic'—hardly!

She *tried*—it was touching, in one so young—she displayed many of the traits of precocity but not the 'gift' that redeems it—so her teachers have attested, with uncanny accuracy. She was not an average child but rather a 'B'-child—sometimes 'B+'—sometimes 'B-.' A dozen times a day we said to each other how *heartrending* it is, this child is *trying so hard*."

There came protests, voices lifted in objection to the mother's words, though these were carefully measured, judicious: "M__ was as 'gifted' and as 'beautiful' as any other child her age, you've been too hard on her. She was only *eleven*—"

"Only *ten*. She was not yet *eleven*."

"Only *ten*. In another year or two she might have—grown, developed . . ."

"—*matured*. God, yes! That seemed to be next. The poor child, so immature mentally, and beginning to mature bodily—that is, sexually. With that sweet, plain face in another nine months *growing breasts* . . . At least she was spared that, as her parents were."

"—I think I'd meant mentally developed. In some ways M__ was a remarkable child, I think you have underestimated her—"

"Oh, thank you! That's very kind of you. Perhaps you are correct, we've been too harsh on M__, we've been judgmental as doting parents often are, but we have not been myopic either—we are not deluded like so many American parents. And it is true, as Don has been telling you, we will miss our little girl *like hell*—"

Here M__'s father interrupted in a voice of raw anguish: "We certainly will! It's been seventy-two hours since we lost her. It's heartbreaking to see her little room, her bed and her stuffed animals we haven't cleared out yet, and to realize that she won't be coming back."

"She was not, as many of you know, a 'planned' child . . ."

The father began to sob. Another adult intervened heartily.

"Well, Don—nothing is 'planned.' Or—'the best-laid plans of mice and men oft-times go astray' . . ."

Nervous laughter. A child whimpered, wanting to be taken home. The mother spoke again, in a firm, forceful voice:

"—but still M__ was a *welcome* child. Once she arrived, and we saw that she was not some sort of freak—we were perfectly delighted with her. Indeed, we *doted*."

"—pretty, with curly red hair, blue eyes—"

"—pebble-blue eyes, mouse-colored hair—"

"—some aptitude for drawing and music—"

"—a sweet girl, at times. Though she could *cry*—"

"—accident-prone! God."

There came startled laughter. Mourners who had not expected to laugh, nonetheless laughing.

Not derisive but affectionate laughter, M__ was thinking.

In the doorway standing with her weight on her good, right leg, as her (left) ankle pounded with pain. Through a buzzing in her ears she'd been listening. With a hopeful smile waiting to be noticed. Oh, by anyone!—but mostly by her mother whom she adored more even than she adored Ms. T__.

Any moment now M__'s mother would glance around to see her, and would give a little cry, and run to hug her, and burst into tears. For there had been some terrible mistake, and seeing M__ would correct the mistake.

As M__ waited for this to happen M__ seemed to understand that it could not happen. For it was too late.

She had stepped into the freight elevator. She had dared to enter the apartment building by the rear entrance which children, especially unaccompanied by adults, never entered. In that instant, it was too late.

In the instant in which she'd stepped into the crack, it was too late.

In the instant before she'd stepped into the crack, already it was too late.

"—lawsuit, absolutely! You are correct. 'Depraved indifference to human life'—'professional negligence'—our lawyer is starting at fifty-five million. The nerve of these crooks leaving an elevator door unsecured—"

"—opened to an empty *shaft*—nightmare—"

"—with children in the building—"

"—an accident-prone child in the building—"

"—at such an age, so young, the poor thing seemed to have no judgment—every decision she made was a poor decision—"

"—biting into a banana, she could *choke*–struggling to swallow a mouthful of raw spinach that had gotten tangled (somehow) around her back teeth—"

"—yes, it is funny—if also sad, tragic—heartbreaking—uncanny, how an intelligent child could make such poor decisions—so often—"

"—yes, it's true—'intelligent'—M__ was 'intelligent'—"

"—but accident-prone. Hardwired in the DNA—"

"—falling from her high chair, falling on the stairs—"

"—hitting her head, turning her ankle—spraining her ankle—"

"—falling *into a crack*—an inch-deep crack—that every other child in fifth grade has managed to avoid . . ."

"—but the elevator shaft, how'd she manage that?—to force the door open—on the eleventh floor—"

"—the damned door didn't require being *forced*. People said it just—swung open . . ."

And on, and on—a litany of remembrances to which M__ stood listening, scarcely daring to breathe.

Me! They are remembering *me*.

But then, no one seemed to see M__ in the doorway. No one seemed even to glance in her direction. One of M__'s mother's relatives had brought two large fruit tarts, that were set on the glass-topped coffee table in the living room; with a silver knife the tart was cut into pieces, and these pieces passed around on paper plates. By this time the sky outside the windows was beginning to darken. Soon it would be dusk. And soon it would be *night*.

Quietly M__ turned, to retreat. Eager to escape before the first of the guests began to leave. Especially, she dreaded one of the girls from her fifth-grade homeroom seeing her. Or two, or three. She dreaded relatives seeing her. And Daddy, and Momma. Their eyes gliding onto her, widening. *Oh. You.*

Limping back through the kitchen M__ paused to take with her, in a white paper napkin, a half-slice of cold pizza, for she'd become very hungry.

Left the apartment, closed the door. Follow the corridor, turn a corner, two corners. The freight elevator, she will find it.

WAITING FOR KIZER

1.

Waiting for his friend Kizer on the outdoor terrace at the Purple Onion Café, Smith is beginning to be concerned.

They are to meet for lunch at 1:00 P.M. on this day, Friday, June 9. Smith is certain. But already it is 1:26 P.M.

Checks his cell phone another time: no email from Kizer, no call. Tries to call Kizer but *call failed*—not even a ring at the other end.

Second time, unless it's the third the teenaged-looking waitress with buzz-cut hair has approached him with an annoyingly cheerful smile—*Excuse me sir shall I bring you something to drink while you wait for*—Smith cuts her off with a glare. Thanks, no! He'd rather wait for his friend.

It is Smith's custom to arrive early to secure a table on the outdoor terrace of the café and to sit facing the entrance so that he can observe strangers without their observing him; also, Smith wants to be in a position to see his friend Kizer approaching before Kizer sights him.

That slight advantage. Inexplicable but unmistakable.

Another time Smith checks his cell phone. Nothing.

It isn't like Kizer to be this late. In their many years of meeting together for lunch—(or sometimes, meeting for a game of squash beforehand at the university gym)—in their many years of friendship, that began decades ago in grade school—Kizer has never been more than ten or fifteen minutes late, Smith is certain.

Well, one distressing time—when Kizer didn't show up at all. (A death in the family?—Smith vaguely recalls.)

Smith leaves his table to inquire of the hostess who has been seating diners on the terrace: has a call come from his friend, for him?—his cell phone doesn't seem to be working, and his friend is a half hour late . . .

"D'you mean 'Nate Kizer'? No, Mr. Kizer has not called today."

"Kizer? Do you know him?"—Smith is taken by surprise.

"No, I don't *know him*," the hostess says. "All I know about Mr. Kizer is that he has lunch here sometimes."

"You mean with me—Nate Kizer has lunch with *me.*"

"Yes, sir. But with other parties, too."

Parties. Not sure what this means.

Tall streaked-blond hostess in long peasant skirt like a wraparound quilt smiling at Smith heedless that his heart has been lacerated.

Ridiculous! Why should Smith care that his friend has lunch at the Purple Onion with others, not always him? Of course, Smith doesn't care in the slightest.

He has lunch with other people, too. From time to time. At the faculty club at the university.

"Are these 'parties' men? Women?"—Smith is innocently curious.

"Men. Usually." But the streaked-blond hostess isn't smiling so brightly as if beginning to wonder if she has said too much.

"Men! I see." Somehow, it seems that Smith would have preferred to hear that Kizer has lunch at the Purple Onion with women.

"But—sometimes women? You said?"

The hostess has not said, exactly. "Well—not for a while. Yes, I think—not for a while. Excuse me, sir—" Clasping the oversized Purple Onion menus to her bosom the hostess is eager to greet new customers.

He has done it again, Smith thinks. Revealed his insecurity, his existential unease, in an imprudent exchange with a stranger. His shameless curiosity for the lives of others that are no business of his—he knows.

Rebuked, Smith turns away. Returning to his table he feels a light tap on his arm and there's a man, a stranger, in olive-tinted glasses seated alone at another table—"Excuse me? Were you talking about 'Nate Kizer'? I couldn't help but overhear."

2.

Where the hell is Kizer?—Smith, the most placid of men, the least impatient, is beginning to be annoyed.

It's 1:38 p.m. Kizer is almost forty minutes late. For the third time at least Smith checks his cell phone: no messages. Tried again to call Kizer's cell. Not even a ring. *Call failed.*

Yet stubbornly Smith isn't going to order his own grim lunch, eat alone and depart. No. He has brought a book to read—*An Anthropology of Time.* Dog-eared paperback he'd picked up on campus, retiring professor (philosophy) emptying his office, stacks of books once diligently read, underlined, and annotated, "taught"—now abandoned on a table in a busy foyer.

But Smith can't concentrate on mere words. Peers again at the God-damned phone cupped in his hand like a talisman.

(Has Smith, like virtually everyone he knows, become compulsive about checking his phone? Good that his family can't know. Scolding fifteen-year-old Trevor for spending so much time on his phone or online, video games up in his room . . .)

Smith has to wonder if something happened between him and Kizer of which he isn't aware. Longtime friendships can become strained, precarious. Tries to recall the last time they saw each other—in fact, here at the Purple Onion a few weeks ago—if Kizer was behaving strangely, Smith noticed nothing.

Resents you. Feels inferior to you. Since you saved his life. No good deed goes unpunished.

It's a fact, no need to bring it up, when they were boys Matt Smith saved Nate Kizer's life. Smith rarely thinks of the incident but guesses that Kizer thinks of it often.

Saving another's life. How it reflects upon your own.

Smith wonders: Was his life altered, at eleven? Suffused with a sense of confidence as his friend's life must have become suffused with a sense of unease, insecurity. Debt.

For the past several years Smith and Kizer have been meeting for lunch at the Purple Onion Café, a relatively new restaurant located midway between Smith's office at the university and Kizer's office at the medical center. The Café isn't either man's first choice but it is moderately priced, unpretentious, specializes in "organic" food, and in warm weather there is outdoor seating.

Good too, that the Purple Onion doesn't have a liquor license.

Today, Smith has driven his car to the Purple Onion. Very likely Kizer will drive, too. Not long ago each was likely to bicycle, walk, or even jog to lunch. There'd been a subtle rivalry between them: who would take the easier course, by driving.

Though he has become somewhat paunchy around the middle, and is sometimes short of breath climbing stairs, Smith considers himself more athletic than Kizer, overall. Taller than Kizer, just slightly. Leaner, more fit. More levelheaded. Less likely to brood, hold a grudge. He thinks so.

Smith's marriage, Smith's children: on the whole, more satisfactory than Kizer's. Possibly, Kizer's career has been more impressive.

Like (identical) twins, in a way. In such relationships there is inevitably the *dominant, stronger* twin.

"Let's play squash next week"—Smith plans to suggest to Kizer. Strange, it has been months since the men have played together . . .

It has become Smith's custom to arrive a few minutes early at the Purple Onion. In this way, he has the advantage. Asks for a corner table shielded from the sidewalk by a wisteria trellis. Always brings a book with him, lowers his head as if reading while observing diners at other tables, arrivals at the entrance. In a familiar reverie fantasizing strangers stripped naked and at his mercy . . . Boldly copulating with the (attractive) women, who never resist his advances; overpowering, humiliating the men. (Of course, Matt Smith is *not like this* at all. The most civilized of men, a gentlemanly man, in fact embarrassed when strangers turn out to be known to him, women friends of his wife's, mothers of his children's friends, the lewd fantasies dissolve at once.)

And he is keen to sight Kizer before Kizer sights him—who can say why?

Owes his life to me. Like no one else in the world. Every heartbeat, every breath—Kizer has to acknowledge.

Born within a few months/miles of each other in San Rafael, California. Grade school, high school. Friends, rivals. Kizer was chess champion of the school district three years in a row but Smith was elected president of the class in their junior year; Kizer barely managed to get onto the track team but Smith still recalls, with a smile, that amazing season when, on the junior varsity softball team, until then just an OK player he'd hit a crucial home run—and earned the grudging admiration of Coach Fenner.

True, both boys were attracted to the same girls. And true, the girls might've preferred Kizer except Kizer was too shy, socially maladroit, to take advantage.

Who had *fallen in love* first?—that remains unclear.

Kizer graduated third in their class of 422; Smith graduated twelfth, but was admitted to UC–Santa Cruz with a full tuition scholarship while Kizer had only a part-tuition scholarship at Stanford.

Away at college they'd lost contact, or mostly. But each returned to San Rafael in their late twenties. Married within a few months of each other. Started families, established careers. Only just coincidental, each man has fathered three children: girl-girl-boy (Smith), boy-boy-girl (Kizer).

At a short distance the wives of Smith and Kizer might— almost—be mistaken for each other but it's strange, at least Smith thinks it's strange, that Lisa (Smith) and Emma (Kizer) have never quite become friends despite their husbands' urging.

When Smith asks Lisa why, Lisa merely shrugs and insists that she likes Kizer's wife *well enough*; possibly, Emma responds in a similar manner if Kizer asks her about Lisa.

One of Smith's (secret) fantasies is Kizer in love with Lisa, which leaves him breathless and excited as well as humiliated, emasculated; while, oddly, Smith feels little attraction for Kizer's wife, Emma, who in turn seems indifferent to him, if not, unless Smith is imagining it, just slightly resentful. *Of course, she is jealous. Her husband's closest friend, to whom he owes his life.*

At the age of forty-nine Smith is beyond adolescent rivalries and so no longer measures himself against Kizer: wife, children, career. House, cars. Kizer is arguably better-looking than Smith, as he'd been the better student in high school, but Smith is in better physical condition, he is sure; though stricken with sciatica last year, which is why he'd cut back on squash. Still, in better condition than Kizer who has been afflicted since childhood by asthma. Surely still a stronger swimmer than Kizer which was why on the rain-swollen San Miguel River, Boy Scout camp, when the boys were eleven years old and their canoe overturned, it was Smith who (desperately) managed to drag (frantically struggling) Kizer back to the canoe so that each boy, skinny, shivering with cold and fear, could hold on to it until help came.

Saved my life! Oh God thank you.

Kizer has never quite said.

Why, Smith can understand. Some memories are so traumatic it is wisest to forget. Amnesia like a spray-washed wall.

Yet: Smith sometimes feels trapped in a dream he doesn't (quite) realize is a dream in which he is trying again to swim to his struggling/drowning friend while simultaneously trying not to let go of the overturned canoe; then, trying to explain to Kizer something both elemental and obscure, crucial for both to comprehend so that Smith's very brain aches with the effort which is the mysterious *effort of the dream: neurological, muscular.* Even as his tongue is thick and clumsy, his words stumble and falter.

Your name is called. You turn, and it is yourself—yet not you.

In actual life if Smith were to stammer such nonsense Kizer would laugh in that soundless way of his, rocking with laughter as if it pained him. For over the years, decades, Kizer has been the one to deflate Smith's existential quandaries. When Smith takes himself too seriously, count on Kizer to puncture the balloon.

Dear God. If something has happened to Kizer, what will you do?

Smith tries to think. Does not dare think.

Looming over him is a waiter asking if he'd like a drink? while he's waiting for his friend?—Smith peers up at a tall lanky-limbed young man, wispy beard, dreadlocks halfway down his back. *White?* Food server with (unwashed, oily) *dreadlocks?*

Damned Purple Onion, hiring freaks. Hippie pretensions, health-food and "gluten-free." Smith glances around searching for the waitress with the buzz-cut hair—or had that been another lunch?

Anyway, the Purple Onion doesn't serve *drinks.* Dreadlocks must mean one of their health-food concoctions—carrot-avocado-yogurt smoothie, pomegranate-lemon-spritzer, "Green Rush" (kale, spinach, broccoli, seaweed liquefied). Next time Smith will insist that Kizer meet him somewhere else.

Smith thanks the waiter but no. He will wait for his friend before ordering.

Turning back to his book, rereading a passage already marked with yellow highlighter. *Time is an illusion in which we "remember" the past but not the future. As quantum physicists have revealed—* but distracted by the fact that Kizer is uncharacteristically late, and hasn't called or texted, possibly Smith's phone is malfunctioning in which case if there's an emergency Kizer won't be able to reach him. Yes, this must be the case! Smith shoves back his chair, hurries to the hostess to explain the situation and ask if his friend might've called and whoever answered the phone inside the restaurant failed to relay the message to him out on the terrace . . .

The hostess listens with a little frown of sympathy. But no—"Mr. Kizer hasn't called today, I'm sure."

"You know my friend's name?"—Smith is taken aback for (he is sure) he hadn't (yet) given it.

3.

Returning to his table Smith feels a light tap on his arm.

"Excuse me? Were you talking about 'Nate Kizer'? I couldn't help but overhear."

Smith is confounded: here is an individual he has never seen before, he's sure, who yet seems familiar to him.

A stranger in his late forties perhaps, in olive-tinted glasses, peering intently, quizzically, at Smith.

"Y-yes. 'Nate Kizer.' We're having lunch together, today."

"*We're* having lunch together, today. Nate and me."

Strained smiles. Stares of disbelief, suspicion.

How is this possible? Smith is thinking—*Obviously, there is some simple explanation. A mistake.*

"Obviously, there is some explanation. A mistake." The stranger speaks slowly with a clenched jaw.

Such a situation would call for levity, one might think. Yet, Smith and the man in the olive-tinted glasses exude an air of hostility, distrust.

Carefully Smith says: "If this is Friday June ninth, there's no mistake. Kizer and I are having lunch today, we were supposed to meet at 1:00 P.M."

"*We* were supposed to meet at 1:00 P.M. Kizer and me."

The two men stare at each other, perplexed and resentful.

Smith sees that the other, the stranger, is gripping his cell phone. No doubt he too has been trying to call Kizer without success.

"Possibly a joke? Or—"

"—a mistake. Kizer's—"

"—he wants us to meet?"

No! Can't believe this. Kizer would've alerted Smith, he'd invited someone else to join them.

Something disturbingly familiar about the man who has dared to touch Smith's arm, to stop him on his way back to his table. His voice is nasal, sounding like Smith's own voice when he has a stuffed head; his manner is awkward, as if his limbs are poorly coordinated, or he has back pain. His not very attractive face is asymmetrical as if there were an uneven crack down the center and half the face has resettled, as after a seismic shift.

His (coarse, sand-colored, graying) hair is receding sharply from his forehead, his eyes appear to be deep-socketed, glistening. Unlike Smith who is wearing, as he often does, a fresh tattersall shirt, clean khakis and running shoes in reasonably good condition, the other is wearing a not-fresh shirt of no distinction, jeans beginning to fray at the knee, sandals that expose bony white toes. His forehead is furrowed and mildly blemished, or scarred, from adolescent acne. His mouth is an asymmetrical smirk that disguises (Smith guesses) an underlying unease.

"And you are—?"

"Matt Smith."

"*Matt* Smith? Well—I'm *Matthew*."

Staring at each other. Slow blinking. Is this a joke?

"Well! What's your middle name?"—(Matt) Smith steels himself.

"'Maynard.' You?"

"'Maynard.'"

"You're joking, right?"

"*You're* joking. Right?"

Surge of belligerence between the men. Rush of adrenaline. One is obviously an impostor, but—which?

"No. I am not joking. If you'd like to see I.D. . . ."

"If *you'd* like to see I.D. . . ."

Now (Matt) Smith realizes: the other's olive-tinted glasses with metallic frames are near-identical to a pair of glasses he'd once had, replaced with the black plastic frames and bifocal lenses he is now wearing.

Smith, that's to say (Matt) Smith, feels a wave of dizziness. As if the terrace floor is beginning to shift beneath his feet. (Earthquake? San Rafael? Not unknown.) He is thinking that something like this has happened before. He has survived, previously. Or had it been a dream, and not real? *Is* this a dream, and not real?

A name is called, it is your name. You turn, you approach—it is yourself, though not (literally) you. He feels a rush of curiosity about the other man that leaves him weak, sickened.

Seeing the expression in (Matt) Smith's face, (Matthew) Smith pulls out a chair at his table. "Hey, man—you're looking kind of pale. Better sit down."

"I—I don't think that—"

"Yeah. You'd better."

(Matthew) Smith is brusque, bullying. (Matt) Smith feels a surge of repugnance for the man, a sensation of dread deep in the gut. Just as he'd felt often as a boy, confronted with older, more dominant boys. Wanting to scream at them *Go to hell. Leave me alone. Don't touch me!* Yet, (Matt) Smith sits at the table as bidden.

Soon it is established: both (Matt) Smith and (Matthew) Smith live in San Rafael, (Matt) Smith on Buena Vista Street and (Matthew) Smith on Solano Street; each was born in San Rafael on July 24, 1969; the names of their parents are identical—"Cameron and Joellen Smith."

Coincidence? Not very likely.

And yet—what else, but coincidence?

In his shock, disorientation (Matt) Smith yet has time for a petty satisfaction—Buena Vista is a much more elegant street than Solano, more expensive houses, quieter neighborhood. Whoever (Matthew)

Smith is, or is presuming to be, he is less affluent than (Matt) Smith as well as heavier, slack-jowled.

"Guess we must be related? Somehow . . ."

"Must be. Yes."

"Except—I've never heard of you before . . ."

"—never heard of *you* before."

"Jesus!"—whistling thinly through his teeth.

As (Matthew) Smith speaks (Matt) Smith glances about the terrace at other tables. Trying to get his bearings. (*Is* the floor shifting? No.) There is the hostess in her striking wraparound skirt, there is the (white) kid with the skimpy beard and dreadlocks tumbling down his back. It's a warm balmy June day, hazy sky like a smudged watercolor. *Sfumato*—is that the technical term? Bizarre that the other diners, mostly women, are chattering companionably together oblivious of (Matt) Smith and (Matthew) Smith in their midst each as confounded by the other's existence as by the appearance of a basilisk. Covertly glancing at each other fascinated, repelled.

(Matt) Smith tries to speak, has to clear his throat: "Well! What're the odds . . ."

(Matthew) Smith coughs, laughs: ". . . fucking coincidence . . ."

Embarrassment settles between them. Sudden shyness.

"D'you think . . ."

"Do *you* think . . ."

"Some sort of—genetic . . ."

"Orphans, from the same family? Adopted—"

"But I'm not—adopted . . ."

"*I'm* not. At least I think so . . ."

"*I* think so, too. I *know so.*"

The men are excited, breathless. Wanting to laugh and yet each feels threatened, endangered. (Matt) Smith worries that it is some sort of bullying contest, the rougher and less civilized will triumph.

But no, not possible. Not on the terrace of the Purple Onion.

(Matt) Smith notices that (Matthew) Smith has been reading a magazine while waiting for Kizer—looks like *Scientific American*. (This, too, is an obscure coincidence, for (Matt) Smith subscribed to *Scientific American* as a brainy high school kid years ago. But he has long since allowed the subscription to lapse.) Seeing that (Matt) Smith has noticed the magazine, (Matthew) Smith says with an embarrassed shrug: "It's a paradox how we 'see' objects with our eyes—objects and one another—yet with a microscope we 'see' a very different micro-reality, magnified. Which is 'real'? Is one 'more real' than the other?"

Why, (Matthew) Smith has intellectual pretensions! (Matt) Smith resents him all the more.

"We see what we want to see."

"We see what we've been told to see."

"What we've been told we want to see—that's what we 'see.'"

(Matt) Smith and (Matthew) Smith laugh together, guardedly. Shyly glancing at each other.

(Matt) Smith concedes: "There's a natural bias in humankind toward the unexamined. For what we think to be common experience. We have to suppress—censor—what contradicts our sense of the 'real.' Otherwise—"

"Of course! 'Otherwise.'"

There is a pause. The men reconsider. (Matt) Smith still finds the situation unnerving but is beginning to feel that yes, he might master it, control it, come out on top somehow with an anecdote Kizer will find wonderfully entertaining when (Matt) Smith recounts it to him.

Not very politely, in fact rudely (Matthew) Smith snaps his fingers at the dreadlocked waiter who has been hovering nearby in the hope that, at last, the men have orders for him. "Hey? Over here? Drinks for both of us."

(Matt) Smith orders a pomegranate-lemon spritzer. Not with much enthusiasm but the spritzer seems the most palatable drink at the Purple Onion. (Matthew) Smith orders a Bloody Mary.

"Bloody Mary? Here? They don't serve Bloody Marys here."

"Of course they serve Bloody Marys here. Why'd we come here, if they didn't? Ask Kizer."

"Kizer doesn't drink at lunch . . ."

"Kizer certainly drinks at lunch. And drinks are served here." (Matthew) Smith appeals to the dreadlocked waiter who laughs politely as if (Matthew) Smith has said something witty. Indeed, on the table is a drinks list.

Drinks at the Purple Onion Café? Since when? (Matt) Smith is amazed.

"Since they reopened. After the renovation. You must have heard, since you live in San Rafael, that a suicide bomber set off a homemade bomb here last fall?"

(Matt) Smith has not heard. Or rather, (Matt) Smith has heard, but—"That was just a ridiculous rumor, Matthew. It never happened."

His heart trips. Just slightly. Calling the other *Matthew*.

"Certainly it happened."

"No. Certainly it *did not.*"

"Look, I live in this town. The bombing was big news. Three people died plus the teenaged bomber. Half the restaurant collapsed, they had to rebuild. It just opened again, when?—in March. I met Kizer for lunch, we sat on the terrace and talked about how strange it felt, to be having lunch here—where people had died . . ."

Lunch with Kizer? Here? Renovation? (Matt) Smith doubts this.

"You can see by the wisteria, there hasn't been any damage. Those trees by the parking lot . . . The Purple Onion was repainted, I think, and some alterations were made, but—not . . ." (Matt) Smith begins to stammer, this is so absurd. Suicide bombing! Purple Onion!

"Someone played a prank, called in a bomb threat but it turned out to be a hoax. The Café was evacuated, in fact Kizer and I were supposed to meet for lunch that day but the area was cordoned off. False bomb threats were called in to the high school and the hospital, too, that day . . ."

(Matthew) Smith retorts: "Those bomb threats came *after* the bomb at the Purple Onion. There was an actual bomb here. A kid from the neighborhood, high school dropout, he'd made a bomb at home and just walked over here with it."

No, no! Nothing remotely like that happened. (Matt) Smith is laughing, frustrated. Trying to remain calm in the face of the other's obstinacy as he has had to do, as a rational person, through much of his life. "It was a stupid prank some high school kids played to get one of their classmates in trouble. This poor kid, innocent kid, he'd been bullied mercilessly . . ." (Matt) Smith's voice is shaking. Recalling those terrible days when Lisa called him in his office sobbing on the phone. *Trevor refuses to go to school. He has locked himself in the bathroom, I am so afraid he will hurt himself . . . Why can't you come home!*

(Matthew) Smith continues to insist that yes, there was a *suicide bomb* here. Asks the dreadlocked waiter who grimaces, smiles nervously, says yes he guesses so, last year, before he'd moved to San Rafael and started working here, yes there was said to be a *suicide bombing*. Here.

(Matt) Smith shakes his head. Ridiculous! His face is hot with indignation but damned if he will continue this fatuous exchange.

It is clear that (Matthew) Smith is a damaged personality. The kind of person who pursues a subject when it is evident that others do not wish to continue. Gratified, vindicated, (Matthew) Smith yet takes a new tack, lowering his (nasal, maddening) voice in a way to suggest sympathy, pity.

"I know, Matt—you don't want to think about it. That is your pre-rogative. That is only *natural.* You and your wife—I would imagine—whoever she is—would rather—rather *not.*" But now (Matthew) Smith has gone too far, uttering the words *your wife.*

"And you? Do you have a wife?"—(Matt) Smith sneers.

Barely can (Matt) Smith bring himself to look at (Matthew) Smith's coarse asymmetrical face. Barely, to acknowledge the watery eyes just visible behind smudged olive-tinted lenses.

"I have an—ex-wife."

"Ah. I see. *Ex.*"

"You don't 'see,' I think." Now (Matthew) Smith's voice is qua-vering, indignant. (Matthew) Smith glances about the terrace with an angry smile. (Where the hell is his drink? How long have they been waiting?)

Next question should be, what is the *ex-wife's* name? But (Matt) Smith refuses to ask this question, just yet.

4.

Damn Kizer! Now forty-five minutes late.

And no call from him, no explanation or apology.

At least, their drinks have been brought by the dreadlocked waiter: Bloody Marys for each.

(Matt) Smith doesn't recall ordering a Bloody Mary but hey, this is fine. Tomato juice for physical well-being, vodka for confidence.

"We might as well order our lunches, too. What d'you think?"— (Matthew) Smith swallows a large mouthful of the neon-red drink.

Not waiting for (Matt) Smith to join him as he drinks. Not sug-gesting a toast to their having, so oddly, met. (Matt) Smith feels just slightly rejected by the other, more blustery man in a rumpled shirt of no distinction while he, (Matt) Smith, makes it a point to wear a freshly laundered shirt each day, often a tattersall, on principle.

Never would (Matt) Smith wear such old, ugly sandals as (Matthew) Smith is wearing! Never would he expose ugly misshapen toes, discolored toenails. His teenaged children would be utterly mortified by him. His wife would recoil in dismay, disgust. And (Matt) Smith thinks too well of himself: his masculine pride.

Seeing again the scattering of minuscule acne scars on (Matthew) Smith's forehead, (Matt) Smith feels a surge of satisfaction. *He* was spared such petty indignities in high school where appearances matter so much.

"Yes. Let's order. If Kizer turns up . . ."

". . . he'll be surprised to see us."

(Matthew) Smith snaps his fingers another time, summons the waiter. Gives his order while (Matt) Smith studies the menu just slightly confused for there are new items listed, not every dish is labeled *organic, local, gluten-free.*

(Matthew) Smith has ordered a hamburger, medium rare. With French fries. (Matt) Smith has not had a hamburger in years, tries to avoid red meat, is tempted to follow his companion but decides no, a cold salmon platter might be better.

(Matthew) Smith remarks that he'd last seen Kizer two weeks ago for lunch, after playing squash. *He* hadn't played as well as usual, sciatica kicking up again, so Kizer had won, but just barely.

(Matt) Smith feels a pang of jealousy. Do (Matthew) Smith and Kizer see each other so frequently? At two-week intervals? Kizer only has time for (Matt) Smith every four, five weeks. And they have not played squash in months.

Feeling an impulse to confide in (Matthew) Smith, he sometimes wonders if indeed Kizer is his close friend as he wishes to think. If indeed (Matt) Smith has any friends at all.

Recalling how sometimes Kizer will tell him he can't make lunch this week, has to postpone lunch next week, plans have changed and he will have to cancel . . . But possibly (Matthew) Smith is lying? Something devious about the hooded eyes behind the olive-tinted lenses, that insidious nasal voice.

Then, (Matthew) Smith's phone rings. (Matt) Smith feels a pang of anxiety, that the call will be from Kizer.

For him. For the other. Not for me . . .

But (Matthew) scowls, listening—the call seems to be of no significance, or a wrong number.

(Matthew) Smith puts away his phone. (Matt) Smith has already put away his phone, in his shirt pocket.

(Matthew) Smith remarks that Kizer never used to be late, until recently. (Matt) Smith denies this: Kizer is never late, at all.

"Well, since that—misunderstanding—with my wife—or whatever it was—Kizer has begun to be less reliable."

"Misunderstanding? With—who? Who is your wife?" (Matt) Smith's heart is beating rapidly.

"My wife? Lisa."

"Lisa! You don't mean—'Lisa Finch.'"

(Matthew) shrugs, grimacing. If this is a joke, it is a just-barely-amusing joke.

"Well, yes—'Lisa Finch.'"

"But—that's not possible? Is it?"

A pause. Neither can quite look the other in the eye.

"'Lisa Finch'—from Petaluma."

"Petaluma? No. I don't think so. Sacramento."

"Well, yes—born in Sacramento. But her parents moved to Petaluma when she was two."

"Five, I think. When she was five."

"*Two.* I'm sure."

Another pause. Breathless.

At last (Matthew) Smith says, in an even voice: "We were talking about Kizer, actually. How—since a 'misunderstanding' with my wife—(at the time my wife, not *ex*-)—he hasn't been so reliable. Though we are still friends—of course. Each of us the other's oldest friend."

"Wait. What was this 'misunderstanding'—"

"Is it possible that you don't know? Yet?"

"Don't know what, 'yet'?"

They stare at each other for a long moment before realizing— *This person is me. Yet—not-me.*

Fortunately, breaking the tension, their lunches are brought to them by the dreadlocked waiter who has been glancing at them, from one to the other and back again, with an expression resolutely neutral.

Also, their drinks are depleted, or nearly. (Matthew) Smith orders another Bloody Mary. (Matt) Smith hesitates, then orders another Bloody Mary.

"Yes, it's 'early in the day.' But one more won't hurt."

"Most sensible thing you've said yet."

(Matthew) Smith laughs, baring big ungainly stained teeth.

He had braces, took care of his teeth. (Matt) Smith thinks. His parents had loved him and provided dental, medical care for him.

"I see that your hair has thinned," (Matthew) Smith says with a sly spider-dimple of a smile, and (Matt) Smith says, not missing a beat, like the capable Ping-Pong player he'd been as a kid, "I see that you've had some skin trouble. Carcinomas?"—in a tone of sympathy.

(Matthew) Smith winces. (Is it so visible?) Conceding that yes, he'd had several small, coin-sized skin cancers removed from his forehead and cheeks a few months ago, in a dermatologist's office. *Not* major surgery.

"Dermatologist? Who's that?"

"Dr. Friedland. A woman."

"Friedland! She isn't a dermatologist, she's our G.P."

"*Your* G.P., maybe. *My* dermatologist."

Wary with each other. Falling quiet as they eat their lunches. (Matt) Smith is feeling slightly light-headed—vodka so early in the day . . . He has noted how thirstily (Matthew) Smith drinks, disapprovingly. The man is an incipient alcoholic.

"You'd said, your wife—*ex*-wife—is named 'Lisa Finch'?"

(Matthew) Smith shrugs, chewing. His mouth is bracketed by lines like fissures. Clearly doesn't want to pursue the subject but (Matt) Smith can't resist.

Saying, with a curious sort of tenderness, "I'd thought you—we—I-loved her—Loved Lisa."

(Matthew) Smith laughs indulgently. "What's 'love'—a matter of perspective."

"What does that mean?"

"It means that we 'love' people to the degree to which we don't know them. Beyond that point, 'love' falters, fails."

(Matt) Smith protests: "I—I am sure—I love my wife very much . . ."

(Matthew) Smith coughs, laughs. Clears his throat.

"It's a matter, as I've said, of perspective. Of seeing the object with the naked eye, or through a microscope."

"But what went wrong? With you and your 'Lisa' . . ."

"Matt, why would you want to know? If you're ignorant of—well, your wife and Kizer—"

"'My wife and Kizer'? What do you mean?"

(Matt) Smith falters. His bolder self meant to exclaim *What the hell do you mean!*

With a curious sort of dignity, or obstinacy, (Matthew) Smith tells (Matt) Smith that he is better off not knowing.

"But—I don't want to remain ignorant. I want to know—whatever it is that I don't seem to know . . ."

"Look, we aren't the same person. We aren't 'identical.' What is true for me isn't necessarily true for you. All I can tell you is what I know—suspected. For years I'd been suspicious of Lisa and Kizer. That softness in her face when she looked at him, spoke of him. The way she went blank sometimes when I touched her, as if she wanted to throw off my hand but didn't dare. The way she would shrug away from me, shivering. Then again she would ask about the canoe accident, how close I'd actually come to drowning, and how my friend Nate Kizer 'saved' me." (Matthew) Smith pauses, brooding. "Those many times she seemed depressed, burst into tears . . ."

"Nate Kizer saved *you*? But—that isn't possible . . . I was the one to save *him*."

A long pause falls upon the men, like vapor. A chill vapor, causing (Matt) Smith to shudder.

For vividly (Matt) Smith remembers: the rain-swollen river, pulling his paddle in water denser than water should be, a boy screaming, panic—then, in rushing water, so much colder than he'd expected . . .

"I was the one to save *him*. I—I saved Nate Kizer's life when we were eleven years old . . ."

(Matthew) Smith shrugs. As if to say *OK so what?*

"I—don't remember Nate ever telling me, he'd saved anyone's life. I mean—if he had, he'd have told me . . ." (Matt) Smith hears his voice faltering, failing. Clearly (Matthew) Smith remembers an episode very different from his. Though they are seated only a few inches from each other, at the wrought-iron terrace table, it's as if there is a chasm between them.

"And my wife—Lisa—she's a very different person from your wife. *Ex*-wife. We are each other's closest friend—or almost. We have no secrets from each other." Though it is true, (Matt) Smith must concede, that from time to time Lisa succumbs to migraine head-aches and doesn't want him to touch her or even to speak to her.

Ridiculous, to imply, as (Matthew) Smith seems to have implied, that Kizer has had some sort of long affair with Lisa. No.

In (Matthew) Smith's own marriage, that might be the case. Why the marriage ended.

"My Lisa is—is not—in love with another man, I am sure."

(Matt) Smith laughs dismissively, as if that were proof.

In a friendly toast, unless it's a mocking toast, (Matthew) Smith lifts his Bloody Mary toward (Matt) Smith, taps (Matt) Smith's glass with his own.

"Here's to *us*. Fuck *them*."

Boastfully (Matthew) Smith allows (Matt) Smith to know that he'd dropped out of college in his freshman year at UC-Irvine, only barely graduated from high school—"Too much weed. Jesus! I think my cerebral cortex turned to vapor." But (Matthew) Smith laughs, indulgently. Better than hanging himself which was the alternative at fifteen, never got over being rejected by Coach Fenner trying out for j-v softball, the blunt way Fenner dismissed him in front of the others, mean son of a bitch not seeming to know how vulnerable a fifteen-year-old boy is, especially a fifteen-year-old with acne. Why he'd spent most of high school stoned. His only friend was Kizer who felt sorry for him, frankly. Wouldn't have had the courage to actually hang himself just like, on the river, when he'd panicked and overturned the canoe he hadn't had the courage to swim to shore and had almost drowned Kizer trying to help him, Jesus!—never live it down, his dying day he'd be remembering.

Well—he'd gone back to college. San Jose State. Lost contact with Kizer until he moved back to San Rafael and started some kind of new life, or tried to.

"Weird thing was they'd known each other in college. I mean,

when they were in college. Though they didn't go to the same college. Kizer and Lisa. They'd—you know . . ." (Matthew) Smith
makes a crude, obscene gesture, of a kind (Matt) Smith has not seen
in decades.

"And you know this, how?"—(Matt) Smith is repelled.

"She told me. When it was over between us. Rubbing salt in my
wounds, like a bitch will do."

(Matt) Smith laughs. (Matthew) Smith is so crude!

(Matthew) Smith stares at (Matt) Smith, considering. "You think
that she—'your' Lisa—wasn't fucking Kizer, off and on for years?
Really? And you know this, how?"

"I won't dignify that by answering."

"Well, good for you! That's what a man like me lacks, fatally—
dignity." (Matthew) Smith laughs.

In truth, (Matt) Smith is fevered with curiosity. Almost, a sort of
sexual hunger. But God damn, *he will not be baited.*

The men decide, it seems simultaneously, to take another tack:
children.

"You have children, Matt? How many?"

"Yes! Two girls, one boy." (Matt) Smith smiles, proudly. A daddy
whose children adore him. "And you?"

"None."

"*None?* Not—even one?"

"'Not even one.'"

"Well—that's too bad . . ."

Awkward words. (Matt) Smith is stricken with curiosity but hesitates to blunder further for perhaps (Matthew) Smith or his wife are
infertile . . .

"You could say 'minus-one.' A miscarriage." (Matthew) Smith
speaks in a voice flat as the tabletop.

"Hey. I'm sorry . . ." (Matt) Smith is taken by surprise.

"Why sorry? It happened a long time ago. Seems like it could've been other people, actually."

(Matt) Smith ponders. Is (Matthew) Smith speaking bravely, to disguise sorrow; or is (Matthew) Smith speaking with an infuriating air of complacency, just this side of a snigger?

Recalling that Lisa had had a miscarriage too—hadn't she? In an early year of their marriage . . .

"At least, that's what Lisa claimed. Frankly"—(Matthew) Smith snorts with laughter—"I had a suspicion at the time that she might've had an abortion. At the women's clinic, in secret."

"When was this?"

"When? What difference does it make? Might've been a year or two after we were married."

(Matt) Smith feels a sensation of cold. Horror. (Matthew) Smith's laughter is inappropriate, bizarre. (Matt) Smith frowns gravely, he will not be drawn into the other's mood. Thinking how if Lisa had lost their first baby, Constance would never have been born. . . . Their daughter, now a senior at USC.

(Matt) Smith loves his daughter Constance. Wanting to gloat to (Matthew) Smith—*You have no idea what it is, the love of a beautiful daughter. Poor bastard.*

"The second pregnancy, or whatever it was," (Matthew) Smith continues, imperturbably, "we'd both agreed should be terminated. The world is a 'terrible place'—'already too many people on the planet'—plus I'd been transferred to San Jose preparatory to being 'downsized.' The saying in our business is—*San Jose, doom on the way.* And we weren't getting along too well, even then. Then," (Matthew) Smith says, with a smirk of a smile, "the bitch dared to claim later that she'd been coerced by me into having an abortion—in fact, more than one—and she'd actually wanted to have children." (Matthew) Smith snorts with mirthless laughter.

"Wait. I don't understand . . ."

"*I* do. It's only required of the husband, to understand."

What this means, (Matt) Smith is not curious to know. Saying quickly, as one might grab a towel to cover one's groin in Boy Scout camp:

"*My* wife—my Lisa—wanted children from the start. Lisa always loved babies. She'd played with dolls—she said. Lisa and I love our kids. Lisa has been a wonderful mother. Can't imagine what our lives would be like without our children . . ." (Matt) Smith hears these words trundle across the table like dull thumping dominoes, falling.

"'Can't imagine'—? Really?" (Matthew) Smith is frankly sniggering now. "I can't imagine what my life would've been like with children dragging me down."

(Matt) Smith protests: "Children don't *drag you down, they buoy you up.*"

His words sound hollow, insincere. Doggedly he perseveres: "When your spirits are low, when you doubt the worth of living, you have only to look at your children, and understand that they are the reason you were born."

As these words issue from (Matt) Smith's mouth he feels a numbing sensation suffuse his mouth, his throat and lungs as if he is breathing in ether.

(Matthew) Smith nods gravely, ironically. As if he has never heard anything so profound.

"'When your spirits are low, when you doubt the worth of living, you have only to look at your children, and see the blessings you've been given . . .' That sounds even more beautiful, Matt. Makes me rethink everything I've believed, or wanted to believe. Maybe I should've made my wife have children."

Seeing that (Matt) Smith blinks at him in astonishment, (Matthew) Smith bursts into laughter.

Loose-jowled, fatty chest, rippling flesh around his waist. How in hell has (Matthew) Smith let himself go, not yet fifty years old? Shame!

"You are despicable," (Matt) Smith says coldly. "You make a mockery of everything decent. You've let your entire life be ruined by—an act of cowardice when you were eleven years old."

"What do you know about me? You don't know shit about me."

"*You* don't know shit about me."

So distracted by their conversation, the men have stopped eating. Each is trembling, indignant.

Oh, where *is Kizer*? Kizer would know what to make of this impasse like King Solomon rendering judgment. (Matt) Smith knows, just knows, that Kizer would rule for *him*.

A precarious moment when each of the men is about to spring up from the table, back away from the other in dismay and disgust, and depart—except—the thought occurs to (Matt) Smith, random and whimsical as the small yellow butterfly drifting past his head, that he has the power to make (Matthew) Smith laugh, even against his will—"What do an atheist and a dyslexic have in common?"

One of his father's jokes. The old man believed in laughter, joking—*Best cure for a broken heart is a broken funny bone.*

(Matthew) Smith furrows his brow. (Matthew) Smith twists his mouth. "'What do an atheist and a dyslexic have in common?'—how the hell should I know?"

5.

In a voice that signals *This is funny, prepare to laugh* (Matt) Smith asks (Matthew) Smith: "What do an atheist and a dyslexic have in common?"

(Matthew) Smith furrows his brow as if the question is profound, crucial.

"Staying up all night wondering if there's a God?"

(Matt) Smith laughs, indulgently. "No. You've got it reversed. 'Staying up all night wondering if there's a dog.'" Waits for (Matthew) Smith to laugh but (Matthew) Smith does not laugh, continues to look puzzled, vexed. "See, the joke is *dog* when people expect you to say *God*."

"But why would anyone expect you to say *God* in any case? Why is this funny? I always thought Dad's jokes were painfully unfunny."

"Dad's jokes were very funny. We all laughed."

"What do you mean, *we* all laughed? I didn't laugh."

"You did. I did."

"I did not laugh."

There is a pause. Both men are agitated, neither can bring himself to look at the other.

"Anyway, the old man is dead. *That* is incontestable."

(Matthew) Smith speaks with such bitterness, (Matt) Smith decides to let this pass. To him his father was *Dad*, to this unhappy person his father was *the old man*.

The one, blessed. The other, accursed.

"The one smart thing Mom did was leave. Just—pick up, pack her things, leave."

"When was this?"—(Matt) is shocked.

"When I was at San Jose State. Should've spent more time with her, helping her deal with him, but—I guess . . ." (Matthew) Smith shrugs, weakly.

"*My* mother is still alive. In a retirement village on Castille Avenue."

(Matt) Smith speaks hesitantly. (Is his mother still alive? She has been failing, steadily. Losing her memory, as his father had lost his. Must visit her soon, before it's too late.)

"*My* mother is still alive, too. I believe."

"When did you last see her?"—(Matt) Smith is skeptical.

"Not—for a while."

There is a pause. (Matt) Smith feels a quiver of righteousness, indignation.

"Our lives have swerved in different directions, it seems."

To this claim—flat, blunt, accusing yet wistful—(Matthew) Smith has no reply.

After a moment (Matthew) Smith clears his throat and says suddenly, reverently, as if he has just thought of it: "Thor."

"'Thor'—?"

"Our dog. Big, beautiful German shepherd . . ."

With a pang of grief (Matt) Smith recalls. Silver—("Silver" had been the family dog's name, not "Thor")—had been a German shepherd and husky mix, with a coat of myriad colors, intelligent eyes that could peer into a child's soul. Through (Matt) Smith's childhood Silver had been a constant companion, a protector.

"'Silver.' Yes . . ."

Stricken to the heart, remembering. A wave of love, loss, regret, pathos. That such a beautiful selfless creature suffused with love for him and for others should have passed from his life . . .

Has to confess, his heart was broken when Silver died. Recalling how Kizer had loved Silver, too, the two had wept together when the beautiful, aged dog died of kidney failure.

". . . never got over . . ."

". . . most beautiful, loving . . ."

". . . unconditionally loving . . ."

(Matt) Smith is deeply moved. His disgust, anger at (Matthew) Smith begins to fade. As if a window has been opened in some closed airless space he is thinking that Lisa must have had postpartum depression, not diagnosed at the time. Accusing him of coercing her into having children, three children in all, when he should have known she was psychologically fragile . . .

But (Matt) Smith had not known. *Had not.*

(Matthew) says, wiping at his eyes: "Kizer loved Thor, too. That's why I forgave him about Lisa. A part of me wanted to murder him but then I realized, I'd lose both my wife and my best friend. And by this time it was over between them, and Lisa had moved to Santa Monica. And Kizer and I have been closer than ever, since."

(Matt) Smith feels another pang of jealousy. But—no: why should he be jealous of (Matthew) Smith, whose marriage has ended in divorce? Who has not the consolation of children, in middle age? In old age, to come?

No. Not jealousy, pity. Sympathy.

(Matt) Smith touches the other's wrist, not knowing what he is doing. But the gesture seems correct, somehow.

Is their lunch ending? The men glance at their watches: 2:15 P.M. Kizer has never arrived.

Where is Kizer? Curiosity in their guts like something livid, living.

Their plates, half-eaten meals, are cleared away. Emptied Bloody Mary glasses, away. (Matt) Smith orders a cappuccino, and (Matthew) Smith orders coffee into which he will heap brown sugar, cream.

A warm, balmy June afternoon. Lavender wisteria in bloom, boxes of marigolds, nasturtiums, geraniums bordering the terrace café and the parking lot. Still the outdoor café is filled with diners, most of them women. (Matt) Smith glances about the terrace, oddly smiling. It's true, Kizer has failed to arrive. And yet . . .

In a lowered voice, as if he is speaking to (Matt) Smith conspiratorially, (Matthew) Smith says: "Remember thinking, as a kid, that the constellations are—insects?"

"The Big Dipper is the Big Praying Mantis. The Pleiades is a necklace delicate as lace—that is, lice."

(Matthew) Smith giggles. "Weevils, beetles, palmetto bugs—all over the sky."

Hours of nighttime scrutiny, years ago. Why has no one else ever noticed? Is humankind too cowardly to confront such knowledge?

Thoughtfully (Matt) Smith says: "We have to feel that there is a creator, and this creator created us in his image. We could not bear to think that the creator is a gigantic beetle."

Never has he articulated this thought so clearly. Not even to Kizer, when they spoke as they sometimes did of abstruse philosophical matters.

Like fitting the final piece of a jigsaw puzzle into place. Or—the penultimate piece.

(Matthew) Smith says, tapping at the magazine beneath his elbow as if it had become relevant in some way, "Darwin said: 'God must have loved beetles, He made so many of them.'"

"Did Darwin say that?"—(Matt) Smith feels a moment's resentment, that the less educated, less intelligent and less *civilized* Smith should know something that he does not.

As in an Expressionist film a shadow falls across the bright-lit table. Both men glance up, narrowing their eyes.

"Excuse me?"—at their table, looming above them, is a coarse-skinned, unkempt middle-aged man, a stranger. His face is ravaged, forehead and cheeks blotched, reddened with scar tissue. Is this a homeless person, a beggar, who has forced his way onto the terrace, pushing through the wisteria, bypassing the proper entrance? (Matt) Smith has been vaguely aware of the disheveled figure making its way across the terrace, rebuffed, ignored by most of the other diners; in another minute, one of the waiters will hurry to escort him from the Purple Onion Café, directed by the frowning hostess/manager. Perhaps the disheveled man comes here often, at this time of day, from the parking lot of the restaurant, hoping to garner a few dollars before he is discovered and made to leave; except now, he seems to have been drawn to (Matt) Smith and (Matthew) Smith specifically, staring at them with the frozen half-smile of a paralytic. His sand-colored, graying hair has nearly receded from his oblong head, except for greasy quills that fall about his face. He wears filth-stiffened mismatched clothes and gives off a pungent odor of unwashed, despondent flesh. Behind badly smudged eyeglasses his small glassy eyes wink in a fever of hectic excitement.

Excitedly telling (Matt) Smith and (Matthew) Smith that they look familiar to him. "D'you think we might be related?—my family used to live around here."

As if the coarse-skinned face is blindingly bright (Matt) Smith and (Matthew) Smith flinch from the unkempt man.

Quickly (Matt) Smith says, reaching for the check, "No. I don't think so."

"*I* don't think so," (Matthew) Smith says, hurriedly taking out his wallet. "And anyway, lunch is over."

6.

"Well!"

"Well."

"The son of a bitch never arrived."

It is 2:23 P.M. (Matt) Smith and (Matthew) Smith are about to leave the Purple Onion Café. Each man is exhausted, exhilarated. Each man is deeply moved, and confused as if he has been taken up and thrown into a spinning barrel.

Each is eager to escape the other, and never see him again.

(Matthew) Smith signals to (Matt) Smith with an ominous grunt: "Look."

"Oh, Jesus."

A disheveled, homeless man has appeared on the terrace of the Purple Onion Café among the chattering women diners who are doing their best to ignore him as he drifts past their tables, pauses to lean over them, an arthritic bird of prey begging for handouts. His face is ravaged. His oblong head is near-hairless, hard-looking with a gunmetal sheen. The skin of his hands and forearms appears jaundiced, like oil scum on water. His body is a sort of landslide or collapse, with thin arms, a thick torso, sagging belly. His small eyes twinkle with a kind of malicious merriment.

(Matthew) Smith whistles thinly through his big teeth.

"*He* didn't get the carcinomas treated in time, poor bastard."

(Matt) Smith and (Matthew) Smith observe the disheveled stranger as he makes his way toward them. Sights them, stares in disbelief, scratches at his neck. Curiosity like raw hunger in the ravaged face.

"Excuse me? Hey—d'you know me?"

"No . . ."

"N-No."

But the stranger is looking so yearning, neither (Matt) Smith nor (Matthew) Smith has the heart to send him away, and so he joins them at their table.

His name, it turns out, is—*Maynard.*

Last name—*Smith.*

(Matt) Smith and (Matthew) Smith have to laugh, this name is both preposterous and inevitable.

Reluctantly they introduce themselves to (Maynard) Smith— *(Matt) Smith, (Matthew) Smith.* There are no handshakes for neither (Matt) Smith nor (Matthew) Smith can bear to grasp (Maynard) Smith's (filthy) hand.

(Maynard) Smith appears disoriented like one who has journeyed a long distance. He tells the men that he is forty-nine years old, no family, no place to stay in San Rafael though he has a bed in a half-way house in San Francisco near the parole office.

Parole. They will inquire about *parole*, though not immediately.

(Matt) Smith asks (Maynard) Smith point-blank: Is he waiting for Kizer, too?

(Maynard) Smith recoils, baring his teeth. His voice is a guttural growl: "'Kizer'! Why would you ask about *him*?"

"Are you waiting for him? We were."

(Maynard) Smith looks from one man to the other. Disfigured face, sunken eyes. Broken and stained teeth. His nostrils are distended, enormous. His breath smells sepulchral. He stares at them as if there is some joke here he should grasp but can't, quite.

"You know that he—him—it's his—'death day' today—like a birthday except it's when you die . . ."

"'Death-day'? Kizer? Kizer is dead?"—(Matthew) Smith is disbelieving.

"'Anniversary' is the word. What I meant to say. Today—June ninth. I saw the date on a newspaper."

"But—Kizer is not . . ."

". . . not dead. He *is not*."

(Maynard) Smith appears to be hard of hearing, or in any case does not hear the others' protests or register their alarm. He tells them that it is his first day back in San Rafael in nineteen years, he'd been released from San Quentin just two days before. His laughter lacerates the ears, the very air, like gravel being roughly shoveled. Rubs his bloodshot eyes with his fists as if he'd like to gouge them out.

"He provoked me—fucking Kizer. It was Kizer or me. They called it 'second-degree murder' but I know better—*he* knew better. If I hadn't done what I did I'd be dead now. *He'd* be here." (Maynard) Smith pauses, drawing a deep tremulous breath. His small mean eyes glance about, seeking food, drink. But the table has been cleared except for the check, which neither (Matt) Smith nor (Matthew) Smith has touched.

"So I'm alone now, I have no friend, no family—nothing except my life." (Maynard) Smith enunciates *life* as one might enunciate *worm*.

(Matt) Smith and (Matthew) Smith glance at each other, trying to absorb what this apparition has told them.

Kizer is *dead*? Today, June 9, is Kizer's *death-day*?

Seeing that (Matt) Smith and (Matthew) Smith seem to be struck dumb (Maynard) Smith speaks harshly yet with a kind of grim satisfaction. His large, dark nostrils contract and expand as he breathes, his very being exudes an air of the grave. As he speaks he picks up a small cucumber slice, a small sprig of parsley, left behind on the tabletop by the careless waiter, and shoves them into his mouth.

"Fucking shadow over my life. Since we were boys. Everything I did has turned out wrong. Mark of Cain on my forehead. So many times I've explained, tried to explain. I didn't have the strength to save myself. *He* had to. That was our secret. I wasn't a strong swimmer. In fact, I was a poor swimmer. My arms had no muscle. My legs were skinny. I was panicked. I clung to the canoe, he had to pry my fingers from it. I was paralyzed . . . So many times I've explained, and no one will believe me. I wasn't the one who capsized the fucking canoe. *He* was."

BLUE GUIDE

1.

When at last the Professor retired from the university he made elaborate plans to revisit the cities of Europe which he'd first discovered as a young Fulbright scholar forty years before. Of the many cities in which he'd lived and undertaken research—which included Madrid, Barcelona, Toledo, Palermo, Rome—it was the medieval city of Mairead, in northern Italy, of which he'd dreamt most persistently; for it was in Mairead that he'd made the discovery that would be the centerpiece of his distinguished career as an historian and translator, in an obscure wing of the Mairead Museum of Antiquities.

And in the Professor's library of more than 20,000 books, among the very favorite books he kept close beside his desk was a tattered and dog-eared *Blue Guide to Northern Italy*, originally published in 1969. In this, the sixteen pages devoted to Mairead were particularly dog-eared and annotated in the Professor's small, precise handwriting, like murmurings of love. This, the Professor glanced into from time to time when his work was stalled or his spirits dashed.

For Mairead was both memory and promise—the repository of his youth, to which he would return one day.

+ + +

"Think of it as a second honeymoon."

The Professor appealed to his wife in that way of his that was both wistful and coercive. His department was making a retirement gift to him of two round-trip business-class tickets to any destination the Professor chose, for the Professor's colleagues knew of his great attachment to Mairead and his wish to return.

He'd had sabbaticals over the course of his academic career but these were usually for single terms, at a time when he couldn't get away from home easily—children in school, a wife with a career of her own. But now, each was retired. His wife was not so enthusiastic about traveling at this time, however, for she'd have liked to stay home with their grandchildren; particularly, she had little interest in traveling to a place in northern Italy in which the Professor had been young, before marriage, children, and grandchildren, about which she'd been hearing for much of their married life.

Still, the Professor persisted, reading to her from the *Blue Guide* of the University of Mairead which had been originally founded in 1390—one of the oldest universities in Europe; of the Basilica di Santo Clemente which was nearly as old; of the Royal Palace and Gardens of Mairead, the Royal Observatory and the Museum of Antiquities, the Promenade beside the magnificent Po River—until at last his wife laughed, and wiped at her eyes, and kissed the Professor's bewhiskered cheek telling him yes of course she would go with him—"I could hardly let you go alone."

The Professor would not have gone alone to Mairead, both knew this. For the days of the Professor traveling alone were over, which neither would have wished to acknowledge.

The journey began in the cacophonous John F. Kennedy Airport, on an overnight flight to Rome, from which the Professor and his wife would take another, smaller plane to Turin and a hired car to Mairead. On the flight across the Atlantic, the Professor could not sleep; instead, as others slept around him he remained awake making further notations in the *Blue Guide to Northern Italy*, planning trips into the mountainous countryside north of Mairead. In all, the Professor and his wife would be in Italy for three weeks, the most ambitious trip of their marriage of nearly forty years.

As dawn neared, the Professor gazed out the window beside his seat, waiting eagerly for the eastern sky to lighten. Though the philosopher David Hume argues persuasively that there is no inevitable reason for the sun to "rise" each morning yet the miracle will happen, independent of human reason or expectation. And how strange it was, being propelled swiftly eastward on the gigantic jet plane at thirty thousand feet! No one seemed to acknowledge the miracle, nor even to observe it. Those who'd wakened, including the Professor's wife, were concerned with other matters, namely the breakfast service which had just begun. The Professor's eyes stared at the horizon beyond the plane's wings—"Like peering into the future, into the maw of time itself." The Professor surprised himself, uttering these solemn words.

"But wouldn't it be the past?" the wife asked, leaning over to peer out the window beside the Professor, at the intensifying light that would soon become blinding. Of the couple, the wife was the practical-minded one. The Professor was drawn to abstractions, the wife to the literal and close at hand. Stubbornly the wife added, "Since it's the east, where the sun is rising."

But the Professor thought otherwise: "It's the future, since it's ahead of us."

"But it's later in Europe. Whatever time it is here on the plane, it's later—earlier—there. It's the past. We are the present."

"*We* are the present, of course. Ahead of us, in Europe, is the future into which we're traveling; behind us, in America, is the past from which we've come."

"No. I don't think so. If . . ."

The Professor was both bemused and exasperated by his wife, who insisted upon disagreeing with him in matters beyond her comprehension, often in company; a habit she'd cultivated as a young woman, as if to distinguish herself as more than merely an attractive young woman of no particular intellectual distinction. Though admittedly the wife was intelligent—among the wives of the Professor's colleagues, one of the most intelligent. She had mastered the domestic world of housekeeping, child-bearing and -rearing while the Professor had become a master of the metaphysical world; among his many award-winning translations were essays on the nature of time by Eco, Borges, Calvino. Whichever side the Professor espoused in an issue, the wife felt obliged to take the opposite side. Sometimes in the midst of their squabbles the wife lost interest abruptly and allowed the subject to fade.

A kind of lovemaking, the Professor supposed. For this, he felt grateful, obscurely flattered.

2.

The Professor had booked them into the Mairead Grand Palace, the most luxurious of the old hotels of Mairead, meriting three stars in the *Blue Guide*. But when they arrived in their hired car, the Professor was dismayed to discover that the elegant eighteenth-century granite facade of the hotel was obscured by ugly scaffolding and that the square in front of the hotel, once so beautifully kept, had a look now of neglect; grasses poked through cracks in the cobblestones, and bits of litter blew in the wind like antic thoughts. Attached to the hotel, it seemed, was a café with few customers, rain-lashed umbrellas above tables with rusted tops.

A family of squat, stout persons in summery tourist attire was descending the steps from the hotel entrance, spreading slowly out to take up most of the steps, like a kind of lava; the Professor and his wife were obliged to step aside, to let them pass. It wasn't clear which persons in the family were adults and which were children for the children were nearly the same size as the adults. Rudely and gleefully they laughed, and would have collided with the Professor if he hadn't quickly stepped aside, protecting his wife with an up-lifted arm—"Excuse me!" But the children snorted with laughter, surging past the Professor and his wife without seeming to see them. Nor did the heavyset adults, descending the steps with annoying slowness, seem to see them, chattering in a language not Italian, indeed no language the Professor could recognize.

The Professor's wife was shaken. She'd had a close look at the children—those brute, blank faces! She dreaded her grandchildren growing up and forgetting her. Between infancy and approximately age ten, children are adorable, and grateful to be fussed over by grandparents; beyond that, they become unpredictable, unknowable. The Professor's wife had a vision of their beloved grandchildren grown into brutes who pushed past their grandparents impatiently without a glance of recognition.

"Are you all right, dear? Take my arm."

"Of course I'm all right! Don't be ridiculous." But the wife took the Professor's arm, grateful to be comforted.

She was shivering, disoriented. Two plane flights had drained her of her customary energy and optimism. In the hired car the Professor had nodded off in sleep but she'd been awake every moment.

I will get through this, and I will bring him back home safely. I will bring gifts for everyone . . .

Checking into the Mairead Grand Palace the Professor was relieved to see that the interior had not greatly changed since his last visit. At least, at first glance it did not seem to have greatly changed. The Professor recalled an opulent foyer with a gold-gilt rotunda ceiling, wine-colored velvet chairs and settees, mahogany furnishings; a pristine marble floor, and a sparkling fountain with nymphs at its center; an elegant tearoom behind tall lush ferns and lacquered Japanese screens, where a string quartet played in the late afternoon and evening. Now, when he looked more closely, the Professor could see that the wine-colored chairs and settees were replicas of the originals, in coarser materials; the marble floor had been replaced with simulated marble, with a plastic sheen; the ferns were still lush, but artificial. The tearoom and the fountain had vanished. The ornate rotunda ceiling had vanished and in its place was a lowered ceiling out of which was piped, not the soothing classical music of Vivaldi, Brahms, Beethoven, but harsh pop-rock music.

"At least, they have our reservation," the Professor remarked cheerfully to his wife, who was pressing the palms of her hands against her ears with a distressed expression. "Our room will be quiet, I'm sure."

Indeed their room, on the eighth, top floor of the hotel, was quiet, with a stillness that seemed unnatural, as in a museum, or a mausoleum; a place where time has mercifully ceased. Both the Professor and his wife were very tired from their long journey but the Professor did not follow the wife to bed immediately; instead, he stood at a window gazing out, searching for landmarks in the darkening city.

At first he wasn't sure where he was, and what had become of the University, the Museum of Antiquities, the Royal Observatory— then he located the Basilica with its tall lighted cross, and the Royal Palace, which was also lighted; there, the shadowy river—the Po; and there, flickering lights along the Promenade. His eyes filled with tears. He would not have wanted his wife to see him in so emotional a state; of the two, it was the wife who was "emotional" and the husband who was "rational"; it would only confuse the wife if she saw him wiping at his eyes for no evident reason.

She is here, somewhere. Agustina!

Sweeping upon the Professor like a flood, the anguish and yearning of his old, lost life in Mairead. How as a young Fulbright scholar he'd journeyed to Italy, to fabled Mairead, knowing that his life would be irrevocably changed. How in the early mornings he'd bicycled to the Museum of Antiquities, where he'd been given a carrel in the Department of Special Collections in which to work; how grateful he'd been, entrusted with precious documents out of the Collection, to translate a twelfth-century Italian exegesis on Aristotle, later revised and refined into his first publication. The kindness of Ricardo Albano, Director of Special Collections, who'd invited him several times to lunch at an elegant restaurant near the University and one memorable evening to dinner in his beautiful old brownstone residence on the Viale di Pignoli, when he'd introduced the young American to his wife and daughter.

Agustina. A girl of sixteen, with whom he'd exchanged only murmured greetings at the time of their first—and only—meeting. How embarrassed the girl had been, to be introduced by her courtly father to the visiting American; a schoolgirl, in a school uniform, looking younger even than sixteen, with an olive-pale skin, dark evasive eyes, unusually thick brows.

How absurd. He did not believe in such a thing, really—*Love at first sight.*

Those many times after the Museum closed he'd drifted past the house on the *viale*. Telling himself that he was—only—going for a walk, to stretch his legs. Clear his head. Glancing up to see a face in an upstairs window of the distinguished old house—just the glimpse of a face, that sent shock waves through his body.

Sick with love: *lovesick*. Chiding himself—*But no. Absurd.*

Of course, it had been absurd. At twenty-four he was much too old for a schoolgirl of sixteen who'd looked (as he recalled) even younger. Proof of that absurdity was, in the years that followed, the Professor made no attempt to contact the daughter of Dr. Albano, nor even to determine what had become of her. Though he'd exchanged letters with Dr. Albano for many years he'd never dared ask personal questions. Then, fifteen years before this return to Mairead, their correspondence ceased. The Professor had not known why, and had not made inquiries. He'd reasoned that Dr. Albano had surely retired by that time. Very likely, the older man's health was impaired. Possibly, he was no longer living.

Though the Professor's wife had heard many accounts of the Professor's privileged time in Mairead as a Fulbright fellow, and knew the name Albano well, she'd never been told of her husband's infatuation with Dr. Albano's schoolgirl daughter. She'd never heard the name *Agustina*, nor was it likely that she ever would.

✦ ✦ ✦

Abruptly wakened by a sound of jackhammers in the square outside!— morning came with a jolt.

The Professor and his wife were obliged to rise earlier than they would have wished, for back home in the States it was not yet 2 A.M.

The Professor had adjusted his watch to the new time the previous day. The wife had not, yet.

The wife shuddered, for she'd had a dream of being cast adrift on a leaky barge, on a river; the worst of it was, she'd been alone, and it was one of the wife's unacknowledged terrors, being alone, and lost, in a foreign place without her husband. The Professor had had a similar dream, of being forced to lie down on his back in water, in a sort of lumpy bed over which cold water rippled in a ceaseless stream like an ingenious form of torture.

The Professor pointed out to his wife that some dreams are explicable as (mere) neurological twitches and twinges, of no more significance than optical illusions. A dream isn't *real* but its neurological processes might be said to be *actual*.

"'Real'—'actual'—what difference does it make, if you are helpless and frightened?"—the wife objected.

Her dreams had been brief, transient, startling visions—(indeed like water rippling over her brain)—from which she'd wakened in a state of panic. She was sure she'd been hearing the faint cries of a boatman. A tall lanky man with a pole, like a Venetian gondolier. The Professor laughed at this odd detail. He could depend upon his dear wife to come up with the most fanciful notions, to dispel tension. "But how romantic, my love! A Venetian gondolier in our hotel room!"

The wife winced at this remark, for the Professor was often condescending, as if she were a bright child not to be taken altogether seriously. She considered, but rejected, telling him that the most frightening part of her dreams was that she'd been alone, without him, in this foreign place.

"As long as you're with me, I can't be lost. So—don't leave my sight, please!"

Very winningly the wife smiled, as she'd learned to do, long ago.

The Professor squeezed the wife's fingers, to assure her.

Imagining the Albano residence on the Viale di Pignoli. A face of wraith-like beauty in a window, awaiting him.

+ + +

When they emerged from the Mairead Grand Palace bright sunshine washed away memories of the night. The café with the stained umbrellas was not yet open, and did not look so derelict as it had the previous night; vendors had not yet opened their stalls, and tourists were not milling about; the cobblestone square glistened as if there'd been a storm in the night.

A short block from the hotel the Promenade was virtually deserted but the river sparkled with light.

By early evening, the Professor said, half the city of Mairead would be strolling along the river. Couples, families, friends walking arm in arm like lovers . . . Forty years ago he'd ached with loneliness. His desire for the schoolgirl daughter of his revered mentor, of which he'd been ashamed. (Though not a soul had known of it, at the time or in subsequent years.) Walking along the Promenade the Professor began to speak avidly, excitedly. His wife saw how he was stroking his whiskered jaws and how his eyes glanced restlessly about, as if seeking a familiar face.

Unlike the Professor the wife knew no foreign languages. It was all she could do to recognize a few Italian phrases and to make herself understood—barely—in carefully enunciated English. She was feeling subdued, slightly dazed. It wasn't like her to cling to the Professor's arm as if she feared him drifting away from her. His excitement was jarring to her for it excluded her. Did he have some particular, secret reason for his excitement? What was he expecting, in Mairead? The city did not seem so beautiful to the Professor's wife as the Professor had described it.

He is looking for——who? Someone.

Everywhere she looked were very old walls that were cracked and crumbling and defaced with graffiti in lurid colors. Simply to see such signs of vandalism registered as a shock, like a shout in the face. Here and there along the Promenade were patches of thistles that had broken through the cracked pavement; jungle-like vines growing like sinewy snakes over walls and railings, some of the vines desiccated and broken. You could see, on the walls, the areas where vines had once been growing and had fallen away, skeletal imprints like outstretched imploring fingers.

Blue Guide in hand, the Professor often came to a dead stop to consult it. The wife tried not to become impatient with these frequent starts and stops. She could see that pages of the *Blue Guide* were annotated in the Professor's handwriting but many of the notations were faded. Also, the Professor was often baffled by discrepancies between the guidebook and the city itself. How embarrassing, his habit of stopping strangers to make inquiries, tapping a forefinger on the map in the book—"The War Memorial is supposed to be here, exactly where we are. But it isn't here. D'you know where it is?"

Strangers whom the Professor accosted in this way usually tried to assist him, though it wasn't clear (to the wife) that they understood him. She wondered if her husband's command of idiomatic Italian, of which he'd long been proud, had deteriorated in the years since he'd used it.

"Maybe you should speak English to them. That might be easier."

"Obviously not! These are Italians, they speak *Italian*."

"Some of them speak English. . . ."

"No. Not most of them. Not in Mairead."

At breakfast in the hotel the Professor had planned a walk along the Promenade that would lead them to one of the historic parts of the city, to the University, the Museum of Antiquities, and eventually to the elegant Viale di Pignoli. But after just a few minutes it was clear that Mairead was no longer a prosperous city: abandoned buildings lined much of the Promenade, as well as boathouses covered in graffiti and boat ramps no longer in use; of the numerous restaurants and cafés listed in the *Blue Guide* only a few remained, and these were not open. The Professor was eager to have lunch at a two-star Michelin restaurant near the Museum of Antiquities, to which Dr. Albano had once taken him; but *Ripetta*, it seemed, no longer existed unless (as the Professor suspected) it had passed into new ownership, and a new name . . .

They were crossing wide, windswept *piazzas* with ornate, but no longer functioning, fountains at their centers, leaf-choked and abandoned. Tall weeds and thistles grew brazenly at the edges of cracked and uneven paving stones. Even tall trees were denuded of leaves, as if autumn had come early. Yet, the Professor was determined to seek out landmarks in the guidebook which he'd marked back in his study at home: the Royal Armory, squares dominated by military/ heroic statuary—lions, eagles, elephants, generals on fiercely grimacing horses, brandishing swords. Another stroll along the Po River where (the Professor recalled) there'd been canoes for rent as well as privately owned sailboats, yachts, motorboats—now much diminished. And there—was that the Avenue of the Apostles?—or had they taken a wrong turn . . .

As the Professor spoke to the wife, or read to her from the guidebook, the wife listened only intermittently, as she had long accustomed herself to listening to only a portion of the Professor's pronouncements. For frequently her husband gave the impression of talking to himself, rehearsing piquant phrases, or thinking out loud; he wanted his wife beside him, for he required an audience, yet he did not really want her to respond to his remarks, and certainly he did not want her to interrupt with questions or comments. Frowning and squinting, stroking his bristling whiskers, the Professor seemed to the wife both pompous and endearing; often she was suffused with love for him, a sensation that could sweep upon her without warning; then, a few minutes later, when the Professor accosted a passerby to ask for directions, not seeming to notice how the passerby was confused by his Italian, she felt exasperation for him. Fiercely protective of her husband yet highly critical of him, intrigued by him yet (sometimes) frankly annoyed by him—the wife knew no one else for whom she felt such conflicting emotions.

Of course—I love him. That will never change.

Back home, in their university community, the Professor had acquired a reputation for eccentricity that wasn't entirely deserved, the wife thought.

His colleagues and graduate students admired him as the most distinguished member of his department even as they regarded him with a measure of (affectionate) bemusement, indulgence. Particularly the younger faculty members noted that the Professor was at times rather absentminded; he muddled their names, and seemed not to hear what they were saying to him so earnestly, to make an impression upon him. He was courteous to the young women in the department without (it seemed) taking them quite so seriously as he took the men. Yet, the Professor was a fount of scholarly knowledge and wisdom; he seemed to know everything in his field, at least up to ten or fifteen years ago, and he could recite long passages from seminal texts in the original languages. He was tireless in his efforts to help their careers—his letters of recommendation were known to be masterpieces of generosity, erudition. It was amusing to observers that the Professor wore, in winter, a wooly black

Astrakhan hat; coarse gray woolen socks with sandals; tweed sport coats with leather elbow patches. He was not handsome but rather what one would call "striking"—"Magisterial." His hair was still abundant, faded to silver-white; his eyebrows were wiry and grizzled and would have obscured his vision if the vigilant wife did not keep them trimmed as she kept trimmed her husband's mustache and whiskers and the more delicate hairs of the Professor's ears and nostrils, with a miniature scissors.

Ridiculous to fuss over his appearance, the Professor complained, embarrassed; but the wife insisted for she could not bear anyone laughing at her dear husband, unless it was herself.

3.

Following lunch (not at Ripetta, which seemed indeed to have vanished), the Professor suffered a rude jolt: the historic district of Mairead, parts of which dated to the eleventh century, had been much altered. Entire blocks of distinguished old buildings (including the southern edge of the university campus) had been razed, replaced by ugly, utilitarian buildings in the raw-cement Brutalist style as well as the most egregious of urban eyesores—multi-level parking garages. At the site of the Royal Observatory, to which the *Blue Guide* had given two stars, and which the Professor remembered distinctly, was a ragged soccer field upon which schoolboys in uniforms ran shrieking as hyenas. The Basilica di Santo Clemente, Mairead's most notable landmark, was not where the map in the guidebook indicated, adjacent to the *Casa di Russie* and its elegant grounds, but several blocks away in a bustling commercial area. And then, to their disappointment, despite the steep admission price, eight euros, only a part of the Basilica was open to visitors, and this part did not contain the great works of art by Bernini and Michelangelo which the Professor had looked forward to seeing for the first time in forty years, and which had lingered in his memory like a potent dream.

In the interior of the great church, in the still stony air, the Professor's wife shivered. She was accustomed to churches on a far smaller scale—New England rural Protestant churches, the most elemental of wood-frame architecture. Here in the Basilica di Santo Clemente, whose pre-Christian foundation had been a ninth-century pagan temple allegedly dedicated to Hera, the scale was distorting, vertiginous. You were supposed to feel important, as if your soul mattered to God, or indeed as if you possessed a soul; but in such a vast space you felt nothing at all, like a frail bubble floating on a turbulent sea. And uncanny to the Professor's wife, disorienting, to feel a compulsion to crane her neck, to stare high overhead at vividly colored stained-glass figures—human, angelic—like gigantic predatory creatures poised to swoop down upon the kneeling worshippers.

In which direction, the wife wondered, were you supposed to *pray*? Or were you supposed to shut your eyes, and *pray* within?

At a side altar at which a few small chubby wax candles had been lit was a primitive wooden cross of about five feet in height upon which the ghastly sculpted figure of Christ, near death, or indeed dead, was suspended by alarmingly realistic-looking spikes through his hands and feet. Red varnish shone like fresh blood. This was *Jesus*—the *Christ* in a transport of agony, before the triumph of His resurrection.

"I don't really enjoy crucifixions"—the wife complained in a lowered voice to her husband.

The Professor laughed. There could be no other rejoinder to such a remark though with a black lace shawl draped over her hair, a veil of Catholic modesty, the wife might have passed for an authentic churchgoer.

"I mean—suffering and death should be *private*. At least, that's how I feel."

The Professor kissed the wife's cheek. What other response, to so practical and female an observation?

For five euros more, visitors could explore the Basilica's cloister, which the Professor recalled as a serenely beautiful place with a grassy interior; but the serenity was sabotaged today by the loud voices of workmen repairing damages.

"Oh, why must they talk so *loudly*!"—the wife lamented, pressing her hands over her ears.

And so, they could not remain long. The Professor vowed to return by himself, to meditate in the cloister as he'd done years ago.

It came to him now: he'd met Agustina in the cloister. He'd dared to take her hand, he'd lifted her hand and kissed the palm, which had made her squirm and giggle, like a child—indeed, he could see close up that Agustina was a child . . . But no. That had never happened.

Of course, nothing remotely like that had ever happened. In the cloister he'd fantasized shamelessly of Dr. Albano's daughter but Agustina had never met him there, or anywhere in Mairead.

"Please! I can't stand it here. It's so noisy, those terrible men are laughing at us."

The workmen were not laughing at them, surely. Scarcely aware of them, an American couple, tourists. If the workmen glanced toward them, their eyes moved through them as if they were wraiths.

Back again on the noisy street the Professor realized he'd forgotten to say a prayer in the cloister. The great Basilica rendered irrelevant matters of mere belief or disbelief. *Thank you, God! Or—is it Jesus?* A sensation of buoyancy filled him. Years ago as a young man on the threshold of his life he'd often come to the cloister with a book, to read in the still, sacred space all the more precious because it was not anything of *his*—he wasn't Catholic, and he wasn't Italian, he was but a visitor to this magical world, where even skepticism dissolved like wetted tissue.

The Basilica had drained the couple of energy, even in its diminished state, badly they wanted to return to the Mairead Grand Palace to take a nap, as they would never have done at home in Ardmore, Pennsylvania; but the Professor would not hear of it, succumbing to such weakness at such a time of day as if he were an elderly man, as surely he was not. And so, the couple merely stopped for cappuccinos at a sidewalk café, so that the Professor could consult the *Blue Guide* another time. After some deliberation he devised a complicated "scenic" route to the University, that turned out not to be scenic at all but to involve crossing streets made treacherous by a continuous stream of vehicles of all sizes, from motorbikes to buses belching exhaust, and brought them to an open-air market at which only a few vendors' stalls were set up, selling cheap-looking souvenirs, handicrafts, and wilting vegetables and flowers. Here, the Professor could not comprehend what was shouted cajolingly at him; if the language was Italian, it was an Italian dialect new and alien to his ears, as the individuals who spoke it were new and alien to his eyes, dark-olive-skinned persons with blunt, sensuous faces, seemingly not ethnic Italians.

"Why on earth are we *here*?"—the wife asked, vexed.

"Because the *Blue Guide* has brought us here. The market is one of the 'essential' points of interest."

The wife was staring at stacks of small cages inside which bright-feathered birds cheeped in continuous terror, and at larger cages in which dull-feathered chickens scarcely moved, resigned to their fate. There came a blood-chilling squeal—a pig? Piglet? The wife swallowed hard, shut her eyes and turned away. A smell of animal panic, pungent, excremental, made her sensitive nostrils pinch.

"Ah!—this was once a place of execution," the Professor said, squinting at the guidebook, "—all of this open square. 'Preferred means of execution were hanging, drawing and quartering, decapitation' . . ."

The wife glanced down at the ground, alarmed. Cracked pavement, not blood-soaked earth. She was spared having to see.

"How recent were executions in Mairead?" the wife asked, supposing the Professor would say *Not for hundreds of years* but instead the Professor said, reading from the *Blue Guide*: "Nineteen forty-three—winter—'Fascist reprisals against the Mairead Resistance'—hanging, firing squad." He paused, then continued: "'The youngest executed were children of eleven, twelve . . .'"

"Oh, stop! Were these Italians who did the killings, or Germans?"

"Possibly—Germans. But maybe not . . ."

"Italy turned against the Nazis, eventually—didn't it?" The wife spoke hesitantly for she dreaded the Professor smiling at her with his superior knowledge. "The Italians were never really—like the Germans—a brutal and barbaric people—anti-Semites . . ."

The Professor was distracted by something he'd discovered in the *Blue Guide*.

"Damn! I see what we've done wrong. At the *Via di Monti*, back there, we should have turned left . . ."

After another twenty minutes of walking (steeply uphill) they reached the stately medieval arch that marked the front entrance of the University of Mairead—only to discover that the main campus was closed to visitors following a *bombardamento terroristico* the previous week. "'Terrorist bombing'! I had no idea . . ." The Professor was astonished. (Why had no one warned him? The airline with whom he'd booked tickets? The hotel? Why hadn't he seen a news report?) Yet, clearly something terrible had happened: they could see a part-collapsed building, heaps of rubble, a devastated tree.

The Professor's wife pressed a tissue against her nose and mouth. Oh, what was that *smell*! Something dry, acidic—scorched hair? Burnt clothing, bones? Terrible.

Seven persons had been killed in the bombing and many more wounded, the Professor learned from questioning a passer-by.

And were the terrorists apprehended?—the Professor asked.

And who were the terrorists?

The young man, seemingly a university student, burdened with a heavy backpack, having grudgingly removed iPods from his ears, was not very forthcoming or friendly—unlike students the Professor had known as a Fulbright scholar.

That is not for us to know at this time—the young man muttered. Almost rudely he pushed past the Professor in his eagerness to escape.

"What did he say? Could you make it out?"

"Yes. But—no. I'm not sure."

"Was he speaking Italian?"

"I think so—yes."

"You *think so*?"

Since the Atlantic flight words seemed to be gliding by the Professor even when he tried to concentrate on them. Water rippling over his brain, paralyzing.

"Maybe he thought you were a journalist. An American . . ."

"*I spoke Italian to him as an Italian would have spoken to him.* Please let's drop this subject."

The wife knew herself rebuked. Very well, then—she would say nothing more for the remainder of the afternoon. Let the Professor talk to himself which was what he most enjoyed.

Still, the Professor's hope was to visit the Museum of Antiquities.

The major impediment was the blocked-off campus: when the Professor tried to make his way on alternative paths he soon became lost, in cul-de-sacs behind buildings. After forty minutes the couple was no closer to the Museum than they'd been at the start, so far as the Professor could judge.

Why didn't they return in the morning, the wife suggested, trying to remain patient. "You're becoming overheated. It isn't good for you to be excitable."

"My dear, *I am not excitable.* I am 'excited'—in a perfectly appropriate way."

The Professor walked on ahead. The wife could follow him, or not—as she wished. He was very vexed with her.

All this day the Professor had been feeling sentimental, soft at the core as an overripe melon. Stick him with a knife blade, he thought, his soft boneless interior would leak out like sticky fluid.

Badly he wanted to return to the main reading room of the Museum—to see if some of the (women) librarians he remembered, who'd been so gracious to a young visiting American, were still there. Badly he wanted to return to his carrel in the interior of the library where he'd spent many enthralling hours reading and translating precious manuscripts as if delving into the mystery of his own soul.

Of course, he wanted most badly to return to the *Viale di Pignoli* where Dr. Albano and his family lived, or had lived, in a dignified old brownstone facing a small park. He'd explained to his wife that he had lost contact with Dr. Albano but might, if he could summon up his courage, ring Dr. Albano's doorbell. "The worst that could happen would be that the Albanos no longer live here."

"'The worst'? No. I can think of 'worst.'"

"What do you mean, dear? Please don't be inscrutable this morning, you know how much Mairead means to me."

The Professor spoke wistfully yet with an air of vexation. The

wife relented at once: "I wasn't being inscrutable. I meant only—
'the worst' could be that the Albanos are home, and are very elderly
and ill. And wouldn't remember you. *That* would be the worst."

The Professor laughed, though what the wife said wasn't funny.
He had thought exactly the same thoughts more than once in the
weeks preceding the trip.

Of course the Professor knew it was improbable that Agustina
would still be living in her father's house after forty years—it would
be likely a catastrophe, if she were.

A middle-aged woman, the schoolgirl Agustina? Not possible!

He could not imagine this. The slender waist, the small but distinct breasts, the exquisite face, dark-lashed evasive eyes . . . If he
shut his eyes he saw, with a stab of excitement, the girl's beautiful
eyes staring at *him*.

Dark eyes, yet exuding a tawny glow, in certain lights. In candle-
light. At the dinner table.

The Professor's wife knew nothing of Agustina. The Professor rejoiced in all the secrets he'd managed to keep from the woman, most
of them small, negligible, yet precious to him, like small coins in his
pockets which, when he wished, he would sift through his fingers.

Still, this was Italy. Northern Italy. Not far from the Swiss border. He'd been noticing very attractive women here in Mairead—
middle-aged, even elderly. These were affluent women, well-groomed,
well-mannered. Venturing on the street they wore stylish clothes, high-
heeled shoes. Their eyes were protected from the bright sunlight by
dark-tinted designer glasses that exuded an air of glamour. Agustina
would have grown into one of these women, the Professor was sure.

Women of other (ethnic) backgrounds did not seem to mature so
attractively, the Professor thought. Catching his eye since he'd come
to Mairead, to his displeasure, like bits of grit.

Like the short squat individuals descending the stone steps of the

Mairead Grand Palace the other day. The Professor had glimpsed them on the Promenade, and he was sure he'd seen them in the Basilica, fortunately at a distance. Where had these others come from? So many of them? Were they guest-workers? Refugees? Northern Africa? Syria? Though they appeared to be tourists, not workers. Though crudely dressed, with no taste, they did not wear work clothes but clothes of leisure. The Professor valued authentic Italian beauty very highly even when he wasn't sure he could define it.

And here was another jarring surprise: the Viale di Pignoli was no longer a beautiful avenue lined with pine trees; most of the stately old trees had been removed, and the once-dignified old houses had become shabby. The Professor recalled lush gardens and carefully tended lawns, but these too had vanished. The park had vanished. Graffiti defaced walls, lampposts. To his chagrin the Professor was not even sure which house belonged to the Albanos for the houses he saw exuded a dispiriting sameness: weatherworn brownstone facades, narrow latticed windows that emitted a grudging light, tiled roofs that looked as if they might leak.

"I—I think this is their house. Here."

The Professor's heart was beating absurdly. *Oh, ridiculous! You are a grandfather. That part of your life is long over.*

"Well, go on, then—ring the bell. What are you waiting for?"

The Professor's wife was resigned to the Professor being disappointed and thought it wisest to get the disappointment over with so that they could hike to the next landmark designated as *not to be missed* in the damned guidebook.

The Professor stood hesitantly before the door of the house. It was painted a dark, agate hue, which the Professor believed he remembered. Yet, he could not bring himself to ring the doorbell. As the wife waited patiently he stood in a kind of paralysis, beginning to sweat as if he'd devoured too much meat at midday.

"Do you want me to ring it?"—for once, the wife spoke gently.

"No. Of course not."

Boldly then, steeling himself, the Professor pressed the doorbell. It wasn't clear that there was any sound within. In any case there was no response.

Another time the Professor pressed the doorbell, and another— no response. Perspiration shone on his lined forehead. He was limp with relief.

"Ah! Look." The wife was peering through a rusted wrought-iron fence overgrown with ivy, beside the front walk. Here was a garden gone wild—a tumult of shrubs, grasses, vines. Once, Mrs. Albano had grown roses here, the Professor was sure; scattered amid the jungle of vegetation were crimson, yellow, white roses in ragged clusters. There were snake-like vines, that seemed almost to be writhing. In the lower branches of straggly trees were raven-like birds with iridescent, slate-colored feathers, acid-bright eyes, long, sharp beaks like ice picks. As the couple peered into the garden the guardian-birds made belligerent shrugging motions with their large wings and emitted hoarse cries of indignation, alarm.

"Maybe this explains it: no one lives here any longer."

When the Professor did not reply the wife added, practicably: "If you go to the Museum tomorrow, you can ask about Dr. Albano. If he isn't there, they can put you in touch with him. If—"

If he's alive. The wife fell silent, the Professor again made no reply.

As the raven-like birds continued to scold out of the trees in the garden, the couple turned away. The Professor closed up the *Blue Guide* for now and shoved it into his pocket.

Though he tried to keep up an air of lighthearted conversation with the wife, the Professor was feeling a sick sort of dread. For— what would he do, now? Had he not journeyed all the way to the medieval city of Mairead to seek out Agustina? While acknowledging the utter absurdity of the quest he had to concede that he'd come these thousands of miles, he'd fantasized how many thousands of times in the past forty years, to catch a glimpse of the wraith-like face at a second-floor window of a house that turned out to be abandoned.

4.

"It's hopelessly out-of-date. I wish you'd buy a new guidebook, and get rid of that damned thing."

"It is not *out-of-date*. No other guidebooks have so much schol-arly information. And my notes are in this copy."

"Your notes! Can you even read that scribbling?"

"Of course I can read this 'scribbling.' It's crystal-clear to me."

The wife had noticed, her husband had begun to scrawl an inde-cipherable signature on checks, credit card receipts. Surely no one could read such a scrawl, that was hardly more than a defiant wavy line, though shopkeepers and waiters had no choice but to honor it.

Next morning after breakfast the Professor and his wife set out another time for the Museum of Antiquities. The wife had insisted that the Professor consult a tourist map provided by the hotel, as well as his beloved *Blue Guide*, and as a consequence the couple found the Museum within a reasonable amount of time though, even with the hotel map, it was farther away than it should have been, in a part of the historic district the Professor didn't recall.

But then it turned out, to their surprise, that the landmark they were approaching wasn't—yet—the Museum of Antiquities but the Royal Garden, which they'd intended to visit after the Museum. Somehow, the two had been reversed on both maps. The wife would have liked her husband to pretend that he'd meant to guide them to the Royal Garden first, and not the Museum of Antiquities, but the Professor merely laughed and conceded yes, he might have taken a wrong turn somewhere—"But it doesn't matter, dear. The Royal Garden is one of the starred tourist sites."

The entrance to the Royal Garden was some distance ahead—a quarter mile at least. Signs covered in graffiti led them along a high wrought-iron fence into an area of the park that was untended, littered. (Indeed, there was a surprising amount of litter in Mairead, which the Professor did not recall from forty years before.) Finally the signs led them to a twelve-foot wrought-iron gate that was not only shut but padlocked. More than just padlocked, the gate had sunk inches into the soil as if it had not been opened in years. Thistles grew abundantly around it.

The Professor's wife gave a little cry of disappointment. "Oh, we've walked so far! The sun is so hot . . . Is there another entrance?"

The Professor consulted the *Blue Guide*. According to which, this was the correct entrance, indeed the only entrance to the Royal Garden.

"I'm afraid not. The signs have led us here."

"Hello? Is anyone inside?"—the wife peered through the gate, shading her eyes against the bright sunshine.

There was no one, evidently. No ticket sellers, no guards. No other visitors.

They would have to content themselves with walking along the tall fence, peering into the garden as best they could. Clearly, the Royal Garden was one of the wonders of Mairead, or had once been one of the wonders. Constructed upon the model, if not the scale, of the great garden of the imperial Roman Forum, this garden had been allowed to grow wild and was overgrown now with a riot of flowers, vividly colored, unusually large, the size of automobile hubcaps. Enormous red multifoliate roses grew in lavish abandon as in a

Fauve painting. Some of the larger plants and shrubs were strangely asymmetrical. Pignoli trees, the most distinctive trees of the region, appeared to be misshapen, stunted. And there, amid weeds, some of the Roman statuary that had once been displayed in the city's historic district. (At least the Professor supposed that these were the original marble statues in their natural state of decay, and not merely copies, though a number had toppled over and were virtually lost amid the jungle of vegetation.)

The wife gave a scream of terror, seeing a white, fallen body, headless, its muscled torso turned toward her and the Professor as in a spasm of agony.

"What is it? What is it? Oh my God—what is it?"

Could the wife not see that the object was a statue?—white marble, if badly weatherworn? Headless, like so much statuary of ancient Rome.

"Darling, don't be frightened! It's just a statue."

"A statue . . . But why? Why there?"

The Professor squeezed the wife's hand, which was cold.

"I suppose they have forgotten it," the Professor said, humbly.

In his seminars, in his lectures, in his consultations with graduate students the Professor was calm and measured in his knowledge, and indeed he seemed to know everything there was to know in his field. In Mairead, he was coming to see that he knew very little; and what he believed he'd known was possibly an illusion.

Adding now, seeing that the wife was staring at him in dismay, "I mean—Time has forgotten it. All of the statues here, that seem priceless to us—Time has forgotten."

"What do you mean—'Time has forgotten'? 'Time' isn't a person— 'Time' can't *forget*. Stop talking like that, it frightens me."

"*You* frighten me, so literal-minded. *You* stop."

The quarrel followed the couple back to the historic district, like a plague of harpies.

The wife wanted to return to the hotel for a rest. The Professor wanted to persevere, for his main goal of the day was the Museum of Antiquities.

"I could go alone, dear. You can return to the hotel."

"You are not going anywhere alone! No." The wife panicked, clutching at the Professor's arm.

Several times the Professor consulted the *Blue Guide*, to bring them back in the right direction. The simpler, cruder, more easily accessible map from the hotel seemed to have been lost, for neither the Professor nor the wife could find it in their pockets.

"You had it last. I saw it in your hand."

"*You* had it last. You lost it on purpose."

"Why 'on purpose'?"

"Because you resent it, not being the damned *Blue Guide*."

They walked on, in resentful silence. For many minutes the quarrel-harpies followed them.

Wistfully the Professor said: "I wonder if I've made a mistake. I've waited too long to make this trip."

Quickly the wife said: "Don't be ridiculous! Of course you haven't 'made a mistake.' When is the last time you've 'made a mistake'?" She laughed. She wiped at her eyes, and laughed, and clutched his arm tight enough to hurt.

5.

In an open square near the Museum were vendors' stalls. The area was much more congested than the Professor recalled. Street musicians, beggars. Scantily dressed young women with crudely made-up, sensual faces. Mimes, with white clown-faces, red wide lips. University students appeared to be a minority here, and many of these were also dark-skinned, not evidently ethnic Italians. As the Professor and his wife approached the Museum the wife cried, "There they are again! The brute children."

Just ahead was the family of short squat persons they'd seen descending the steps of the Mairead Grand Palace on their first night in Mairead. The Professor had caught a glimpse of these creatures (they did not seem fully human to him) on the Promenade and even in the Basilica the previous day, but had not spoken of them to the wife and hoped she hadn't seen them. (In fact, in the Basilica the wife had seen several of the creatures [they did not seem fully human to her] at a distance, females who'd somehow gained entry to the church bare-headed, bare-armed, wearing shorts that fit their fleshy bodies tightly, as female visitors were forbidden to do; the wife, obeying rules clearly posted at the ticket kiosk and noted in the guidebook, wore a black lace shawl over her head, brought in her suitcase for this purpose, as well as a skirt that fell below her knees, and a shirt with long sleeves. She was deeply resentful of those ignorant tourists who'd violated the rules.)

Adults, adolescents, children? You could hardly tell them apart. Blank, brute faces, vacuous eyes that turned sneering in an instant. "But they aren't 'children'—are they?"

The wife was trying not to stare. *She* was a polite, civilized person— *she* did not stare at strangers no matter how crass.

But it was so, the children were large and ungainly, like dwarves grown to an unusual size. You could only tell the children from the adults by their behavior: the children ran, jostled one another, gibbered like monkeys. The adults moved stiffly, as if their brains and their limbs were ill-coordinated. Their mouths seemed oddly hinged in their lower faces, like the mouths of ventriloquists' dummies. And what coarse language were they speaking? Harsh consonants, grunts. Not melodic fluid Italian. Not Spanish, and certainly not French. Whatever admonitions the adults shouted at the children, the children ignored them. The children's cries were loud, joyous. These were the sounds wrestlers might make, the Professor thought, as they struggled to slam their adversaries to the floor and break their backs.

"Come! Let's go into the Museum. They won't follow us . . ."

As soon as he stepped into the Museum the Professor felt a swoon of nostalgia. Ah, the beautiful faded mosaic ceiling!—he remembered. A glass display case of ancient Greek artifacts. A spiral staircase leading down—a staircase he'd taken many a time. (His carrel had been on the ground floor of the Museum, a shadowy place in which young scholars from foreign countries had found themselves in a congenial little community of outcasts.) When the Professor identified himself (in Italian) to a receptionist as a former Fulbright scholar who'd once worked with Dr. Ricardo Albano, and asked if Dr. Albano was still head of Special Collections, the woman told him with a broad smile yes, Dr. Albano was at the top of the stairs, in his place . . . The Professor wasn't sure what the receptionist meant by this odd usage but as he and his wife ascended the creaking stairs he was astonished to see, on the first-floor landing, Dr. Albano waiting as if he'd been expecting them. The distinguished scholar stood smiling and poised with his right hand extended as one might pose in expectation of greeting a friend.

Almost, you could hear Albano's warm, welcoming voice—*Ciao come stai mio caro amico!*

Ricardo Albano was shorter than the Professor recalled, by several inches; he'd lost weight, considerably, though the dignified gentleman wore, as always, a dark three-button suit with a vest, white

cotton shirt and gold cuff links. His once-handsome face had become deeply creased, his once-abundant black hair had thinned and
grayed. Thick-lensed glasses reflecting light from a nearby window
obscured his kindly eyes.

"Dr. Albano! This is a—this is so—"

Breathless from the stairs the Professor held out his hand in greeting. Seeing then that there was something wrong with the man's
face: his demeanor was congenial, patient; his smile was familiar;
but his eyes were not focused upon the Professor's face. Instead, he
was gazing affably over the Professor's shoulder into a corner of the
ceiling.

"But, Dr. Albano—what is wrong?"

The Professor shrank away in shock and revulsion. What had he
touched? What was this hand?—could it be *wax*? *Ricardo Albano*
was not a living human being but a mannequin of some sort, de-
ceptively lifelike at a distance but up close, obviously only a replica
of a man.

"Oh, God! He—it isn't—real," the wife stammered, "—it's something like a dummy. Look at the eyes . . ."

"But—this is impossible . . . Why would anyone do such a
thing . . ."

Other tourists did not regard the lifelike figure on the landing
labeled DR. RICARDO ALBANO as revolting or alarming, nor indeed
as a figure of esteem, but rather as a novelty to be photographed.
They crowded past the Professor and his wife exclaiming in delight.
No idea who *Ricardo Albano* was but eager to take his photograph. A
group of young Asian students posed with the figure, taking selfies
on iPhones.

Several seconds were required for the stunned Professor to absorb
this information. With a part of his mind he could see that his former
mentor stood before him transformed as a clever replicant, not as a

living being; with another part of his mind he yearned to believe that this was indeed his mentor, waiting for him in the Museum, sure to invite him and his wife to dinner. The face was disconcertingly realistic, as if it had been treated with an embalming chemical. The cheeks were artificially plump, which gave the face a youthful air, though the eyes behind the reflective lenses were glassy—indeed, glass.

On a brass wall plaque the Professor and his wife read that the figure was not a sculpture but the actual "mummified" body of the longtime head of the Special Collections of the Museum of Antiquity of the University of Mairead, Ricardo Albano. The "mummification" by a renowned Italian artist had been commissioned to commemorate one of the university's greatest scholars.

The wife laughed, saying that the figure was very lifelike, but had not fooled *her*.

The Professor laughed, shakily. He could not deny it—he'd been deceived by the figure. The hesitant, so-realistic way in which the mummified Albano stood on the landing, one hand slightly extended; the courteous smile, that was both welcoming and unassuming; the kindly eyes, with their glassy glint. But how horrible, the *actual body* of the deceased man had been transformed into a mannequin, positioned in this public place. Why had the Albano family given permission for such a spectacle? Had Albano himself given permission, before his death?

Curious tourists continued to ascend the stairs, to exclaim and take pictures on the landing. Only a few climbed to the second floor to view the Museum's permanent exhibit of ancient Greek and Roman artifacts. Very few troubled to read the plaque, that listed Ricardo Albano's achievements and awards. And now the Professor was feeling light-headed, and had not the strength to continue.

Fortunately, his wife made the decision for them: "No more for today. *Basta.*"

As they descended the stairs, gripping the railing, more tourists were making their way up. The Professor did not want to think that his old, revered mentor was a money-making property for the University; for, to gain entrance to the Museum, you had to pay five euros.

A lurid spectacle, the Professor thought. He hoped his university would not do the same for him when he died.

+ + +

Next morning the Professor realized that he'd left the Museum so eagerly he'd forgotten to visit his old carrel on the ground floor, in a remote wing of the Museum.

Another time, he thought. Just not now.

6.

"Here—the 'Royal Aquarium.'"

"Oh! What is that smell . . ."

In the dank interior of the Aquarium immense water tanks emitted a greenish phosphorescence. The glass sides of the tanks were covered in scum, though not evenly, so that you could see into the interior in patches: bearded faces of great, glum fish, luminous blind-glaring eyes on stalks, or eyeless faces; rows of serrated teeth, in cavernous mouths; sea creatures that appeared to be translucent guts, lengthy tangles of guts, with abbreviated heads and tiny gills; eerily beautiful scales of the hue of Mediterranean sunsets, or reflecting moons. There were sea-creatures that were spheres attached to hose-like tendrils with suction cups, and there were sea-creatures that were bony spikes, star-shaped, whorled shells the size of basketballs.

Some creatures glided gracefully, and some darted; some, on the murky floor of the tank, scuttled along raising clouds of muck in their wake. The major activity of the tank-life was eating—that is, brainlessly devouring; those who were not eating, were being eaten. In the interior of the Aquarium most of the tanks were empty, to the wife's relief—no reason to peer anxiously into them, to discover what horror resided there.

In a courtyard were open ponds with fountains, that kept the murky water circulating, to a degree; though even some of these were choked with a virulent-looking bright green seaweed, and emitted a fetid odor. Seeing the shadows of visitors pass over them large carp thrust themselves up in the water, thrashing, ravenous to be fed. The wife shrank away, frightened. Was that orange-stippled *koan* large as a full-grown cat trying to attack them?

The Professor laughed at her alarm—"*Koi*, dear. Not *koan*."

"'Coy'—what?"

When the Professor continued to laugh affectionately at her the wife pushed away his hand. *I hate you. I can't wait until we are both dead.*

But no, the wife was only sleep-deprived. The wife did not mean a syllable of such a thought. Each night was a torment of rippling water over her supine and paralyzed body, the unwanted solicitude of strangers calling to her. Badly she wished she might beg the Professor to cut short their Mairead adventure, and fly to Venice. Or better yet home where her grandchildren awaited her, their adoring *Gran'ma.*

"What do you mean—'coy'?"

"The exotic fish are *koi*, dear. Not *koan*."

"Of course—*koi*. That's what I said. And they are hateful—so gross, so hungry. Can we leave here soon? This place smells of—*fish*."

How like *death, fish*. The very words, as well as the odors.

The Professor had been telling his wife about visits to the Royal Aquarium years before, when certain of the tanks had contained the most exquisite tropical fish, some of them as large as the aggressive *koi*, but others smaller than minnows. Every color of the rainbow— such luminous beauty! The trickling sound of the water had been soothing, he recalled. There had been no foul smells of which he'd been aware, in those days.

No way to exit the Aquarium except to return through the inner, dimly-lighted room like a vast mausoleum. No visitors had entered since their arrival nor were there security guards visible. In the foulest-smelling tank lifeless bodies of fish floated on the surface of the water with open-staring eyes, gills that appeared to be breathing but were not.

The couple had no choice but to pass close by a skein of bulging bobbing eyes, pressed against the scummy glass of a tank. No eye-sockets, only just staring eyes.

Outside, the wife was overcome by a wave of faintness. The Professor urged her to lower her head, to stimulate blood coursing into her brain, to revive her, and this was helpful, to a degree.

"Don't make me go into the Aquarium," the wife begged, "—where all the creatures are eating one another, without end. Please."

"We've already visited the Royal Aquarium, dear. We've just been there. You will be all right."

"It's that they have nothing else to do. But eat one another. In the Aquarium, and in the ocean. That's the terrible part of it. But we don't have to see them doing it. Please."

The Professor laughed affectionately, and assured his wife: no. They would not enter the Royal Aquarium ever again.

In the *Blue Guide*, checking off the Royal Aquarium. As, one by one, the major landmarks of Mairead were being checked off.

✦ ✦ ✦

But here was a pleasant surprise: two pages of the Professor's copy of the *Blue Guide* were stuck together. He had never perused these pages describing the Royal Bird Sanctuary, for his meticulous notations were not to be found here. *Travelers to Mairead will not want to miss one of the great attractions of northern Italy . . .*

The Royal Bird Sanctuary was located, according to the *Guide*, adjacent to the Royal Garden which the couple had visited, or had tried to visit, the previous day. Though, retracing their steps, the Professor and his wife discovered signs for the Royal Bird Sanctuary, by chance, sooner than they expected, at the edge of a derelict playing field.

Unlike the Royal Garden, the Royal Bird Sanctuary appeared to be open to the public. A ten-foot wrought-iron fence surrounded it but the fence was broken and discontinuous and its gate had fallen partway off its hinges. No one was around: no ticket sellers, no guards, no other visitors in sight. Overgrown gravel paths led into a marshy area of several acres, lush with tropical-looking flowers and vegetation, buzzing with butterflies, bees, wasps, mosquitoes. Trees whose roots had died but were still standing, with skeletal branches. On the paths were remnants of abandoned bird nests, some of them with broken eggs inside, or what appeared to be the tiny corpses of fledglings. The air was pierced with bird-shrieks— the Professor's wife felt as if someone were jabbing at her ears with ice picks. No songbirds were in evidence—no smaller birds at all. Everywhere the eye could see, large ungainly birds (crows, ravens, hawks, vultures) were perched on tree limbs or flying agitatedly out. Coarse feed had been tossed to them, bits of bone, gristle, raw meat.

Birds were feeding ravenously on the ground, jabbing at one another with their beaks, squawking. The smallest birds were grackles with long blunt-edged tails. The largest were vultures. Birds tore at hunks of suet with their beaks and claws, cocking their heads as they swallowed. Within a few harried minutes the wife was more than ready to retreat from the bird sanctuary but the Professor insisted upon following one of the paths into the marshy interior.

On the lower branches of a skeletal pine tree were slate-colored birds the size of ravens—the very species the couple had seen the day before at the Albanos' former home. Among these ungainly birds was one smaller and more slender than the others, not so ugly, with silky iridescent feathers, eyes that glowed with light as if lit from within. Indeed, this bird exuded an air of extreme alertness, awareness of the human couple. Its feathers shone fiery-blue, its head was cocked in the Professor's direction.

How strange, the wife thought! As if the bird recognized her husband . . .

Entranced, the Professor stumbled ahead. Unlike the other slate-colored birds emitting hoarse cries, the slender bird emitted cooing seductive sounds. It shrugged and shifted its wings suggestively, lifted its clawed feet from the limb and lowered them again in a ritual-like dance. Its acid-bright eyes were fixed upon the Professor who, without realizing it, had left the path and was walking on marshy soil, into which his crepe-soled shoes were sinking.

Is it you? Agustina?

My dear. My darling . . .

Do you remember me? I've become so old . . .

To the astonishment of his wife the Professor began speaking to the bird in Italian, incomprehensible to her, somehow shameful, with an air of pleading.

To a bird! Speaking Italian, gesturing with his hands.

The wife was terrified that something might happen to her husband, so far from home . . .

Within the past year he'd had "episodes"—just one or two. (That she knew of.) Not strokes, or rather not quite strokes. Blackouts lasting for a few seconds. By his account he did not seem to lose consciousness but became light-headed, dazed. *A vastation. It awaits us all. There will be a time, a place.* At such moments the Professor stood very still as blood drained from his brain and his knees grew weak, just barely his legs managed to support him. As his heart thudded like a fist rapping against a door shut against it, and the moment passed, or perhaps did not pass, entirely.

You! It is you, Agustina—isn't it?

But what has happened to you? To me? To our lives?

Clearly he could see, the eyes of the slender slate-colored bird with the iridescent feathers were the beautiful dark eyes of Agustina, glowing with a fierce, fiery light. Staring at him boldly, defiantly. *Yes, it is me. But you—what has happened to* you?

Agustina did recognize him, then. She'd been aware of him years ago—the anguish of his desire for her. When he'd hoped to speak with her, to murmur some awkward little joke out of earshot of her parents, perhaps even, daringly, to brush his hand against her bare arm, to feel the soft hairs stiffen, she'd turned abruptly from him. And then she'd fled to another part of the house.

Yet, days later she'd been awaiting him at the window. That pale face at the window, he had never forgotten.

What you did to me—tried to do . . . I could not bear the shame.

He cupped his hand to his good ear. What was Agustina saying? His heart beat quickly in alarm, opposition.

I—did nothing! I loved you and would never have hurt you . . .

"Leonard, please! Stop this."

His wife spoke sharply, despairingly. She plucked at his arm trying to hold him back but he brushed away her hand as he might have brushed away a fly. In his excitement he dared to approach the base of the tree where the raven-like birds were shrieking and shaking their ungainly wings.

The smaller bird had become agitated too, no longer cooing but emitting hoarse cries like the others. A female bird it seemed to the Professor's wife, in its fright and agitation. Eyes bright as acid. Silky slate-gray feathers. The bird fluttered panicked to a higher branch of the tree, out of reach of the Professor, excreting a pale, soft liquid that glistened along the tree trunk, and splattered onto the Professor's head and shoulders. You could see that bird lime, greenish-white, covered much of the tree's lower branches, and was encrusted on the ground.

"Leonard, please! Do you even hear me?"—the Professor's wife pleaded with him to return to the path. Yet stubbornly the Professor continued to address the smallest bird, in Italian, in an effort to speak cajolingly, seductively, swiping at the bird's droppings on his head, hands, clothing. His glasses were askew on his face, splattered with the milky-white liquid. Desperately his wife pulled at him, stopped his flailing hands, held him tight. The largest of the birds, nearly the size of a hawk, swooped furiously at them, jabbed at the Professor's head with its sharp beak, drew blood. The wife screamed. In the scuffle the Professor's glasses fell into the marshy soil but the wife snatched them up before they were broken.

Managing to pull her husband away from the shrieking birds, to walk him forward with her arm around his waist. All of the wife's senses were keenly alert, she knew herself under attack, threatened. She knew that she must protect her husband, his life was at risk. Somehow, by some miracle, the distraught man did not lose his balance and fall into the marsh where the birds might have swooped upon him and pecked out his eyes.

At last they were back on firmer soil, and out of the nightmare bird sanctuary. The wife wept with distress and relief, dabbing a tissue against the Professor's bleeding scalp as the Professor stood stooped, obedient and unprotesting.

The wife hailed a taxi to return them to their hotel for it was too far for the Professor to walk, in his condition.

Once at the hotel, safely in their room on the eighth floor, the Professor's wife undressed her exhausted husband. In the bathroom she washed his befouled hair, face, hands. She then led him to their bed, and pulled a sheet over him, and prayed that he would sleep, sleep, sleep as long as his stunned brain required, even if they should miss dinner that evening which the Professor had planned at a three-star restaurant recommended in the *Blue Guide*.

The wife made no attempt to sleep. The wife wondered if she would sleep for the remainder of the trip.

Thinking—*If he should collapse, or die. In this hateful place. What will I do!*

Arrange for the body to be shipped home. For the children would wish to see their father a final time.

But no. In his will Leonard requested cremation.

In which case does the wife make the arrangements, or will someone at the Royal Grand Hotel make the arrangements for her, for a fee? And would she then be allowed to bring the ashes home, in a proper receptacle?

Imagining returning through U.S. customs. Having to declare her husband's ashes. Having to show the urn (if it was an urn) to the customs inspector. (And what is that mixed in with those ashes? Could it be cocaine?) The wife—the widow—is arrested, taken away weeping by airport police as fellow travelers stare at her with curiosity, pity, revulsion.

7.

One of Mairead's major attractions, according to the *Blue Guide*, is a gondolier cruise on the river, along the Promenade, just before sunset. This, the Professor is determined not to miss.

They are leaving Mairead in the morning, earlier than planned. But the Professor is determined not to miss the cruise along the river.

Sir! Madame—an aggressive gondolier calls to them in heavily accented English particularly annoying to the Professor, for its suggestion that he has been mistaken for an ordinary American tourist. *Only five euros! Hurry before desk.*

Desk?—must mean *dusk.*

Bobbing on the water the gondola is sleek-black as a polished shoe. Plainer than the fabled gondolas of Venice, as the gondolier is not costumed but dressed in a white muslin shirt, oak-colored trousers. His hair is black as pitch with a faint iridescent streak, stiff-moussed on his head as a wig; around his neck is a crimson scarf, knotted.

As the couple strolls along the Promenade the gondolier calls to them to climb inside, he will assist them, but—*Hurry! Almost desk.*

The Professor's wife shudders. Though the late-afternoon air of Mairead is very warm, steamy-humid. Pulls away from the Professor who is looking at her expectantly. "I—don't think so. Not just now. No." She has begun to breathe with difficulty.

The Professor has been reading in the *Blue Guide*, how "spectacular" the view of the Royal Palace and other historic buildings of Mairead is from the river. One of those experiences *not to be missed.*

But the wife balks, frightened.

"But why not, darling? We've been in boats together before. The river current isn't swift. There are other boats around, nothing could possibly happen to us . . ." The Professor speaks patiently, he is determined not to become exasperated with his wife, on their final evening in Mairead. He has fully recovered from his collapse of the previous day, in the Royal Bird Sanctuary; so far as his wife can determine he has forgotten his mortifying encounter with the silky-feathered raven-like bird. If he wondered at his clothes encrusted with bits of chalky birdlime that can't be scrubbed out, he has said nothing about it to his wife who will arrange discreetly for the clothes to be dry-cleaned, when they return home.

And today, *Blue Guide* in hand, the Professor has been enlivened, exhilarated, on the eve of their (premature) departure from Mairead which will be (the wife surmises) something of a relief to him as well as to her.

In lowered voices the Professor and the wife discuss the gondola ride. The Professor is puzzled by the wife's reluctance, as the Professor's wife is vehement; she doesn't have to explain or defend herself, she insists. "I just don't want to climb into that 'gondola.' I don't want to be taken on a river cruise *at desk*."

The Professor points out that they have come so far to Mairead, and this is the eve of their departure. The wife points out that they have no idea if the gondolier is even licensed—"He could be anyone. A criminal."

The Professor laughs. He is trying not to become seriously annoyed. "Darling, you say such ridiculous things."

"Stop it. Stop laughing at me. I'm going back to the hotel. I will go back home—alone. I don't need you."

"But—what on earth are you saying?"

"I don't need you. I never have."

The wife is breathing strangely. Can't catch her breath. The air is humid, hot. Feculent-smelling. For (of course) the river that gleams and glitters with light like the scales of a great beautiful fish is polluted from industry upriver.

The wife hates the gondolier staring at her, avid and eager. That hunger in the eyes of strangers, she has come to recognize, and to dread. She presses her hands over her eyes. Her vision oscillates. Hurt by her words, the Professor says that she can return to the hotel if she wishes but he is going to climb into the damned gondola, and see Mairead from the river, which is the only way to truly see it.

The wife cries, "No! No."

But in the end, the wife will not be able to leave the husband. Her dread of the river is less than her dread of abandoning him to the river and of being abandoned by him. Nor could she make her way back to the hotel alone, though it is only a few blocks. She takes her husband's arm, trembling. Of course, it is nothing. There is no danger. The Professor holds her hand affectionately. Turns her hand palm upward, kisses the clammy-cold skin as he has not kissed it in—how many years? Isn't this something they have done many times in their long marriage?—a journey of some sort together, embarked upon with innocent enthusiasm, naivete, misguided perhaps, a mistake, never quite so wonderful as they'd anticipated, but worthwhile nonetheless, as they will agree in retrospect? Why would this forty-minute cruise on the Po River be any different from their previous adventures? *Why* is the wife behaving so irrationally on the very eve of their departure from Mairead?

"Darling, come."

The solicitous gondolier helps the elderly couple into the sleek-black gondola polished like a shoe. Even before they are settled in the hard seat, that hurts their buttocks, the gondolier begins poling the vessel, with long ravishing strokes, making the murky water ripple, lap, splash. Within minutes they are well out into the river which is wider and windier than they would have expected. And colder. Swiftly they are moving away from shore and staring now at the facade of the Royal Palace, pale gold in the waning light. From this angle the palace looks ancient and heraldic, like aged ivory.

The many windows of the Palace flash thin blades of light. There is no movement at any of the windows or on the stone steps beside the Promenade—the Promenade itself has become deserted. Where have the other pedestrians gone? It is hardly sunset. The sky is a bright pale waning orange, an exquisite watercolor, rapidly fading to dusk.

"Oh! It is beautiful," the wife says, deeply moved. She is beginning to cry, tears leak from her eyes though (she would have said) she has no tears to spare, no more tears in this lifetime. Gently the Professor kisses her cheek, squeezes her thin fingers—"Didn't I promise you, dear? Why do you always doubt me?"

ASSASSIN

Assassin. Hissing sound like snakes. First came to me through the steam radiator. Waking open-mouthed and the inside of my mouth raw and festering from what had been done to it while I'd been made to sleep a drugged sleep in this terrible place.

Then, the whisper of hope—*Assassin. Assassin!*

The room I was assigned at Saint Clement House, this was the first insult. This was unforgivable. The room, the bed, the bed with a lumpy smelly mattress, on a high floor of the House. Had to climb stairs. With my swollen ankles, weight. Panting like a dog. Had to make my way along the winding corridor like a rat in a maze. Insult at my age. *Pre-diabetic* was the diagnosis. *Hypertension.* To be assigned such sleeping-quarters, in a bloody attic, low ceiling, no privacy, I would have to share a dreary dripping lavatory with strangers, it was not fair or just.

Saint Clement House where residents are the staff, and the staff are residents. You will look out for one another, they told us. Smug bastards all of them. There are (paid) nurses, nurses' aides, attendants but not many of these and so we are all obliged to assist one another (unpaid) when required. Dr. Shumacher is the resident psychologist but Dr. S. does not reside in the House and does not linger in the House any longer than is necessary for the bastard is clear of us by 5 P.M. and on his way. I was meant to be an equal of Dr. S. (for I am educated) but was cheated of my destiny by reason of my sex (female). Also, unacknowledged enemies in the government. After my discharge from the "hospital" where I was kept (against my volition) for eight months. Deemed not ready to return to a normal life and so sentenced to a *halfway house* as it is (laughably) called. *Half-arsed halfway house* it is. And now, the worse insult, to be assigned one of the fifth-floor dormer rooms where at fifty-three I am old enough to be the grandmother of most of the residents. And I am not a junkie, or a souse. I am not gaga like some. I am not a filthy slut—hardly. But forced to cohabit with such crippled specimens of humanity for the sake of a bed and food to eat until I am well enough again to live by myself and tend to my own needs.

My only friend does not live here. My dear friend like a sister I have known since St. Agatha's grade school is Priss Reents who is my age and stout like me and with a plain honest face like raw bread dough. When I am well enough again, Priss Reents has said I might live with her, in a room in her house if I could pay just a few dollars a week to help with rent and expenses. It is very surprising— Priss Reents is a cleaning woman for the P.M. himself, would you believe that?—yet it is so, for thirty years Priss Reents has worked for the same cleaning service that is assigned to the P.M.'s residence at Queen's Square. But if you ask the woman what the P.M. is like she will blink and stammer and seem not to know.

Guess I don't see much of him, or any of them.

A dull female, not like *me*.

Well, I'd known that Priss Reents cleaned the P.M.'s residence and had done so for many years but it never struck me much until the other day waking like I did stunned and swallowing not knowing at first where the hell I was. Hissing in the radiator—*Assassin.*

Love the sound of that word—*Assassin!*

Not *killer*—not *murderer.* Those are common words. Not even *executioner.* (Though there is something about this word, I am beginning to admire.)

Assassin. Executioner. In the service of fairness and justice.

The insult of my room on the fifth floor and how we are fed here in the *half-arsed halfway house.* Cold gluey oatmeal one morning and when I spat out a mouthful onto my spoon, disgusted to see what resembled a small wizened piece of meat.

Your own heart—the whisper came to me, laughing.

Yet, the idea of *assassination* did not occur to me for some time. I have lost track of the days since that time but it might have been a month at least. What began in the hissing, in a dream, and spread out of the dream, like a potato sprouting roots in dank soil—*Assassin.*

Somehow it came to me that I would saw off the head of the arrogant bastard P.M. This would be my destiny, not the other—not to be Dr. S. and lord it over the mentally enfeebled, addicts and sluts, for I'd been cheated of that career. But this, I would not be cheated of and would go down in history like the Hebrew Judith in her triumph over Holofernes.

Assassin. Assassin! I was slow to realize and to accept as you would be if you won a lottery and did not dare to believe. *Have I—won? The winner is—me?*

Almost, I could hear the crowds applauding on the TV.

Hateful arrogant son of a bitch the P.M. was, you saw clearly on TV. A bachelor, he was—never married. No worse than any of them

in any of the "political parties" but the P.M. is the top dog deserving of his bloody head sawed off. And fitting, the very person who
scrubbed his filthy toilet should be the one to saw it off.

You see, no one notices us. This will be our revenge.

Short squat middle-aged female like Priss Reents/me moves through
the world invisible. She/I have bunions, varicose veins, swollen ankles. She/I are short of breath making our way upstairs. Hell, we are
short of breath making our way downstairs. Not five feet three, 170
pounds. No one has glanced at us in decades. Not a man or a boy
in memory. We are deserving of respect as any of you yet we do not
receive your bloody respect so bloody hell with you.

In fact, this is our strength. An *assassin* in the figure of a middle-
aged cleaning woman flush-faced and panting on the stairs, breasts
like balloons collapsed to her waist, fattish thighs and buttocks in a
nylon uniform—who'd suspect?

*What, are you daft, man? That cow? That's the cleaning woman for
Christ's sake, man. Let 'er through.*

Something like this it was, that transpired that morning. Very
cleverly I ground up a half-dozen sleeping pills to dissolve in Reents's
coffee which the woman so dilutes with cream and sugar it is not
even coffee any longer but some disgusting sugar-concoction. And
they are trying to say to me, that I am the one who is *pre-diabetic*.

And so, there was no difficulty for me to put on Priss Reents's
uniform when she was fast asleep and snoring with her vast mouth
agape, and indeed the stretch-waist nylon trousers fitted me like
a fist in a glove. No difficulty for me to impersonate Priss Reents
who is near-enough to me to be a twin sister. So that even if a security guard had thought to actually look at me, he'd have seen Priss
Reents and not me for it was Priss Reents's I.D. photo pinned to my
bosom slumping to my waist and he would not have given that
I.D. photo a second glance either out of repugnance for that sort

of female bosom. Also, Priss Reents wore an insipid knitted cap to disguise her thinning hair, which suited me, too. *OK, ma'am. Go on through.*

If a man does glance at you, if you are Priss Reents/me, his eyes are glazed with boredom. Not for an instant does he *see.*

Waved through security without a hitch. Exactly as planned. Dragging a vacuum cleaner on wheels, mop and bucket, canvas bag in which were stuffed sundry cloths, brushes, and cleaning materials. From innocent queries posed to Priss Reents I had ascertained which corridor to take into the P.M.'s private rooms, and there swiftly I left behind the cleaning items and sought out the bloody bastard in the swanky interior, for whom I was feeling a fierce hatred as if, in a dream of the night before, the P.M. had insulted me to my face as so many others have done. You would be surprised as I was, how swiftly I moved on my swollen ankles. Which would make me realize, in reflecting back over this episode, how the *assassination* was a foregone conclusion, like a final move in a chess game, except until just recently the *assassin* had not been named. And I would wonder if they had sought out others as the *assassin* in this case, and these others had proved inferior, and so they had settled upon me with the knowledge that I would not disappoint. For they must have known of me—my previous life, my education that had come to nothing, the sharpness of my intelligence blunted by myriad disappointments of which not a single one was my fault. In the man's bedroom, in his (black silk) stocking feet, there the P.M. stood before a three-way mirror frowning as he buttoned a crisp-ironed white cotton dress shirt with his back to the door unsuspecting, for Priss Reents would never have dared enter any room in the residence without knocking meekly beforehand and if there was no knock, there could be no intrusion; if no intrusion by a stranger, there could be no sudden blow to the head from behind, so swift rushing into the penumbra of the mirror there was no chance for the targeted one to draw a breath, to escape the hard blow of a pewter urn selected from a mantel, fairly cracking the eggshell-skull in that moment. *You will know what to do, as you do it*—the hissing voice had instructed out of the radiator, and so it was, in an adjoining kitchen there were fancy sharp knives on a magnet-board, and of these I selected a knife with a double serrated blade, and for the next half hour or more I was engaged in sawing off the head of the bloody P.M. as he lay helpless on the floor on a fancy thick-piled carpet. This "career politician" (as he was known) who had so many enemies in our country, any number of them would rejoice in my actions and thank me for my patriotism. To sever a (living) head from a (living) body is no easy task and it is very bloody and tiring as you might imagine but the P.M. was deeply unconscious from the blow to his skull and could put up little resistance.

The Head (as I would call it) was mine as soon as the Head was cleanly severed from the body. It was larger than you would think, and it was heavier. And very bloody, with veins and sinews and twitchy nerves dripping nonstop from the ragged neck. And the skin of the face was coarse and darkening, as with chagrin. And the eyes were half-shut, droopy-lidded like a drunkard's. And the hair which was thin, grizzled-gray, and not a handsome whitish silver such as you are accustomed to see on the P.M. in his public appearances—a hairpiece which (evidently) the P.M. would fix upon his head when he left his quarters.

"Missing your hairpiece, are you, love?"—the wisecrack issued from my lips, unbidden.

I wondered if this would be a new trait of mine—a coquettish sort of wit. For it was very unlike my usual self in the presence of men, I can testify.

The Head was too stunned to respond. Of the eyes, the left had all but disappeared inside its socket while the right was trying very hard to fix me in focus, to determine what was what. For the P.M. had not gotten to his position in the government without being sharp-witted. Out of kindness as much as mischief I sought out the hairpiece in an adjoining bathroom, and this I placed upon the near-bald scalp, and adjusted as best as I could, for even in his decapitated state the P.M. was something of a lady's man.

Almost you have to smile, to register a man's vanity at such a time.

Soon then, I would exit the P.M.'s chambers trailing vacuum cleaner, mop and bucket, canvas bag. And in the bag, wrapped in plastic to prevent the blood from soaking through, the Head. And a dollop of disinfectant to make the nostrils pinch.

Leaving the P.M.'s residence, you are not scrutinized. There is only precaution against bringing a deadly instrument into the residence and when you exit it is by a different door.

Still, it was early—not yet 8 A.M. If they'd had their wits about them they might've wondered why the cleaning woman was leaving so early but indeed they took no more notice of her than of a fly buzzing to be let out.

From Priss Reents I knew that the shiny black limousine to bear the P.M. across town to the capitol building would not appear until 8:30 A.M. and so no one would miss the deceased until then.

The headless body I had left covered with a quilt from the disheveled bed. Being *headless* a body is of not much interest and interchangeable with others of its sex, it seemed to me.

In Priss Reents's rubber-soled shoes, with Priss Reents's I.D. photo removed from my bosom, and a coarse-knit nylon cardigan of an unusual shade of lavender, that resembled nothing of Priss Reents's, and the insipid knitted cap removed, I took the Land's End trolley to the end of the line. There is a place here I know, that I have not

visited in years, but I'd once known well, down behind a boardwalk by the beach, in an area of the beach that is no longer much
frequented, and here the Head would not be easily discovered. My
plan was to bury it in the coarse damp sand with care, for this part
of the *assassination* seemed to be left to me, to devise; as it often
happens, a know-it-all will instruct you what to do but neglect to
include the complete instructions, so you must supply them yourself. Women are familiar with this, it was not surprising to me. The
Head comprehended my plan, for the right eye was fixed upon me
with alarm. Though luridly bloodshot that eye was sharp-focused.
Don't abandon me—it begged.

Such nonsense! I wasn't about to listen to such nonsense. In life
the P.M. had had a wheedling way about him, that was often remarked upon. A right proper bastard, the P.M. One-quarter Scots
blood it was said of him. One of those sly ones who would *get his
bloody way* if you were not careful.

So, I hid the Head in a safekeeping place behind a shuttered stall.
Still in the canvas bag but it was so grimy a bag, in the most desperate eyes not worth stealing. By this time I was very hungry and so
went out to have a snack on the boardwalk, then returned, and there
inside the bag was the Head flush-faced and chagrined and the left
eye adrift but the right eye blinking in the harsh oceanside light and
accusing. *Don't abandon me. Please! Your secret is safe with me—I will
not tell them what you've done.*

And, most piteous—*Don't bury me like garbage, I beg you.*

The Head most feared being buried alive. I took pity on the Head,
for I could understand how it felt in such circumstances.

In a few days I would come to a decision, I thought. In the mean-
time, the Head is doing no harm. We are in a sheltered place where
there is no one to hear it, and it cannot escape (of course). I have set
it on a platter, with some moisture beneath, to keep it moist, as you

would keep a succulent plant moist, now the bleeding has stopped, or mostly stopped. Atop the scalp I have affixed the silvery hairpiece, as the Head is anxious not to be seen without it.

Soon, the Head has become a familiar presence. Like a husband of many years. (Once, I'd had a husband. I think I remember this. But not the actual man, and not myself as a wife, I don't remember.) *Please have pity on me. Please love me. Don't bury me*—the Head dares to whisper.

And—*Kiss my lips! I love you. Please.*

But at this request, I just laugh. I will not *kiss your lips*, or anyone's bloody lips. I am calculating where to bury you, in fact. Farther out the pebbly shore but deep enough so the gulls don't smell you and dig you up and cause a ruckus. No, I am too smart for that. Fact is I am just sitting here having a rest, and I am thinking, and when I am finished thinking I will know more clearly what to do, and I am not taking bloody orders from you, my man, or from any man ever again.

2.

SINNERS IN THE HANDS OF AN ANGRY GOD

1.

This matter of the face mask, for instance.

Well—just a half-mask, a green gauze mask, of the kind medical workers wear.

Not a *full-face mask*—that would be ridiculous.

Before the floods, landslides, firestorms of the past several years Luce had (sometimes) worn a gauze mask. Not in public! Just at home.

When it seemed to her that the wind "smelled funny"—"Smelled wrong."

Especially from the south. Industrial cities to the south. Hazelton-on-Hudson in Dutchess County is two hundred miles north of New York City, which means a near-equivalent distance from the industrial cities of Rahway, Elizabeth, Edison, Newark, New Jersey, and an even shorter distance, depending upon wind currents, from the notorious power plant at Wawayanda, New York, with its majestic white plumes of poisonous smoke sometimes visible to those residents of Vedders Hill who search the sky with binoculars on the alert for (visible) air pollution when the Hudson Valley Weather Air Quality Alert for Ulster and Dutchess Counties has reported a red alert.

This mask, acquired at a medical supply store in Kingston, Luce hurriedly removes if Andrew returns home unexpectedly for her husband disapproves of what he calls her *overreacting—catastrophizing.*

(Is that even a word—*catastrophizing*? Luce understands that Andrew means to suggest a comical tone, a sort of cartoon-rhetoric, to soften the mockery and the annoyance he so clearly feels; yet, *catastrophizing* also acknowledges the very real, the (surely) imminent— *catastrophe*.)

Today, Luce is not wearing the mask. (Though the wind from the south does indeed smell *funny, wrong*. And the rank smell of the soil close about their house has returned, in fact stronger this spring.) Luce has scanned the scene with her binoculars and has discovered nothing to alarm her unduly except that repairs on the higher stretch of Vedders Hill Way, recently washed away in a mudslide, seem to have temporarily stopped. Ugly yellow construction vehicles parked haphazardly at the side of the narrow road, God-damned eyesore.

And a fleet of jets from the military base at Fort Drummond, pass overhead with earsplitting noise tearing a seam in the sky.

Her violin! Luce runs into her room to fetch it, quick before Andrew returns, hasn't touched the instrument in weeks, desperate suddenly to take it up, cup it to her chin, wield the bow—snatch from oblivion a few minutes of a Bach partita she'd first memorized as a music student at Columbia, nothing more exquisite, soothing to the soul, of course her playing has deteriorated but not nearly so badly as she'd feared.

2.

"We will give a dinner party. It's been too long."

"God, yes! But better hurry."

This is a joke. A mild joke, as Andrew's jokes go. Still, Luce winces. For perhaps it isn't funny, entirely. Luce resents such humor from her husband, at such a precarious time in all of their lives.

In the distance, on the farther side of Vedders Hill, a rolling sound of thunder.

Putting her in mind of the thunderous game of ninepins played by the demonic old Dutch-colonial dwarfs in the legend of Rip Van Winkle. For on their mountainside above Hazelton-on-Hudson they are living in what was once the Kaatskill Mountains, now the Catskills; in an earlier incarnation, as the Dutch village of Vedders, Hazelton-on-Hudson was likely the setting for the story of Rip Van Winkle's near-fatal enchantment more than two hundred fifty years before.

3.

It isn't that they are *old*. Not by the calendar. Not essentially. Not most of them. Edith Danvers, for instance, Luce's colleague at Bard College, one of their few remaining neighbors on Vedders Hill Way, recently diagnosed with stage three colorectal cancer, is only fifty-one—Luce's age exactly. And Andrew's lawyer-friend from Yale, Roy Whalen, a former Olympic swimmer and longtime resident of Hazelton-on-Hudson, afflicted with worsening stenosis of the spine, is only fifty-seven. Todd Jameson, Andrew's tennis partner, cofounder of Dutchess County Greenpeace, stricken last year with a mysterious autoimmune disorder which mimicked certain of the symptoms of lupus but was not (evidently) lupus, is just sixty—a youthful sixty. Heddi Conyer, Luce's closest friend in the Hazelton Little Chamber Orchestra, recently diagnosed with Crohn's disease, is only fifty-six. Lionel Friedman hadn't been *old*—a youthful sixty-four. (Indeed, it is usually healthy young men, swimmers and divers, who contract the deadly *N. fowleri*—brain eating amoeba.) Others in the Stantons' approximate generation whom they'd known in the Hazelton-on-Hudson/Red Hook area since the mid-1980s are reporting cases of diverticulitis, stomach cancer, pancreatic cancer, lung cancer (in one who hadn't smoked for thirty-seven years), leukemia and lymphoma, failing kidneys, failing hearts, inflamed joints, neurological "deficits," even stroke—at such (relatively) young ages! And there is the latest, shocking news of Jack Gatz, longtime Dutchess County district attorney and the best player in Andrew's poker circle, last week diagnosed with early-onset frontal-temporal dementia at just fifty-nine.

"As Jack deteriorates at poker the rest of us will greatly improve," Andrew says, "—but it will hardly give us much joy."

"I should hope not!" Luce says, shocked. "And I hope you haven't told Jack that."

With the air of an actor to whom the script has assured a perfect rebuttal Andrew says: "That was a joke, darling. In fact it was Jack's joke, when he told us the news last week."

Rebuffed, Luce retreats. Laughs awkwardly, apologetically.

In marriage as in tennis, one player is inevitably superior to the other.

After nearly thirty years of marriage Luce is never altogether certain of her husband's tone, nor of the meaning of his facial expressions. *Disdain for her obtuseness, sympathy for her naivete, affection for her good heart?*

Or all, or none, of these?

✦ ✦ ✦

Thirty years ago they'd met on the steps of Butler Library, Columbia University.

Descending the icy steps carefully yet she'd slipped, turned an ankle, would have fallen except a tall young man ascending the steps deftly gripped her arm at the elbow and held her upright— *Hey! Got you.*

Blurred with tears from a cold, wet wind—(the Hudson River was only a few blocks to the west, though invisible from where they stood)—Luce's eyes lifted in surprise and gratitude. The strong fingers gripping her elbow did not immediately relax.

Thirty years. Her life decided for her.

By what circuitous and vertiginous yet (seemingly) inevitable course from that moment to this as chastened wife retreats from the husband's expression of veiled triumph—*Hey! Got you.*

4.

Initially the question is—*Who in our circle will die first?*

Then—*Who is next?*

Then—*Don't ask.*

Luce lies awake in the night thinking of their afflicted friends in Hazelton-on-Hudson. Beside her, his back to her, Andrew sleeps the heavy blissful sleep of the oblivious.

Luce is concerned for her fellow-violinist Heddi but she is more concerned for poor Edith Danvers for (she reasons) colorectal cancer is more life-threatening than Crohn's disease, which can be controlled with medication, if not cured; and Edith has long been Luce's yoga companion, as well as her (adjunct) colleague in the English

Department at Bard. Edith has been Luce's confidante in the matter of husbands, marriage, children—her companion at Code Pink protests in Manhattan. Since her cancer diagnosis Edith has become obsessed with fear that her husband will "never touch her again," for she will not only have to endure extended chemotherapy, she will have to wear a colostomy bag—a revelation that makes Luce tremble with indignation. (Yet: a fear of Luce's own for she has seen that fleeting expression in Andrew's face, of something like repugnance, at times when Luce is less than beautiful, sneezing, graceless, unkempt. When Luce looks *her age*.) (She has seen, and looks quickly away.)

Andrew feels more sympathy for swaggering Jack Gatz whom—frankly—he'd always admired. For Jack Gatz had the most prominent public career of anyone in the Stantons' Hazelton circle. The Gatzes' house—glass, stone, redwood, burnished copper—loosely described as *in the manner of Frank Lloyd Wright*—was the most spectacular house on Vedders Hill, indeed anywhere in Hazelton-on-Hudson, until it was reduced to an ignominious pile of rubble in the firestorm of the previous fall.

No, Luce thinks. It isn't that they and their friends are *old*. Or that they haven't taken good care of themselves—their medical insurance allows for a generous array of mammograms and prostate screenings, colonoscopies, electrocardiograms and echocardiograms, biopsies, CT-scans, and PET-scans, MRI's and fMRI's . . . Roy Whalen has undergone a week of intensive tests at the Mayo Clinic, Todd Jameson at Johns Hopkins. Pete Scully, first violinist and conductor of the Hazelton Little Chamber Orchestra, is said to have dialysis three times weekly at the Kingston Dialysis Center. And their friend Samantha Plummer is scheduled to undergo the most complicated and expensive medical procedure of all—a stem-cell transplant involving a barrage of chemotherapies followed by quarantine

in germ-free isolation for a minimum of six weeks in a specially constructed apartment owned by Sloan Kettering in Manhattan.

Their friends and neighbors are collapsing all around them!—in
mimicry of the collapsing roads of Vedders Hill, mudslides, flash
floods, and flash fires of the past several years. It had once seemed
natural that droughts, hurricanes, tornadoes, torrential rainfall, cat-
astrophic blizzards were a way of life in Western and coastal states
but now such extremities of weather are afflicting even Dutchess
County.

5.

"'The God that holds you over the pit of Hell, much as one holds
a spider, or some loathsome insect over the fire, abhors you, and is
dreadfully provoked: his wrath toward you burns like fire; he looks
upon you as worthy of nothing else, but to be cast into the fire.'"

Andrew is very entertaining, and Andrew is very chilling, channeling the voice of the eighteenth-century Puritan minister Jonathan
Edwards who'd reputedly terrified congregations with his infamous
sermon *Sinners in the Hands of an Angry God*. (Not aligned with any
college or university, Andrew Stanton is a self-styled private scholar;
his most renowned book is the Pulitzer Prize–winning *An Intellectual History of America from the Puritan "City on a Hill" to the "Great
Society."*)

It's Andrew's (half-serious) opinion that in the twenty-first century damnation isn't a matter of Hell but not having adequate medical insurance.

"We are spiders dangled by fate over the fires of hell, and the
slightest slip will plunge us into an eternity of misery—kept alive by
machines for which we may have to pay 'out of pocket.'"

Andrew's listeners laugh, uneasily. He may be joking—or half-joking—but this is the nightmare everyone in America dreads.

Educated and enlightened individuals who have no fear of a wrathful God. No need for Jesus Christ to rescue them from this God but they do fear the tyranny of medical bills even as their medical ailments seem to be increasing.

"The more tests, the more diagnoses. The more diagnoses, the more illnesses and 'conditions.' The more illnesses and 'conditions,' the more treatments. The more treatments, the more hospitalization and the more hospitalization, the more medical bills."

Oh, Andrew Stanton is very funny! With the others Luce laughs, and winces.

We know what our punishment is, but what was our sin?

6.

Despoiling the one earth we were given, of course.

7.

Where once the soil was a solace to her, now the soil is becoming fearful to her.

Outdoors, bright, blinding sunshine. Frantic need to *get outside.*

With a hand trowel digging in rich dark soil Luce has created herself over many years of composting, but that now smells strange to her nostrils, rotting-feculent, as if teeming with microscopic virulent *life.*

Global warming, Luce thinks. The hairs at the nape of her neck stir. There is no longer a guarantee of protracted sub-zero temperatures in this part of North America, that once killed off such virulent *life*.

If she wears gloves, Luce reasons. If she never actually touches the earth with her bare fingers . . .

Her mask? That Andrew has ridiculed, and that looks (she acknowledges) silly on her, should she wear *that*?

Sufferers of depression are recommended gardening, music.

Not so much reading, certainly not writing, for such exercises of the brain activate *thinking*. Not a good idea.

A sensation of despair as of sand fleas crawling up her legs, a very bad memory from girlhood of long ago.

Deciding she won't work outdoors this morning after all.

8.

"Luce, darling! If you've started inviting people to our dinner don't forget Lionel Friedman and—" (forgetting the wife's name, taking for granted that Luce will provide the name, and indeed Luce murmurs *Irina* in a way she has perfected to inform her husband without interrupting his train of thought)—"It's been a really long time since we've seen them, I think."

"Well—yes. It has."

"I've always liked Lionel—he's very impressive if sometimes a little pompous. And—what's her name—"

"—'Irina'—"

"—very smart, as I recall. And a good cook. We owe them a dinner, don't we?—I seem to remember."

"Yes, I think so. I think you are right."

"So, then—invite them, please."

"Y-Yes. I will."

No need to upset Andrew at this time of morning. Just as he is about to enter his study for a morning of work.

It isn't just that Lionel Friedman died eight months ago but that Andrew seems to have forgotten. And not just that Andrew has forgotten, but Luce dreads his questioning her, as frequently he does when she reminds him of something he has forgotten, suspiciously, irritably, as if she'd kept such information from him out of deviousness—*Why on earth didn't you tell me?*

Nor does Luce want to be obliged to (re)tell her husband the ghastly details of Lionel's death, so rare and obscure a virulent infection of the brain that there was a paragraph about it in the science section of the *New York Times* beneath the lurid headline *Increase in Brain-Eating Amoeba Cases in US Traced to Gradually Warming Temperatures.*

9.

Do they dare? After such a long time? Not a single musical performance by the Hazelton Little Chamber Orchestra in the (disastrous) season 2018–19, and the *little quartet* as they call themselves, four musicians, members of the Orchestra, haven't gotten together to play in—how long?—five, six months?—where once they'd played together every two or three weeks, and sometimes more frequently.

First violinist of the Little Orchestra, Pete Scully. Violinist, Luce Stanton. Cellist Tyler Flynn, violist Heddi Conyers. All of them non-professionals for whom music was the unattainable career and other careers, however successful, second choices.

Luce and Heddi have decided, the *little quartet* must play at the Stantons' dinner party. Such private musical evenings were frequent years ago, everyone had seemed to enjoy them, why not resume?

The *little quartet* has been working for years on several Schubert string quartets. The most challenging has been the last, most exquisite quartet—#14 in D-minor, *Death and the Maiden*. Often for small audiences in private homes they'd performed less rigorous quartets by Dvorak, Borodin, Brahms, but they'd never quite brought the more ambitious, emotionally grueling *Death and the Maiden* to a point where they'd have been comfortable with anyone else hearing it. But now, as Heddi says with a wild little laugh—"Time may be running out."

Luce gives no indication of having heard this remark. She shivers, and laughs—"Do we *dare*? So much has happened lately . . ."

"Which is the point. *We* must take back control."

"Scully has been sick . . ."

"*I've* been sick. But I'm stronger now, and I think that Pete is, too."

Luce hears the quaver in her friend's voice. She doesn't want to question whatever Heddi says, not just yet.

"I called Ty to invite him and Glenda to the dinner and he sounded—well, surprised to hear my voice. Maybe he thought I'd been killed in the firestorm?"

This droll remark Heddi ignores.

"But did he say 'yes'?"

"Yes to the dinner party, and then when I brought up the subject of playing a little music for the guests he hesitated, then said, 'Oh, what the hell! *Yes*.'"

"That's just like Ty! I love Ty. What about Pete?"

"Oh, I'm sure—*yes*."

"You and I can start practicing today. Tonight!"

"Tonight? Really?"

"Yes. Come to my house. Andrew won't mind in the slightest, he watches MSNBC and CNN after dinner, till midnight, and I just *can't*. No more! So please come, we'll get a head start on the guys."

"But—Schubert? *Death*—?"

"We have three weeks, two days. We can do it."

"We can?"

"We *can*."

Breathless, laughing together, Luce Stanton and Heddi Conyer. Like girls clasping hands on a high platform, preparing to dive together into the murky water below.

"God, I've missed you. I've missed our evenings. I hardly listen to classical music any longer, I don't know what has happened to me."

"To all of us! I don't know, either."

"I don't even read books. I mean—real books. Tried to reread *Anna Karenina* when I was in the hospital, and afterward at home, and just—*could not*. Like that part of my brain is wizened. Five-, ten-minute 'reading' on a screen is what I do now, mostly."

"Well, we already know *Death and the Maiden*. We've practically memorized it and we can practice together. Before we all meet to rehearse. We can listen to the Takacs recording, I've heard it dozens of times and it always breaks my heart."

"Oh God, yes! My heart, too."

Heddi hugs Luce impulsively. Luce is struck by how thin her friend has become, and how ivory-pale and papery-thin her skin, but still Heddi grips Luce tight, her breath is warm against Luce's face. A single jolt of happiness runs through the women's bodies like an electric shock.

10.

Is it the earth, the water, the air?—*contaminates*.

Something is poisoning them. Seeping into their lungs, into the marrow of their bones.

Brain-eating amoeba. Or is it flesh-eating bacteria. Luce doesn't want to think.

Jesus, darling! Don't catastrophize!

When they first moved from West 78th Street and Columbus Avenue, New York City, to Hazelton-on-Hudson in 1986 the air in the Hudson Valley was cleaner, the sky a brighter and clearer blue— Luce is certain. The white oaks and birches had not shed their leaves prematurely, in hot September. That maddening chemical odor wasn't borne on the wind, and the soil on Vedders Hill seemed more solid, substantial. Mudslides were unknown, still more firestorms were unknown. An excess of pollen was a far more serious problem than a depletion of ozone. True, there were reports of acid rain in the Adirondacks and the Hudson River had been seriously polluted, like Lakes Ontario and Erie upstate, but the media didn't make a fuss over it and social media, the vehicle for channeling outrage, did not yet exist. Everyone sailed, canoed, kayaked on the Hudson River. Fished! The river's steely beauty prevailed.

What have we done, what have we done!

What have we failed to do.

She began to have difficulty breathing at night, in bed. Sometime in her mid-forties. Lying on her back she felt particularly oppressed, as if something were squatting on her chest. But if she lay on her side, her heart beat uncomfortably.

In the night she seemed to lose track of her identity. That she was a *wife*, that a sentient being slept beside her that was a *husband*, became an elusive fact.

Light rippling sleep like shallow water over rocks streamed across her brain. She was trying to walk in the water—lost her balance, stumbled—woke abruptly, heart pounding in panic.

How deep the husband's breathing, like the breathing of one who has been transformed into pure being—unnamed, unknown to her.

She must stumble to keep up with *him*—whoever *he* was.

Her protector. Her superior. Though not her father sometimes in sleep he was conflated with her father.

She was terrified of the man leaving her. Terrified of losing him.

Recalling how on the icy steps of the library she'd slipped, turned her silly ankle, fell heavily and cracked her skull. Shiny glossy chestnut-blond hair, wet with blood. Whoever it was, the male, the husband-to-be, squatted and scooped up her suety brains in his hands.

Laughing, for you have to laugh. All thinking matter—all of Schubert, Mozart, Beethoven—all that's *human*—is but fragile brain matter encased in a crackable skull.

In a sieve, some of the brain would leak through. Most would not, meaning—what, exactly?

What isn't suety, soupy—that is the soul. Gnarled like nuts. Immortal.

Waking with a start. (Was it sleep apnea?) (Luce feared that she might be falling asleep/waking dozens of times in the night as her father had done in the last decade of his life. Injurious to the heart as to the brain, such stumblings into sleep.)

Worse: there came a recurring dream in which Luce found herself in an airless bunker with other women, girls. Her age was uncertain. Even her name. She and the others wore shapeless uniforms of a vaguely military sort. They were required to sleep together in un-made beds. They were required to fit gas masks over their faces when sirens routed them from sleep—but Luce's gas mask turned out to be solid rubber lacking openings for her nose and mouth, hideous.

She struggled, tried to scream. "Luce! Darling! For Christ's sake wake up"—Andrew shook her, alarmed and exasperated.

Another time Luce woke panting and sobbing, having pulled the sheet up over her face as a mask to filter toxic air seeping into the room from a vent.

"You've got to get control of yourself," Andrew said grimly. "This *catastrophizing* is wearing us both out."

Luce offered to sleep elsewhere but Andrew would not hear of it. Though their lovemaking had become infrequent in recent years there was always the possibility of lovemaking, the husband in his vanity did not like to relinquish.

Then one hot September morning before dawn they were both awakened by crackling heat, sirens, no dream but a firestorm raging above them on Vedders Hill dry as tinder from weeks of drought. Smoke, suffocating white smoke, screams of neighbors, a hysterically barking dog next door. On the narrow private road, in stretches of the most prestigious real estate in Dutchess County, fire trucks and emergency vehicles could barely move; residents fleeing the Hill were forced to abandon their vehicles and descend on foot. The Stantons grabbed clothes, shoes, wetted cloths to hold against their astonished faces. Fled the firestorm on foot descending a half-mile into Hazelton like refugees and returned five days later, when Vedders Hill was reopened to civilians, to discover a ravaged landscape—more than half the hillside houses had burnt to the ground while others, eerily, including their own, remained standing scarcely touched except for smoke-stained facades and broken windows.

"Oh, God! Why have we been spared!"—Luce burst into tears, stricken with guilt and shame.

Andrew, staring grimly at the devastation that surrounded them, his face ashen and his eyes bloodshot, did not seem at first to have heard. Then, uttering, without his usual jovial irony: "*We* have been spared? Is that what you think?"

In the acrid air the question hovered between them. Luce thought—*We will be sick with guilt. No one will forgive us.*

Accompanied by volunteer firefighters they'd been allowed to walk through the rooms of their house holding damp cloths against their faces, allowed to retrieve a few essential items—Andrew's laptop, notebooks, checkbooks and financial records; Luce's violin, lesson plans, student papers. The smoke-stench lay like a haze about them and would not fade for months. (Has it ever disappeared? Or have they simply become accustomed to it, and no longer notice, as they have ceased noticing, or at least being jarred by, the ruins of their neighbors' houses?)

Above the Hudson River a grayish haze hovered like a crouching beast. Yet beyond this haze, a perversely ceramic-blue sky. To a blank-faced young volunteer firefighter Andrew joked that, in Christian theology, it's a feature of salvation that the saved, in Heaven, are allowed to gaze down upon the damned in Hell—but Andrew's remark was lost in a fit of coughing.

Even on windless hot-summer days, on Vedders Hill there was likely to be a stirring of the air, which was sure to help disperse the smells, in time. Luce took heart, there was no need for her and Andrew to consider moving away, not just yet; even neighbors with badly damaged houses vowed to rebuild, not to "give up"—"Abandon the Hill." Others declared bravely their intention to "rebuild"—"Reclaim." Property on the Hill had always been absurdly high-priced, now it would be more fairly appraised, taxes would have to be lowered, a new school bond issue for Dutchess County was out of the question this year . . .

Classes at Bard were suspended for two weeks. Luce was restless in their temporary quarters in a Marriott Inn in Poughkeepsie, with others evacuated from the Hill. She could not wait to begin the effort of clean-up, repair; with shifting crews of mostly strangers she went on missions distributing food and clothing at the Hazelton community center, driving people without cars to hospitals, clinics. Luce was particularly good with the elderly, who were grateful for any kindness, and clutched at her hands as if she were, not a middle-aged woman with a predilection for melancholy, but a young person, suffused with purpose and energy, radiantly smiling. How good it was, in these quarters, to be *seen*!—for even her students did not seem to see her, and her (adult) children had long ceased trying. She would even take a grim pleasure—well, not so grim: festive!— in cleaning their house, washing walls, vacuuming—simple chores for years surrendered to Guatemalan cleaning women, by Andrew's edict. And what an ideal opportunity to toss out shabby old things—furniture, art by local artists now deceased, books unread for decades—without Andrew quite knowing; for Andrew, fatigued by the evacuation, his nerves shot, did not care to revisit the house, just yet. In the aftermath of the firestorm there were new friendships to be made among the volunteers: like matches struck simultaneously in the dark, individuals discovered one another who'd forgotten one another for years. (Even members of the Hazelton Little Orchestra who'd long taken one another for granted, or had somewhat disliked one another. What a pleasure to greet one another, and to embrace!) Luce liked it that everyone you saw on the Hill wore gauze masks, and that Andrew, if he even knew, couldn't possibly have accused her of *catastrophizing.*

Soon they were able to reclaim their house. Even the windows were sparkling-clean—Luce had washed them herself. With an air of genuine pride Andrew praised Luce: "What a great job you've done, darling!"—not seeming to notice what was missing in the house, that had made it cluttered and shabby before.

With relief Andrew retired to his study with the spectacular, if now partially ravaged, view of the Catskills and the Hudson River, shut the door quietly but firmly as he always had, resumed his work. He'd brought his laptop with him to Poughkeepsie, of course, but few of the books he needed; disrupted from his routine he'd been disoriented, irritable, but now he could immerse himself again in his work, and detach from his surroundings. All that really mattered, Andrew joked, was that power was restored to the Hill, and Wi-Fi.

In time, Thursday poker nights among the survivors would be resumed.

11.

Yet, from this day Luce begins to perceive that Andrew is sometimes short of breath ascending stairs. He isn't so likely to charge ahead on their hikes as he has been; indeed, Andrew less frequently suggests hiking with Luce on their favorite hiking trails in the Catskills. Though he has been proud of completing three New York City marathons, and often speaks warmly of the experience, it seems to Luce that Andrew has virtually stopped running even on the flat jogging trail beside the Hudson River.

More recently, returning home from an evening rehearsal of the *little quartet* in Hazelton, letting herself quietly into the house not wanting to disturb Andrew, Luce happens to see, through a doorway, her husband as he rises from his desk chair, but rises unsteadily. Ah, Andrew has lost his balance!—a startled look in his large handsome face.

Soon then, within a few seconds, Andrew regains his balance. He has reasserted control, no need to flail his hands in panic.

By now Luce has eased out of sight. Shortly she will call cheerfully to Andrew, informing him that she's home, and Andrew will respond, "And how was the rehearsal, darling?"—in his affable way, not troubling to listen to Luce's reply but wanting to establish that yes, Luce is *home*; as Andrew is *home*. Despite the possibility (Luce thinks) that the very earth beneath *home* is shifting.

Luce has seen nothing to disturb her, not that she will recall.

Forget what you have seen—it never happened.

12.

Waking to a thrill of—is it *hope*?

Beginning to feel again her old excitement. A stirring of curiosity, anticipation. Preparing for the dinner party. Rehearsing the Schubert quartet with her dear musician-friends.

True, their playing has become somewhat ragged since the last time they've been together. Scully seems annoyed with Luce, as a music instructor might be annoyed with a star pupil. Tyler is easily winded and Heddi continually forgets to turn off her damned cell phone. *Death and the Maiden* is (possibly) a naive choice, why hadn't they settled for something easier?

But they don't feel the dismay and exasperation they'd have felt in the past, enduring one another's mistakes. Scully's bad temper, Tyler's self-disgust, Luce and Heddi trembling with anxiety. Now they are forgiving of one another's flaws as they are forgiving of their own.

Look, we're amateurs. Let's face it, OK?

Luce is feeling hopeful. Luce is feeling that they are not—yet—beyond surprising one another.

And Andrew. Andrew has surprised Luce, too.

Discovering in their online checking account that her husband had evidently transferred twenty thousand dollars from his private savings account into the joint account, subsequently donated to several Dutchess County disaster funds, without informing her. Luce is shocked, but Luce is impressed. (As an adjunct instructor at Bard she barely makes that amount of money per term, after taxes.

Fortunately Andrew's books are bestsellers that continue to sell well in paperback.)

Luce thinks of Andrew with renewed tenderness. She has felt concern for his health. His breath—often quickened. High blood pressure? Heart trouble? Andrew will keep his health issues to himself, Luce supposes, until such time when he no longer can.

She will take care of him, she realizes. No doubt, she will outlive him, for that purpose perhaps.

This, the destiny for which she was born . . . Is that possible?

Obsessively Luce consults websites for the latest data on air, earth, water pollution in the Hudson Valley. She would not want Andrew to know how compulsive she has become—how prone to *catastrophizing*. The long-term effect of pesticides, additives, hormones on the human brain. Organic foods vs. farm-factory foods. A chart graphing degrees of toxins in fish and seafood. Luce is outraged reading in *Consumer Reports* that fish is often mislabeled—tilefish (high in mercury) sold as halibut, farmed Atlantic salmon sold as wild-caught Pacific salmon, tilapia masquerading as "sole" or "bass." Types of tuna are cynically mislabeled, "red snapper" is rarely red snapper. Luce hasn't bought swordfish in a decade—swordfish is saturated with mercury. Luce pitches her voice to make a wry observation, not to complain, for Andrew dislikes complaining and whining— "It seems that everything we eat, and any air we breathe, is 'toxic.'"

"Does it!"—Andrew agrees, vehemently. As if Andrew has been listening.

13.

Andrew is absorbed in selecting wine for the party, that is his chief responsibility, along with choosing several very good cheeses from the Cheese Board in town. To much that Luce utters, no matter how carefully it is pitched, not complaining, not a *cri de coeur*, Andrew pays little heed. But he is pleased that Luce has followed his suggestion and (re)washed the crystal wine glasses by hand, that are usually left with chalky streaks from the dishwasher.

"About time, some festivity on the Hill! As if we've all died and gone to Hell but different regions of Hell, that don't overlap."

It's clear as the first guests arrive at their house that the Stantons have been missing their friends more than they knew. Luce finds herself reduced to tears, even Andrew is touched. There are exclamations, handshakes, embraces. These are friends of many years. Once, young married couples, young parents, middle-aged parents, now grandparents—most of them.

Two (recent) widows, one (recent) widower. Ken Jacobs, once a brash young research chemist who'd warned of global warming thirty years ago, and is still writing articles on the subject. Clive Turner who'd gloomily predicted a "white nativist" revival in the United States at the very outset of the Obama administration, long before Trump erupted on the political scene. Jaqueline La Port, poet/ feminist/ anarchist now wheelchair-bound with multiple sclerosis but looking beautiful and brave in a flowing scarlet sari. Ben Ferenzi and Dannie Kozdoi, divorced from their respective wives and now married to each other. Another widow, and a divorcee. A distinguished Bard musicologist whom Luce doesn't recall having invited to the party, indeed a professor emeritus she is certain died sometime last year, arrives in pinstriped seersucker propelling himself on a walker, haltingly but in good spirits, with a bottle of champagne for his hosts—"Hello, friends! Am I late, or am I early?"

Parking on Vedders Hill Way is difficult, so most drivers let out their passengers and park some distance away. Here is Glenda Flynn depositing Tyler at the foot of the gravel driveway, up which he limps gamely with a cane in one hand and his cello case in the other, thumping against his thighs.

Wheelchairs, walkers, canes. Little knitted caps on (bald) heads. A contingent of chemotherapy walking wounded, of whom two are total surprises to Luce—she'd known of Edith Danvers of course, but not Sallie Klein and Gordon Jelinski. Jack Gatz arrives blank-blue-eyed and smiling broadly but with a muttered aside to his host: "Why the hell's so many people here for poker night?"

And here is Gregory Cardman, one of Andrew's marathon-runner friends, gleaming scalp, hairless head, no eyebrows, eyelashes—skeletal-thin, but shaking Andrew's hand, hard.

"Jesus! It's been so long."

"Is it—Greg? It *is*."

Handclasps, hugs. Kisses.

Kisses near the mouth. Wet kisses boldly on the mouth.

". . . yes, sometimes we feel very lonely on the Hill. 'Survivor's guilt' is real. We feel uneasy that we have been singled out for a reason, our house untouched while so many of our neighbors have lost their homes, though (in fact) we don't *really* feel we've been singled out for any reason—for who, or what, would do the 'singling out'? This isn't Puritan New England—we don't believe in a God of wrath. But you can see how people become superstitious—trying to make sense out of chaos. There is such a powerful human yearning to imagine our lives 'destined'—'purposeful.' No one wants to think that our lives are random tosses of dice."

". . . but are tosses of dice *random*? Isn't there a statistical predictability? If you have enough data, won't an algorithm predict—something?"

More crucially, what sort of world will younger generations inherit?

Talk of children. Grandchildren. Boastfully. Wistfully.

Well, some of the children are activists. Grandchildren too. Pro–
gun control. Ecology, environment. "Animal liberation." But some
of the grandchildren are not so involved, frankly. Some of the grandchildren are barely literate. Video games, cell phone games, nonstop
social media.

"Vaping"—e-cigarettes.

"'Vaping'—what exactly is 'vaping'?"—Andrew asks with a faint
sneer.

*Do I have to take any of this seriously? It will all pass away in time,
won't it?*

Luce has hired a twenty-year-old from the college to help with
the party. Long straight blond hair, oversized T-shirt, jeans. Deftly
moving among them, a darting silver minnow among thicker slower-
moving fish.

"Oh!—look . . ."

Dazzling-beautiful-bloody sunset beyond the mountains like a
cluster of burst capillaries.

✦ ✦ ✦

Having reconnoitered in a back bedroom for a harried half-hour the
little quartet appears on the deck, gleaming instruments in hand.

Violin, violin. Viola. Cello!

Encouraging applause. (Though some guests continue talking,
laughing. Not all can hear acutely.) Luce feels her face flush hot.
What on earth was she thinking, arranging for this *musical evening*!

It takes a certain *chutzpah* to perform in front of your closest
friends. Much more difficult than public recitals.

"I always forget how small a violin is!" Audrey Jameson foolishly
exclaims.

"Yes! They are so exquisite, like toys."

The musicians are seated. A curt nod of Pete Scully's head and abruptly the music begins. Such urgency in the familiar opening notes of *Death and the Maiden* are struck, even the musicians seem to be taken by surprise. For how frail a vessel, music! On this ravaged hill where half the landscape seems to have disappeared and the sky beyond the mountains is a fireball.

Though the *allegro* movement begins shakily the musicians gather strength as they press onward like rowers in a skiff on rough water, keenly aware of one another, yet never glancing at one another, determined to maintain the pace set by the swiftest rower.

Luce is dazed, light-headed. Her fingers move of their own volition, it seems—her hand wielding the bow, her arm in a continuous motion. Though every cell in her being warns her *no!* she glances sidelong at Scully seeing, or imagining she sees, in the violinist's gaunt face a look of fierce concentration raw as sexual pain. Luce is stunned, distracted—*No. Don't show us that face. What are you thinking!*

Luce feels exposed, eviscerated. As if the man's anguish is her own.

Yet somehow it happens, even with a perceptible faltering of Luce's bow, and a mistake—or two—from the cello, and missed notes from the viola, the first brilliant movement of *Death and the Maiden* comes to an end. Not a triumph but neither is it a disaster. Its violent shifts of mood have disguised the musicians' jerky playing. A wave of visceral relief ripples through the gathering. Tyler wipes his perspiring face with a white cotton handkerchief. Heddi glances sidelong at Luce daring a small conspiratorial smile. *So far, so good!* Scully, hunched forward frowning at the music on the stand before him, is grinding his teeth.

Another nod of Scully's head and the second, *andante* movement begins, more gracefully than the first. At least, the instruments are together! With schoolgirl posture Luce fixes her gaze on the bars of music before her, she is determined not to be distracted. She is not frightened, she is not abashed, she is thrilled to be playing Schubert with her musician-friends. The small gleaming instrument in her hands is the most beautiful object imaginable, yet somehow it has come into her possession—hers! A gift from a doting grandmother many years ago, and a responsibility. She grips the violin tight, for it thrums with life. She leans into the music, above the violin, embracing the violin to her breast. *Oh God! What we live for. Is there anything else.* As the musical theme gathers power there is— abruptly, rudely—a sudden spasm of coughing, one of the guests in the very first row, God-damned coughing the musicians try to ignore, who the hell is it?—at last the afflicted individual slips away to cough elsewhere, sounds as if he's coughing out his guts, as the movement lurches to an end. God *damn.*

Scully is furious. Scully does not dignify this audience by glancing out at them. Tyler too is flushed with annoyance, blowing his nose loudly in the vivid-white handkerchief that looks to Luce like a flag of surrender. Heddi looks as if she is about to cry, fussing with her instrument as one might fuss over a fretting child.

In the brief interlude Luce dares to look for Andrew—where is Andrew?—for a fleeting moment Luce is frightened, her husband has abandoned her, he and blank-blue-eyed Jack Gatz have drifted off together to play poker in Andrew's study . . . But then Luce sees him, seated at the edge of the circle on a foot stool, almost out of her range of vision. Andrew has a glass of red wine in hand, and Andrew is drinking steadily. Which is not like Andrew. Luce hopes that his mind hasn't been drifting. Luce hopes that she has not humiliated herself, in her husband's eyes, by this rash if unwitting act of self-exhibition. It seems ominous to Luce, Andrew isn't making much of an effort to meet his wife's gaze, encourage her. *Hey! I love you.*

With the sharp—"Demonic"—*scherzo* the quartet resumes. This is a breathless movement that rivets the audience's attention until—

unfortunately—the harsh cries of birds interrupt. Circling hawks, at dusk. Swooping, plunging on widened wings to capture their (shrieking) prey in the lower air, or on the ground, distracting the listeners, in this way distracting the musicians. At least, the *scherzo* is short. Damage is minimal.

There is even a light smattering of applause, a nod to the musicians that the audience is *on their side*, not the birds'.

This is not quite the *little quartet* Luce recalls from their early robust days. Each of the musicians in their twenties, then! Even Tyler, the eldest. An intense erotic awareness among them, tight-strung, utterly absorbing and thrilling though (as Luce recalls) indefinable, thus unspeakable. Was she sexually enthralled by the imperial Scully, or was she romantically drawn to the more gentlemanly Tyler; possibly, was she infatuated with Heddi Conyer, the most beautiful freckle-faced individual she'd ever seen, close up? Or was it the music they played, or attempted to play? Like climbing a mountain together, attached to one another by life-lines, each dependent upon the others? Was it the actual, literal violin that has been Luce's (secret) life, entrusted to her hands? Was it the mere feel, the smell, the *beingness* of that violin? The sounds of the music the musicians' strings created together, a heart-aching swelling, a pulsing deep in the groin, indeed unspeakable? How happy they'd made one another, though often how exasperated, furious! Like siblings, struggling together for dominance, clarity. Jealous, bitterly so. Euphoric, ecstatic.

Now Luce wields her recently restrung bow, a new woman, in some ways (she wants to think) a younger woman, less dependent upon the (elder) men. She will outlive them, she knows. She will outlive her husband. That will be her fate, she must accept—it is what the gathering intensity of Schubert's music tells her.

Tyler's head is bowed, he too is leaning into the music, drawn into its swift skimming momentum. Scully, longtime concertmaster of the Little Chamber Orchestra, rumored to be reluctant to relinquish his position despite his illness, is playing now not so aggressively, as if, beside his companion violinist he is willing to acquiesce to her; as if thrice-weekly dialysis has rendered him something less than what he'd been, but something more as well: a crystalline transparency where once he'd been opaque, elusive. Pale-freckled Heddi too seems altered: an undercurrent of passion, possibly rage, in the dulcet sounds of the viola, where previously the violist had been tentative as if feeling herself unworthy of the music.

And Luce too, by consensus the weakest of the musicians, the most impulsive, least disciplined and least reliable, yet the most devoted to the *little quartet*, is being buffeted by the music as by waves that rush at her to drown her; yet she will not be drowned, she will persevere, chin lifted, heart beating calm with a wave of adrenaline, though what risk, she is thinking, what exposure, the terror of mortality that is *Death and the Maiden*, yet acquiescence to this terror—the acquiescence more appalling than the terror, because more final.

The terror of beauty, Luce thinks. Like the terror of mortality, it is what links us.

Nearing the end of the *presto*, in a white-water rapids plunging forward, downward, manic intensity, wild flying notes in a tarantella, suddenly it happens that the *little quartet* is lurching again, someone has missed a beat, missed a crucial note, there is a stumble, a teetering on the brink of collapse—yet no time remains for such mistakes to be registered, hesitation in the viola, or in the cello, for the final bars of *Death and the Maiden* rush at them, loom before them majestic and intransigent as the closing of steel petals—perfection!

The musicians' bows are stilled. Schubert's Quartet #14 in D-minor has been accomplished.

And then—silence. . . .

The little audience is stunned. In the startled hush someone coughs, or laughs—sheer embarrassment, nerves. *Scully, Tyler, Heddi, Luce*— these mortal beings, familiar faces shining with triumph, having played for the audience as if their very lives were at stake . . . "Bravo!" Andrew Stanton is on his feet leading the applause, with an air of genuine surprise, relief and delight, and in another moment others join in.

Bravo! Bravo! Those guests who can stand easily, who are not discouraged by arthritic joints, or bad knees, rise to their feet in homage to the *little quartet.* Luce is blinking back tears, Heddi wipes her face on a sleeve of her sleek black shirt. Tyler seizes both the women's hands in his and kisses them wetly in turn, palm up. Scully's nostrils pinch in Olympian contempt, Scully is ashen-faced, yet triumphant too. *See, you bastards? I am not dead yet.*

More cries of *Bravo!*—by far the most spirited applause the *little quartet* has ever received for any performance.

Yet: behind the musicians the sky has been steadily darkening. There are flashes of heat lightning like fire. Deafening claps of thunder like the (mock) applause of giant hands.

Within seconds a storm moves in from the northeast. Low rumbling rolls across the sky like a sound of celestial bowling. Vedders Hill itself seems to be shaking.

"Oh Jesus, is it us? Another landslide?"

"Is it *us*! We would know, if it were."

14.

Inside the Stantons' glass-walled house, the long oak refectory table has been set with a colorful Native American tablecloth. Waxless candles have been lit, their flames high and tremulous. Now rain is pelting against the windows. Rain in steely sheets. The thunder continues—then, an earsplitting crack. Flashes like strobe lighting that stun the brain. Guests press hands over their ears. Shield their eyes. They are laughing, though they are also frightened. They are white-faced, stricken. Some of them are not certain where this place is—where they have been brought. But here comes their affable host Andrew Stanton brandishing a wine bottle in each hand— "Chardonnay? White?"—to the rescue.

Overcome by emotion Luce has fled into the kitchen clutching her violin as if to shield it from staring eyes. She has exposed herself, she thinks—her very soul outside her body, but perhaps it is her body as well, unclothed, naked. If Andrew has heard the music clearly, then Andrew knows. Everyone who has heard, must know. And there is Scully close behind her. Scully, daring to follow Luce into the kitchen! He isn't drinking tonight, he has announced. He wants ice for his God-damned Diet Coke.

Not meeting his eye Luce drops ice cubes into Scully's glass. "Thank you, Luce"—Scully touches Luce's wrist lightly.

Luce shrinks away. Doesn't want to see how the concertmaster's eyes, tarnished, bloodshot, fix upon her with that look of yearning she remembers from years ago—that look she'd believed she would never again see in any man's face.

No, no!—never again. Go away.

You are Death, but I am not the Maiden. No.

Still, the man's touch has burnt her skin. The spark of that touch will long smolder in Luce's heart.

15.

In bright-blinding sunshine. In the green-gauze face mask, and on her hands newly purchased garden gloves. Digging in the remains of last year's garden. She has purchased flats of petunias, pansies, black-eyed Susans to plant in the moist earth.

But how vile, the smell! After last night's heavy rain it is worse than ever, a miasma lifting from the soil like ether.

Brain-eating amoeba, flesh-eating bacteria breeding in warming earth.

But surely Luce is protected by the mask, and certainly she is protected by the gloves which are thick and unwieldy, made not of cloth (which can wear out) but a sort of plasticized rubber.

Except for the smell Luce is actually very happy. Luce is smiling, Luce is thinking—*What a triumph!* The *little quartet* surprised everyone the previous night but particularly the *little quartet* surprised themselves.

Next, they are daring to consider one of Beethoven's late quartets. Why not?—as Heddi has reasoned. Time is running out.

"Hel-lo!"—unexpectedly, Andrew calls to Luce from the side door of the house.

It is unusual for Andrew to venture outdoors at this hour of the day. Usually Andrew is at his desk by 8 A.M., in his spectacular study surrounded by three solid walls of books, staring into a computer screen, that stares back at him. And the surprise is—Andrew is wearing a green-gauze face mask of his own!

Must've purchased the mask in town, without telling Luce. A joke, unless it's something more than merely a joke. Luce stares at her husband, smiling uncertainly. Not knowing if Andrew is mocking her or whether, smelling the befouled earth close outside their house, Andrew is acknowledging at last that something is grievously wrong.

Andrew joins Luce in the ravaged garden. Luce sees that Andrew's mask is askew, giving him a wry, rakish air.

Half their faces hidden, each has become tantalizingly unfamiliar to the other. Their eyes seem different, somehow. Wife, husband? Masked by gauze, their voices are muffled. They begin to behave in antic fashion, like mimes. They begin to laugh together, giddy. Perhaps they are still drunk from the festive night before that did not end, for some of the hardier guests, until after midnight.

"Oh, darling!"

Luce adjusts the mask on Andrew's face as she often adjusts a twisted shirt collar of his, a strand of sand-colored graying hair out of place. Careful not to be overly familiar with her thin-skinned husband, not to offend; yet, she means to protect him from looking foolish.

Can masks *kiss*? It is not expected, but of course.

HOSPICE / HONEYMOON

Hospice."

Once the word is uttered aloud there is a seismic shift. You will feel it.

Like a (very short) thread through the eye of a needle, swiftly in and swiftly out.

The very air becomes thin, steely.

At the periphery of your vision, an immediate dimming. As the penumbra begins to shrink.

In time it will become a tunnel. Ever diminishing, thinning. Until the remaining light is small enough to be cupped in two hands. And then, it will be extinguished.

For when "hospice" is uttered, it is at last acknowledged—*There is no hope.*

No hope. These words are obscene, unspeakable. To be *without hope* is to be without a future. Worse, to acknowledge that you are without a future—you have "given up."

And so when the word *hospice* is first spoken—carefully, cautiously, by a palliative care physician—probably neither of you will hear it. If you hear, you don't register that you have heard.

A low-grade buzzing in the ears, a ringing in the ears as of a distant alarm, an alarm in a shuttered room. That is all.

For if you don't hear perhaps it has not (yet) been uttered.

For if neither of you hears perhaps it will not (ever) be uttered.

Yet somehow it happens, *hospice* comes to be more frequently spoken as days pass.

And somehow it happens, surprising himself, your husband begins to speak of his *final days*.

As in *I think these might be my final days*.

As if shyly. On the phone very early one morning when he calls, as he has been calling, immediately after the oncologist making rounds in the hospital has seen him.

On the phone so that he is spared seeing your face. And you, his.

A new shyness like the first, initial shyness. Finding some way to say *I love you*.

For some, an impossible statement—*I love you*.

But your husband managed it, and you'd managed it—somehow: *I love you*.

And now years later it is—*I think these might be my final days*.

These words you hear over the phone distinctly, irrevocably yet (you would claim) you have not heard. No!

But yes, you've heard. Must have heard. For the walls of the (bath) room reel giddily around you, blood rushes out of your head leaving you faint, sinking to your knees like a terrified child stammering— *What? What are you saying? That's ridiculous, don't say such things, what on earth do you mean*—"Final days" . . .

Your voice rises wildly. You want to fling the cell phone from you. For you can't bear it. You don't think so. Not knowing, at this time, the vast Sahara that lies ahead of all that you cannot bear that nonetheless will be borne, and by you.

For always, each step of the way, you resist.

It is a steep uphill. It is natural to resist. Or, if you grant the steep-uphill, console yourself by thinking that it is just temporary. The plateau, the flatland to which you've been accustomed, that awaits you, both of you, you will return to. Soon.

Until a day, an hour. Always there is a day, an hour.

When you began to speak of *hospice* yourself.

At first you too are shy, faltering. Your throat feels lacerated as by lethal metal filings.

Gradually you learn to utter the two syllables clearly, bravely—*hos pice.*

Soon then, you begin to say these (distinct, deliberate) words: *our hospice.*

Soon, you draw up your vows. Quaintly state to yourself as to God, a formal decree.

It is my hope: I will make of our hospice a honeymoon.

My vow is to make my husband as comfortable as it's humanly pos-sible.

To make him happy. To make us both happy.

To fulfill whatever he wishes, that is within the range of possibility.

First: a new setting for him. NOT the Cancer Center.

As soon as he is stabilized. Our hospice will be in our home.

He loves our home!—the atrium flooded with morning light.

A foreshortened horizon for the house is surrounded by trees. But always there is the sky—flotillas of sculpted clouds.

Your husband can lie on a sofa staring at the treeline, and at the sky.

Comfortable on the sofa with pillows behind him and feet (in warm socks) uplifted.

Or, what is more likely your husband can lie on a (rented) hospital bed positioned in such a way that he can easily gaze out the window. Some furniture will have to be rearranged but that can be done. And you can lie beside him, as you have done in the hospital.

Holding hands. Of course you will hold hands. His hands are still warm—strong. When squeezed his fingers never fail to squeeze in return.

As his lips, when he is kissed, never fail to kiss in return.

You will sleep beside your husband holding him in your arms which have surprised you recently, not strong arms, in fact rather weak arms, which nonetheless can be made to behave as if they are strong.

Scatter seed on the redwood deck outside the window. Not ordinary seed but the more expensive "wild bird seed" your husband purchases.

Thrilling to watch the birds. Taking time, not distracted, really watching birds for once . . .

And the husband loves music! You will bathe him in the most beautiful music through his waking hours.

Holding hands. Fingers laced together. So long as it is not uncomfortable for him you will lie on the bed beside him holding him listening together to Beethoven's Hymn to Joy, *Rachmaninoff's* Vespers.

Falling asleep together. Even during the day. Your head on the pillow beside his head.

From the bookcases in the house select art-books, his favorite artists, books from his photography shelves—Bruce Davidson, Edward Weston, Diane Arbus, Eliot Porter. Turn the pages slowly, marvel together.

His favorite foods . . . Well, you will try!

When he is stabilized and at home possibly then his appetite will return. When you are the one to prepare his food for him, his appetite will return.

Of course, family will come to visit. Relatives, friends. Old friends from grammar school, he hasn't seen in fifty years. Some surprises for him—you will negotiate.

It will not be merely hospice, it will be our hospice. *Not sad but joyous, a honeymoon.*

You will be happy there, in your own home. For both of you the final days will be a honeymoon. You vow!

IN FACT, nothing remotely like this will happen. How could you have imagined it could happen!

Hospice, yes. *Honeymoon,* no.

SUBAQUEOUS

So densely constructed is the old, urban campus of the state university, so labyrinthine the interiors of the high-rise cinder-block buildings secreting A, B, C levels underground at the foot of Pitt Street South, it is hardly to be wondered that cell phone reception is poor to nonexistent here; and so, on those cheerless Thursdays when you venture into the city, and descend underground to C-level of Building H (Humanities) to teach in a fluorescent-lit windowless classroom containing twenty-five careworn vinyl chairs arranged in a haphazard, asymmetrical, and unpredictable pattern, in effect you step off the grid, or rather you are expelled from the grid, or expunged from the grid, for several hours floating in a sub-aqueous element like a deep-sea diver dependent upon air supplied by an invisible source that though (surely) oxygen-deficient is yet breathable, life-sustainable. And though at the conclusion of the three-hour class, and before your office hours (C-level), you might make an effort to align your cell phone with the university's WiFi, or better yet exit Building H, to sprint to a nearby park where your cell phone would spring into life like a reanimated heart, out of inertia you usually remain in Building H, only ascending to a café on A-level where you sit at a table facing a cinderblock wall gaily festooned with glossy reproductions of Parisian-café scenes by Toulouse-Lautrec, spreading papers out before you with the hope not to be interrupted before you are expected in your office two floors below. In the brightly lit café are students at long formica-topped tables, hunched over laptops, with intense eyes, furrowed foreheads, grayish skin like parchment; though you try not to stare at these near-immobile figures you are inclined to think that they rarely leave Building H for each Thursday when you return you see them, or figures who closely resemble them, in the same positions at the long tables, hunched over their laptops; and though your title is Visiting Professor in the College of Arts and Sciences, with all that that implies of distinction (and transience), you find yourself gravitating toward the same place also, to the café that is really not a café but (merely) a bright-fluorescent-lit stretch of windowless cinderblock corridor perversely festooned with Parisian scenes of a bygone era and outfitted with humming vending machines, overflowing trash containers, recycled air eking from narrow-pinched vents overhead. Occasionally in the Parisian café (as it is known in Building H, though it is not a café and there is nothing Parisian about its vending machine drinks and food) other patrons seem to recognize you, for indeed it's likely that they are "your" students, as you are "their" professor, but you and they greet one another cautiously, with awkward smiles, for it's difficult to establish your relationship outside the classroom in which the class meets as if the four walls of the room were a kind of clothing, to hide nakedness; and so like a creature that has grown comfortable inside its underground burrow, even as its eyesight is weakening, even as its lungs are shrinking, even as its heart is beating ever more weakly you return to the same table, the same chair, the same vending machines; pressing your fingertips against your forehead to forestall the onrushing cluster headache; staring at your watch to calculate how many minutes you can remain here on neutral terrain, before you must descend to the windowless office assigned to you on C-level.

And here you are overcome by a sudden need to call your husband with whom you have not spoken in some time. Why this is so, why you have not spoken in some time, is not clear. It seems that you and he are separated, yet, from your perspective at least, you have no idea why. Yearning for the absent husband is constant as a heartbeat but like a heartbeat unnoticed, unremarked, unacknowledged, for only the aberrant defines itself; what is constant can be easily lost; and so with slightly trembling fingers you remove your cell phone from your canvas bag, suddenly eager to hear your husband's voice, that is like no other voice; it's bizarre to you, inexplicable, that out of pride perhaps (his or yours?—you don't know) the two of you have drifted apart, have failed to mend a misunderstanding or a rupture; but even as your fingers grip the cell phone you realize that you've forgotten that the Parisian café is underground, and there is no cell phone reception here; when you try to call your husband the device rebukes you immediately—*call failed*.

Desperate now, unable to grasp why you haven't made more of an effort to speak to your husband, uncertain where your husband is, or why he is apart from you in another city perhaps, or perhaps he is traveling, in a subaqueous zone too in which there is no cell phone reception, unable to comprehend how you can have allowed this *drift* to separate the two of you; why you seem to have filled your life with every kind of diversion, and digression, and distraction, and derangement, as if Time were a vast empty windswept space, a cheerless plaza between high-rise cinderblock buildings that has to be filled, in any way possible filled, cluttered with vinyl chairs so lightweight they are blown about in gusts of wind, clattering and rattling, filled with long formica-topped tables at which motionless figures sit hunched over gray-glowering rectangular screens; you are suffused with the desire to tell him *I love you, where are you, I want so desperately to see you, I want to speak with you, I want to hold you, kiss you, comfort you, and I want to be comforted by you but—where are you?* And the yearning is so strong, the heartbeat so pronounced, it is revealed to you as the most profound fact of your life, which you have not fully understood until now, and now in your face this revelation must show, no wonder that strangers glance at you in surprise and alarm, and pity; some of them look away quickly, in embarrassment at such raw unfettered yearning, and some of them cannot look away, for it's as if you are holding a lighted candle before your face, shielded by a hand as the candle's tremulous flame is borne through a jostling crowd; shielded from drafts of chill air from overhead vents in labyrinthine corridors, that stir unspeakable yearnings, regret, remorse, vivid-red as mercury rising in a thermometer. And so, needing to acknowledge that yes, the man who is your husband has broken you utterly, your deepest and most secret self he has pierced, as one might pierce a melon with a sharp instrument; your limbs he has broken, your neck and your spine he has shattered, your soul he has broken as one might break an egg; the sudden joy in such breakage, the spilt yolk, exhilaration as one might feel at last—finally!—slashing the most precious arteries in the arms with any instrument sharp enough for the task.

By this time you have made your stumbling way to the solitary elevator, which moves with maddening slowness, always there's a disgruntled gathering of persons awaiting this elevator including at least one individual in a wheelchair; all wait in silence, resigned; but you are not resigned, for you are desperate to hear your husband's voice; desperate to escape the subaqueous below-ground; and

so losing patience, breathlessly ascending stairs to the first floor
of Building H and through a revolving door into the filtered gray
urban air of winter; hurrying now along a traffic-clogged street,
breaking into a run, desperate to get to the park, running the last
block to the park, threading your way past pedestrians who glance
at you with expressions of surprise, annoyance, wonder that a mature woman is running in such a public place, glancing after you as
you pass panting and determined, finally crossing into the small urban park that smells of damp chill earth mixed with acrid exhaust,
where—suddenly, like a revelation—you feel the cell phone gripped
so tightly in your hand vibrate with life like a resuscitated heart as a
stream of emails floods in, you have returned to the grid, lifting the
phone eagerly to call your husband even as the realization comes to
you that your husband is no longer living, of course your husband
has died, he is no more, in April of the previous year your husband
died, in your arms he died, and now it is January of a New Year.

That is it. There is no mystery—why your husband has been silent, and why he has drifted from you. He has died, he is dead.

In the bleak little wintry park where you stand on a pathway
with a useless cell phone in your hand the paralyzing knowledge
sweeps through you from the tips of your toes to the crown of your
head, a great wave that cauterizes even as it obliterates.

THE HAPPY PLACE

Professor! Hello.

White winter days, sunshine on newly fallen snow. You have come to the happy place for it is Thursday afternoon.

Another week, and you are still alive. Your secret you carry everywhere and so into the happy place.

So close to the heart, no one will see.

✦ ✦ ✦

Not a happy season. Not a happy time. Not in the history of the world and not in the personal lives of many.

You wonder how many are like you. Having come to prefer dark to daylight. Sweet oblivion of sleep to raw wakefulness.

Yet: in the wood-paneled seminar room on the fifth floor of North Hall. At the top of the smooth-worn wooden staircase where a leaded window overlooks a stand of juniper pines. In the wind, pine boughs shiver and flash with melting snow. The *happy place*.

Here is an atmosphere of optimism light as helium. You laugh often, you and the undergraduates spaced about the polished table.

Why do you laugh so much?—you have wondered.

Generally it seems: the more serious the subjects, the more likely some sort of laughter.

The more intensity, the more laughter.

The more at stake, the more laughter.

The *happy place* is the solace. The promise.

Waking in the morning stunned to be *still alive*. The profound fact of your life now.

✦ ✦ ✦

Already at the first class meeting in September you'd noticed her: *Ana*.

Of the twelve students in the fiction writing workshop it is *Ana* who holds herself apart from the others. From you.

When they laugh, Ana does not laugh—not often.

When they answer questions you put to them, when in their enthusiasm they talk over one another like puppies tumbling together— Ana sits silent. Though Ana may look on with a faint (melancholy) smile.

Or, Ana may turn her gaze toward the wall of windows casting a ghostly reflected light onto her face and seem to be staring into space—oblivious of her surroundings.

Thinking her own thoughts. Private, not yours to know.

You feel an impulse to lean across the table, to touch Ana's wrist. To smile at her, ask—*Ana, is something wrong?*

But what would you dare ask this girl who holds herself apart from her classmates? *Are you troubled? Unhappy? Distracted? Bored?*—not possible. One of the others in the seminar might take Ana aside to ask such questions but you, the adult in the room, the Professor, don't have that right, nor would you exercise that right if indeed it were yours. Still less should you touch Ana's wrist.

It is a very thin wrist. The wrist of a child. So easily snapped! The young woman's face is delicately boned, pale, smooth as porcelain, her eyes are beautiful and thick-lashed but somewhat shadowed, evasive.

You have noticed, around Ana's slender neck, a thin gold chain with a small gold cross.

The little cross must be positioned just so, in the hollow at the base of Ana's throat, that is as pronounced and (once you have noticed it) conspicuous as your own.

(What is it called?—*suprasternal notch*. A physical feature aligned with thinness, generally conceded to be a genetic inheritance.)

Indeed, Ana is a very diminutive young woman. To the casual eye she would seem more likely fourteen than eighteen and hardly a *woman* at all.

Ana must weigh less than one hundred pounds. No more than five feet two. You see, without having actually noticed until now, that she wears loose-fitting clothing, a shapeless pullover several sizes too large, and the thought strikes you, unbidden, fleeting, that Ana may be acutely *thin*. Her diffident manner makes her appear even smaller. *As if she might curl up, disappear. Cast no shadow.*

How vulnerable Ana appears!—to gaze upon her is to feel that you must protect her.

Yet, you suppose that there are many who would wish to take advantage of her.

When the others speak of "religious belief"—"Superstition"— with the heedlessness of bright adolescents wielding their wits like blades Ana sits very still at her end of the table, eyes downcast. Touching the cross around her neck.

Why doesn't Ana speak, intervene? Defend her beliefs, if indeed she has beliefs?

Yes. This is a superstitious symbol I am wearing. What is it to you?

The discussion has risen out of the week's assignment, a short story by Flannery O'Connor saturated with Christian imagery and the mystery of the Eucharist, and Ana, like the others, has written an analysis of the story.

But Ana remains silent, stiff until at last the discussion veers in another direction. Glancing at you, an expression of—is it reproach? hurt?—for just an instant.

✦ ✦ ✦

The *insomniac night* is the antithesis of the *happy place.*

Unlike the *happy place* which is specifically set, and unfortunately finite, as an academic class invariably comes to an end, the *insomniac night* has no natural end.

If you cannot sleep in the night, the night will simply continue into the next, sun-blinding day.

✦ ✦ ✦

You have thought *Is she a refugee* for her spoken English is hesitant, imperfect. You have not wanted to think *Is she a victim. Has she been hurt. What is the sorrow in her face. Why is she so unlike the others.*

Ana's face, that seems wise beyond her years. (You are certain you are not misinterpreting.)

Oh, why does Ana not *smile*? Why is it Ana who alone resists the *happy place*?

In twenty-seven years of teaching you have encountered a number of *Anas*—surely.

Yet, you don't recall. Not one. And why should you, students are impermanent in the lives of teachers. There is nothing profound in this situation. Ana has done adequate work for the course, she has never failed to hand in her work on time. You have no reason to ask her to come and speak with you, no reason at all.

Ana's reluctance (refusal?) to smile on cue, as others so easily smile—this is a small mystery.

Is it your pride that is hurt? But how little pride means to you, frankly.

You are conscious of the (unwitting) tyranny of the group. Of any group no matter how congenial, well-intentioned.

That all in the group laugh, smile, agree with the others, or "disagree" politely, or flirtatiously. The (unwitting) tyranny of the classroom that even the most liberal-minded instructor cannot fail to exert. *Pay attention to me. Pay attention to the forward-motion of the class. No silences! No inward-turning—this is not a Zen meditation. A small class is a sort of skiff, we are all paddling. We are all responsible for paddling. We are aiming for the same destination. We are aware (some of us keenly) of those who are not paddling. Those who have set their paddles aside.*

Perhaps Ana has not clearly understood that enrollment in a small seminar brings with it a degree of responsibility for participation. Answering questions, asking questions. "Discussing." The workshop is not a lecture course: students are not expected to take notes. Perhaps it was an error in judgment for Ana to enroll in a course in which (it seems apparent) she has so little interest as, you are thinking, it was an error in judgment for you to accept her application, out of seventy applications for a workshop of twelve.

Why had you chosen Ana Fallas? A first-year student, with no background in creative writing? Something in the writing sample

Ana had provided must have appealed to you, a glimpse of Hispanic domestic life perhaps, that set it aside from others that were merely good, conventional.

Though now, as it has turned out, Ana's work has seemed less exceptional. Careful, circumspect. Nothing grammatically wrong but—nothing to call attention to itself.

As if Ana is trying to make herself into one of *them*—the Caucasian majority.

It is likely that Ana is intimidated by the university—its size, its reputation. By the other students in the writing class. She is but one of only two first-year students, and the other is Shan from Beijing, a dazzling prodigy intending to major in neuroscience.

The others are older than Ana, more experienced. Three are seniors, immersed in original research—senior theses. Most of them are Americans and those who are not, like Shan, and Ansar (Pakistan), and Colin (U.K.), have studied in the United States previously and seem to have traveled widely. Ana is the only Hispanic student in the class and (you are guessing) she might be the first in her family to have enrolled in college.

Is Ana aware of you, your concern for her? Sometimes you think *yes*. More often you think *no. Not at all.*

I CAN'T.

Or, *I don't think that I can . . .*

At the age of twenty-two you were terrified at the prospect of teaching your first class.

English composition. A large urban university. An evening class.

More than a quarter-century ago and yet—vivid in memory!

You had never taught before. You had a master's degree in English but had never been (like most of your graduate student friends, and your husband) a teaching assistant. Amazing to you now, that the chairman of an English Department in a quite reputable private university had hired you to teach though you'd had no experience teaching at all—had not once stood in front of a classroom. (He'd said afterward that he had been impressed by the written work of yours he'd seen, in national publications. He'd said that, in his experience, teaching was best picked up *on the fly*, like learning to ride a bicycle, or like sex.)

It had been thrilling to you, to be so selected over numerous others with experience, older than you. But it had not been so thrilling to contemplate the actual teaching. At twenty-two you would not be much older, in fact you would be younger, than many of your students enrolled in the university's night school division.

English composition! The most commonly taught of university courses, along with remedial English and math.

Your husband, young himself at the time, just thirty, had tried to dispel your terror. He'd tried to encourage you, tease you. Saying—
Don't be afraid, I can walk you into the classroom on my shoes.

Such a silly notion, you'd laughed. Tears of apprehension in your eyes and yet you'd laughed, your husband had that power, to calm you.

Between your young husband and you, in those years. Much laughter.

You think you will live forever. Always it will be like this. You don't think—well, you don't think.

Your husband had a Ph.D. in English. He was an assistant professor at another, nearby university, he'd been a very successful teacher for several years. Gently he reasoned with you: What could possibly go wrong, once you'd prepared for the first class?

What could go wrong? Everything!

They won't pay attention to me. They will see that I am too young—inexperienced. They will laugh in derision. Some of them will walk out . . .

Your husband convinced you that such fears were groundless. Ridiculous. University students would not walk out of a class. Especially older students would not walk out of a class for which they'd paid tuition—it was a serious business to them, not a lark.

In this class, so long ago, were thirty students. Thirty! Over-large for a composition class.

To you, thirty strangers. You broke into actual sweat, contemplating them. The prospect of entering the classroom was dazzling. A nightmare.

For days beforehand you rehearsed your first words—*Hello! This is English one-oh-one and my name is*—which you hoped would not be stammered, and would be audible. For days you pondered—what should you *wear*?

On that crucial evening your husband drove you to the university. Your husband did not *walk you into the room on his shoes* but he did accompany you to the assigned classroom in the ground floor of an old redbrick building. (Did your husband kiss you, for good luck? A brush of his lips on your cheek?) How breathless you were by this time, seeing your prospective students pass you oblivious of you.

Wish me luck.

I love you!

And so it happened when you stepped into the classroom, and took your place behind a podium in front of a blackboard, and introduced yourself to rows of strangers gazing at you with the most rapt interest you'd ever drawn from any strangers in your life—an unexpected and astonishing conviction flooded over you of *happiness.*

Knowing you were in the right place, at just the right time.

YOU FEEL HER absence keenly.

This day, a particularly wet, cold day Ana is absent from the workshop.

Reluctant to begin class you wait for several minutes. (For other students are arriving late.) Then, when it is evident that Ana will not be coming, you begin.

You have noticed that Ana sits in the same place at the table each week. She will arrive early, to assure this. Such (rigid?) behavior is the sign of a shy person; a person who has had enough upset in her life, and now wants a predictable routine; a person who chooses to rein in her emotions; a person who knows that, like internal hemorrhaging, emotions are not infinite, and can be fatal.

Tacitly the others have conceded Ana's place at the (farther) end of the table. No one would take Ana's chair, just as no one would take the Professor's usual seat.

Yet, no one mentions Ana's absence. So little impression has she made on the class, no one thinks to wonder aloud—*Hey, where is Ana?*

You ask for a volunteer, to provide Ana with the assignment for the following week. At first no one responds. Then a young woman raises her hand—*Sure! She's in my residence hall, I think.*

You might email or text Ana yourself. But you are thinking you would like someone from the workshop to volunteer, to forge a connection with Ana however slight.

✦ ✦ ✦

That evening Ana sends you an email, apologizing for her absence. *Flu, infirmary sorry to miss class. Will make up missing work.*

+ + +

Ridiculous, you are *so relieved*.

Smiling, your heart suffused with—what? Hope like a helium-filled balloon.

When Ana returns to the workshop you tell her—*We missed you, Ana*.

True, to a degree. *You* missed her.

Naturally Ana has completed the assignment: the reading in the anthology, and the weekly prose piece. Though Ana is not one of the more imaginative writers Ana is the most diligent of students.

Hers has been good work, acceptable work so far this semester. It is careful work, precisely written English, surprisingly free of errors for one whose speech is uncertain. Is this the utterance of clenched jaws?—you wonder. Maybe Ana would like to scream.

You will encourage her to write more freely. From the heart.

You will tell her—in fact, you will tell the class—*Write what feels like life to you. It need not be "true"—your writing will make it "true."*

Ana frowns distractedly, staring down at the table. She knows that you are (obliquely) criticizing her work, which the others have discussed politely, without much to say about it. For all her pose of indifference Ana is highly sensitive.

You have encouraged your students to write, not memoir, but *memoir-like* fiction. You do not (truly!) want these young people to open their veins and pour out their life's blood for the diversion of others but neither do you want them to attempt arch, artificial fiction derivative of work by the most-read fiction writers of the era—for that they cannot do, and certainly they cannot do well.

Others in the class take up the challenge, excited. *Write what feels like life to you.*

Ana takes back her prose piece from you. Ana's eyes slide away from yours and will not engage.

You had written—*Promising! But something that anyone might have written. What does "Ana" have to say?*

Away from the seminar room which is the *happy place* you ponder your obsession with this student. For the first time acknowledging the word—*obsession.*

Telling yourself that now you've made the acknowledgment, the *obsession* will begin to fade.

✦ ✦ ✦

And then, in the seventh week of the semester, long past the time when you'd have thought that any undergraduate could surprise you, Ana hands in something very different from the cautious prose she has been writing.

The assignment is a dramatic monologue. Just a page or two. In the "memoirist" mode.

Here is urgent, intense work by Ana. Not cautious at all—a bold plunge into stream-of-consciousness speech uttered (seemingly) by an adolescent daughter of (Guatemalan?) (illegal?) immigrants stranded in a nightmare detention center at the Texas border in Laredo.

The other young writers take notice. It is requested that Ana read the monologue aloud.

Oh, I—I can't. . . .

Stammering *no*, blushing fiercely but the others insist.

✦ ✦ ✦

From a prose poem of Ana's:

> I thought the eucalyptus had burst into flame, I'd seen it
> and ran away screaming. And then—years later they laugh
> at me and told me no, that had not happened to me but to
> my little sister.
> And when I remember my brother beaten by our father with
> his fists they tell me no, not just my brother but me, as well.
> But they are not laughing.
>
> In the foster home there are three girls named Mya.
> Those acts perpetrated upon one of the Myas are perpetrated
> upon the others.
> We do not know your name but your face will always be
> known to us.

✦ ✦ ✦

Astonishing and wonderful—Ana is writing with such passion now.

Less guardedly, and less circumspectly. Wonderful too, how others in the seminar take up her work with excitement and admiration.

This is not conventional "fiction"—there are few "characters"—minimal "description"—"Settings." All is dreamlike, rapid-fire.

In fragments it is revealed that a girl named "Mya" has lived in one or more foster homes in the Southwest. Albuquerque, Tucson. In the home are (illegal?) Central American immigrants. There are bribes to be paid. There are hopes for visas, green cards. There are knives, guns. Brutal beatings when debts are not repaid. Shootings, woundings, blood-soaked mattresses. A ghastly scene in an emergency room where an eighteen-year-old Guatemalan hemorrhages to death, and a laconic scene in a morgue in which a drug-addled woman attempts to identify an estranged and badly mutilated husband. Hiding from law enforcement officers, rummaging Dumpsters for food. Shoplifting. Unexpected cruelty in the foster home, and unexpected kindness.

Homeless children, adolescents. A girl seeking out a younger sister who has been sent to live in a foster home.

There was no choice. My mother believed our father would kill her if she did not leave.

. . . first there were three Myas in the foster home. Then there were two Myas. Then there was one Mya.

Then, none.

† † †

You are filled with dread, you have gone too far. Your shy, unassertive student has begun writing *what feels like life*—she has thrown off restraint.

It is true, you have triumphed—as a writing instructor. But this is a precarious triumph—(maybe). As if you have prized open a shell, the pulsing life of the defenseless mollusk within is exposed.

One of the most imaginative writers in the class, whose name is Philip, whose major is astrophysics and whose favored writers are Borges, Calvino, Cortázar, declares that Ana's prose poetry is *beautiful and terrible as a Möbius strip.*

Ana is deeply moved to hear these words. You have seen how Philip has been casting sidelong glances at Ana, over the weeks; now Ana lifts her eyes to his face.

Much attention is paid in the workshop to Ana's prose. Her sentences, paragraphs—headlong plunges of language. There is praise for Ana's spare, elliptical dialogue which is buried in the text as if it might be interior and not uttered aloud at all.

No one cares to address Ana's powerful subject matter. Desperate persons, domestic violence, a hint of sexual assault. *Three girls named Mya in the foster home.*

Amid their admiration the others are uneasy. It is considered bad manners—the violation of an implicit taboo—to ask if anyone's work is based upon her experiences, at least when the work is so extreme. And you have taken care to instruct the students, memoirist writing is *not memoir.* Even memoir is not "autobiography" but understood to be more poetic and impressionistic, less literal and complete.

At the end of the discussion Ana is flushed with pleasure. Unless it's an excited sort of dread. Never have you seen Ana so intense, so involved in the workshop.

You would not dare reach out to touch her wrist now, her burning-hot skin would scald your fingers.

+ + +

The following Thursday Ana is not in the seminar room when you arrive.

Everyone waits for Ana's arrival. The chair in which she usually sits is left unoccupied. But she does not appear.

Your heart is seized with dismay. You are sure it's as you'd feared—Ana regrets what she revealed to the class, she regrets being led to such openness.

Having written what she has written, that cannot now be retracted.

I am so sorry, Ana. Forgive me.

You don't write such an email. Never!

From your husband you learned never to impose your emotions upon students. Never to assume to know what they are thinking and feeling, that is (but) what you imagine they are thinking and feeling, unless they tell you; and it would be rare indeed for them to tell you.

You are the adult. You are the professional. You must prevail.

+ + +

And then: by chance you encounter Ana in a store near the university.

Indeed it is but *by chance*. Indeed *you have not been following Ana*.

Seeing too, another time—how alone Ana appears. How small, vulnerable.

Inside an oversized winter coat falling nearly to her ankles, that looks like a hand-me-down.

Her face is flushed from the cold, her eyes startled and damp. Faint shadows like bruises in her perfect skin, beneath her eyes.

Though you can see that Ana would (probably) prefer not to say hello it is not possible for you to avoid each other. You greet Ana with a friendly smile as you would any student, ignoring her nervousness; she stammers *Hello Professor. . . .*

Ana is embarrassed, awkward. Still, Ana manages to smile at her professor.

Telling you apologetically that she'd meant to write to you, to explain why she'd had to miss another class: there'd been a family emergency, she'd had to spend time on the phone with several relatives. Ana speaks so rapidly, in faltering English, you halfway wonder if she is telling the truth. Yet in her face an expression of such genuine dismay you are sure that she must be telling some part of the truth.

You are thinking *If this were a story . . .* You would invite Ana to have coffee with you, perhaps you would walk together in the lightly falling snow, and talk. Ana would confide in you at last, directly; as, it has seemed to you, she is confiding in you indirectly, in her writing. Ana would reveal herself the survivor of abuse, a broken and devastated household. A traumatized child in need of advice, protection . . .

But that does not happen. Will not happen. For this is not a story, and not a fiction. This is actual life, that does not bend easily to your fantasies.

The moment passes. You move on. You do not glance after Ana, as, you are sure, Ana does not glance after you.

It is true, you are desperately lonely. But you understand that yours is an adult loneliness that no adolescent stranger can assuage.

RECALLING YOUR SHOCK, and subsequently melancholy, when the first class of your teaching career came to an end.

How you'd actually wept . . . *I will never have such wonderful students again.*

For they had come to seem like family to you. Even those at the margins, not so fully engaged as others, the distracted ones, the annoying ones, the ones with quirky mannerisms, yet you'd come to love them all—their final smiles, their handshakes at the end of the final class, devastating to you, such loss.

Your husband had not laughed at you, not exactly. But assuring you, *Yes. You will.*

Twenty-seven years ago.

+ + +

As abruptly as it began, the semester has ended.

The final workshop in the wood-paneled seminar room at the top of the smooth-worn staircase in North Hall.

And then, "reading week"—between the end of classes and the start of exams. Through this week you will see students in your office, individually.

Following these conferences, which are sometimes intense, it is not likely that you will see most of the students again.

After such intimacy, abrupt detachment. The way of teaching—semester following semester.

Professor! Hello . . .

There is Ana, in the doorway of your office. Accompanied by two tensely smiling adults—parents?

You don't expect this. You are totally surprised. You'd thought—what had you thought?

A lost girl, an abused girl. An orphan.

Though Ana appears to be virtually quivering with nerves, or with excitement, she has brought her parents to meet you—*Elena and Carlos Fallas.* Ana's pride in the situation, her thrilled face, shining eyes, the way she clasps her parents' hands in hers, urging them to enter your office—it is very touching, you are moved nearly to tears.

Ana's parents are so *young.* Especially the mother who is Ana's height, small-boned, with beautiful dark eyes. Haltingly the parents speak to you in heavily accented English. They are visiting from San Diego, they say. They have heard much about *you.*

Through a roaring in your ears you hear Ana speaking of her favorite class, her writing class, how you helped her to write *as if your life depended upon it.*

How you'd told her—*It need not be true, your writing will make it true.*

Ana is breathless, daring. What an achievement it has been for your shyest student to have brought her parents to meet you! How long has Ana been practicing these words, this encounter . . .

The scene seems impossible to you. Unreal. How had you so misread Ana Fallas? Her seeming lack of interest in the seminar, and in you . . . Her sorrowful expression, her isolation . . .

Had you misinterpreted, and Ana is not telling the fullest truth now? But rather, performing for her parents? And for you?

The melancholy was not feigned, you are sure. The sorrow in her eyes. Yet—here is a very different Ana, laughing as she discreetly corrects her parents' English, vivacious and sparkling, happy.

Ana has plaited her hair into a sleekly black braid. She has painted her fingernails coral. She is wearing, not baggy clothes, but attractive bright-colored clothing that is a perfect size for her small body. The little gold cross glitters around her neck. Ana is very pretty, and she is adored by her parents. She is not an abused child, she is certainly not an orphan.

Astonishingly, you hear—*My favorite professor.*

You are determined not to betray this astonishment. You are determined to speak despite the roaring in your ears. Assuring Ana's eager parents that Ana has been an excellent student. A very promising writer. Like few young writers, Ana can learn from criticism—constructive criticism. Ana's imagination is fertile, seemingly boundless. You are giddy as a drunkard. Words tumble from your mouth, you are shameless. You will say anything to please these people, you want only to make them happy, to make them less ill-at-ease in your professorial presence.

You will not confess—*I have been so mistaken about your daughter. I am ashamed . . .*

She is not the person I had imagined. You are not the people. For-give me!

Ana's parents have brought you a beautifully wrapped little gift. Your heart sinks, you hope it isn't expensive. (That size? Could be a small clock. A watch.) You have not the heart to decline their gener-osity but it is considered a breach of academic ethics, at least at this university, to accept gifts from the parents of students, even small gifts.

The card from Ana you will accept, with thanks. The gift you will pass to the departmental secretary.

Ana's parents are less nervous now. They tell you how proud they are of their daughter, the first in the family to attend a four-year college. How grateful for the scholarship that brought her here— though it is so far from home. How honored to meet you.

When they leave you stand in the doorway of your office staring after them, still disbelieving, dazed. *So mistaken. How possible . . .*

The little gift you leave on your desk for the time being. The card from Ana you open: *Thank you, Professor, for giving me the key to my life.*

✦ ✦ ✦

And then, returning home later that evening.

A mild shock—the door is unlocked.

Turn the knob, and the door opens. Not for the first time since your husband has died. It is a careless habit, away for hours and the house unlocked and darkened.

You have become careless with your life. Indifferent.

Entering an empty house from which all meaning has fled.

Once, this was a *happy place.* That seems like a bad joke now.

Each room in this house is a kind of exile. You avoid most of the rooms, you keep in motion. Difficult to find a place to sit, a place where you are comfortable sitting. Almost at once you feel restless, anxious. Your fingers clutch at the hollow in your throat, you have difficulty breathing.

He has been gone how many months. Still you cannot—quite—acknowledge the word *dead*.

Once, you'd known precisely how many weeks, days. Down to the hour.

But the house is still as deserted. This place from which happiness has drained like water seeping into earth.

You have tried to explain to your husband, as you try to explain to him so many things, for he is patient, unjudging—how you were mistaken about Ana, for so long. The stubbornness in your misperception, the *hurt*. You have tried, and failed, to explain to him why Ana has meant so much to you. And why it has all ended, as it has ended.

It is frightening to you, in this empty and darkened house—*What else has eluded you, that is staring you in the face? About what else have you been mistaken?*

NIGHTGRIEF

No need to speak of it. By mutual consent, no words, no speech, no language and scarcely the complicity of touch, instinctively they began to shun the day, which is to say light—*day-light*. For there was, for them, the solace, balm, oblivion of *night* that coursed through their parched arteries and quickened their hearts grown wizened as prunes.

As in a reverse tropism each began to shrink from the glare of *day-light*. Independent of the other each began to crave, with an almost sensual appetite, *night*.

During the day, too much noise, commotion. You could see much too clearly, and too far in any direction. *Day-light* was blunt, raw, vulgar. *Day-light* was exhausting.

Too many children in *day-light*. Kids on bicycles. Shouts, laughter. At the 7-Eleven, in the drugstore parking lot, on the steps of the branch library—loitering teenagers. The wife hurried past them eyes averted like a tightrope walker on a high wire, no net below.

And afterward, collapsed in her car, sobbing, choking in a rage at herself—*No. Stop. You will be seen, pitied. Just—stop.*

Anywhere in the vicinity of sprawling Englewood Park and particularly the southeastern corner which was the softball field—sinkholes to be avoided. In *day-light* it had become treacherous to drive on certain streets, roadways. Past the beige-brick Florence Howe Middle School on Riverdale and past the redbrick Mt. Olive High School on North Main. In *day-light* these (ordinary, terrible) buildings loomed freakish-large, blotting out the sky. Never (again) Northway Mall including the streets leading to it. Without needing to confer each understood: none of these routes was possible any longer by *day-light*.

By *night*, one might drive anywhere. Or nowhere.

Day-light in any part of the urban landscape had begun to cause eye strain, aching eyes, squinting eyes, visual malformations caused by an excess of (stinging) tears. Fugues of near-blindness in bright sunshine, and then in not-bright sunshine, and then in dull-opaque daylight, finally in any degree of *day-light* at all.

Debilitating headaches—cluster headaches, migraine. As if the very skull had been struck by an ax baring the moist quivering vulnerable brain.

Sunglasses helped temporarily, at the start. The wife purchased stylish new prescription grayish-pink lenses of the kind called "progressive"—meaning that the lenses darken with the brightness of the sun. The husband purchased new prescription olive-tinted glasses, also "progressive."

Yet even with "progressive" lenses their eyes grew ever more sensitive to light. And so each began to wear lenses so dark that their eyes were hidden completely, like the eyes of the blind; and the frames of these glasses were large, masking one-third of their faces, like the faces of the guilty who wish to pass among us incognito.

So disguised, if they dared to venture out in *day-light* it was not surprising that people who knew them did not (seem to) recognize them. That people who knew them, or had once known them, might glance toward them without seeming to see them, as if, singly or together, they had become invisible.

Not surprising, no one to blame, if friends/acquaintances/neighbors did not smile bravely at the couple—*Why, hello! How are you! We have been thinking about you and meant to call* . . .

Solace came only with darkness. When dusk yielded to the sweet oblivion of *night*.

✦ ✦ ✦

Whatever it was that had happened, however it had happened, in the bedroom at the top of the stairs in the late winter of the year, had happened at night.

Happened was how they spoke of it. Passive, past-tense.

Like rain, hail, dripping eaves. Earthquake. Act of God.

Yet, what had happened in the night was discovered only in the morning—"Just after seven A.M. We are an early-rising family."

By which time it would be calculated that what had happened, that could not ever be reversed or undone, had happened approximately eight–nine hours before. Which was to say, between ten P.M. and eleven P.M. of the previous calendar day.

Through the (long) night unguessed-at by the adults of the household.

A rude surprise, at breakfast. The earthquake, at breakfast.

The wife had been the one to make the discovery. Of course, it would be the wife. For it was nearing seven-thirty A.M. and there'd been no sound, no footsteps overhead or on the stairs. The wife, who'd called upstairs. The wife, who'd then gone upstairs to see.

"Breakfast-time was always our happiest time . . ."

Never again breakfast, not even the possibility of breakfast, the very word *breakfast* an obscenity not to be muttered aloud.

In fact any meal contemplated during *day-light* was likely to provoke nausea, breathlessness, choking. Loss of appetite came to be associated with *day-light*—the very smell of food repulsive.

Day-light itself repulsive. Treacherous.

The only solace came to be sleeping through *day-light* and only after dark rousing themselves sleep-engorged and bloated like ticks that have feasted on blood not always knowing where they were, or when it was, or who the other was; for the consumption of alcohol (in her case, white wine; in his, whiskey) as well as barbiturates ("sleep aids") had become the primary means of self-medication.

Waking to find themselves in the room quaintly, comically, cruelly designated "master bedroom" of a size and dignity (bathroom adjoined) to set it apart from other, smaller, mere bedrooms in the house of which there were several including the room at the top of the stairs which was no longer used as a "bedroom" nor even as a "room." Waking groggily, reluctantly in the (master) bedroom that soon began to exude the smells of a sickroom though neither the husband nor the wife was (they would have insisted) *sick*. A double bed rarely changed now, that had been routinely, even religiously changed each Monday, with fresh-laundered fine-spun cotton sheets in (matching) colors and prints, and (matching) pillowcases. And a quilted green-satin comforter atop the bed now soiled, mysteriously grimy as if with food-, blood-, vomit-stains, seen now solely by lamplight which is a forgiving sort of light unlike the raw unsparing light of day. Bedclothes dampened from sweaty dreams, sheets twisted by twitching legs, pillowcases grown sodden beneath heads leaking shame and anxiety like mucus. Underfoot in the perpetual twilight were miscellaneous socks, T-shirts, underwear—*his*; though similarly worn, soiled, *hers* were never tossed onto the floor with that cavalier air (the wife thought, observing her husband covertly) of mockery, derision.

Her soiled things were hidden away in a hamper in the bathroom, in a proper reflex of shame. *Her* towels, though chronically damp, dirtied, beginning to fray, were yet hung properly on towel-racks in the bathroom, while *his* were likely to have fallen to the floor in a heap and this heap kicked into a corner of the bathroom.

Like a (small, sodden) body it was. Roadkill, possibly. Tossed to the side of the road.

Yet, the husband was correct in such deportment. What did cleanliness, propriety, even a pretense of cleanliness and propriety, *matter*?

If the wife should pick up the husband's tossed-down laundry, holding her breath reaching beneath the bed to retrieve a dirt-stiffened sock, if she should take up the moldering towels in a heap in the bathroom, would such good-wife self-abasement *matter*?

Of course, it would not.

✦ ✦ ✦

What *mattered* was sleeping through the day. Not so very easy, to sleep through an entire day.

Especially in hideous light-filled months: April, May. Pinnacle of *day-light* horror: June 21.

What had happened in the room at the top of the stairs in the season of melting snow, dripping eaves, thunderous skies had seemed at the least to be fixed, permanent. *There is that*—the wife might say with a bitter sort of joy. For here was a promise of finality, the worst that might happen, that had happened, had the power, or should have had the power, to stop time. Yet—time had not stopped.

Not in the slightest had time stopped. What a joke, to imagine that there was an entity—Time—that might choose to *stop*.

Instead late, wintry March yielded by degrees to a warmer season. Befouled snow, dripping icicles at last—disappeared. Hard-frozen earth thawed, miniature shoots began to appear, the wife stared in disbelief at—what could these be?—a scattering of *snowdrops* vivid-whitely blooming amid the debris of winter beside the rear door of the garage . . . As the brain-damaged are not likely to comprehend the blow of the sledgehammer that has damaged their brains so the wife and the husband could not comprehend this stunning betrayal—a new season?

Where in a late winter of occluded skies a stuporous kind of dark-muck sleep was possible, this sleep became, even with self-medication, ever more elusive in a season of obscenely bright skies. Eight hours of sleep was a challenge. Nine, ten hours a fantasy-wish. Eleven hours, a triumph rarely achieved.

By mutual consent, neither chose to swallow a half-dozen chunky white barbiturates, or more. Neither chose to obliterate obscene consciousness altogether. No words, no speech, instinctively they shrank from such a remedy for the pain of *nightgrief.*

Someone has to remember. If there is no one . . .

Waking too soon, the heart pounded in dismay, disgust. If the light of late afternoon was still discernible through minute cracks in the venetian blinds.

Tightly the blinds were drawn to prevent light leaking in. Tightly in all the windows of the house, not just in the (master) bedroom. A savage tightness as the husband readjusted the blinds to draw them *tighter.* The wife whimpered as if the husband were drawing something *tight, tighter* around her neck—but to no avail, the husband did not hear. *Day-light* was the enemy, the husband would defeat. Slats in the blinds broke and had to be mended with duct tape.

A kind of radioactive light was indeed leaking into the house, an obvious poison. The wife began to wear the oversized dark-dark glasses in the house, during the (obscene) hours of the day when sleep failed her and cast her out forlorn as a mangled creature on a littered beach when the tide has gone out. The husband cursed at infinitesimal motes of light glimmering through blinds drawn to the windowsills and stomped from room to room nailing blankets over the windows, the darkest blankets he could find, the largest bath towels to keep out the despised light.

Hammering!—the husband did love to hammer. (Was this love new? The pleasure of gripping the wooden handle of the claw hammer, certainly new. Having taken leave of his *day-light* work to sink into the more exhausting labor of *nightgrief* the husband had energy to spare.) The wife cringed, pressing her hands against her ears. Pain darted inside her skull like lightning. Such fury in the husband's hammering, the wife feared he was striking at her head with the claw hammer as he pounded nails into the wall securing a blanket or a towel in place. The husband was methodical, precise. There is a particular fury in precision.

Yes I am the one, the one to blame. Yes you are blameless.

Yet, one day the husband was heard, in a distant room, calling "Help! Help me!"—his voice ringing through the house like something buzzing and careening in terror, striking walls.

The wife froze where she stood. That's to say, where she stood the wife froze.

That's to say, the wife did not precisely *freeze* in place, though she was shivering with cold, a chronic sort of clammy-damp cold that had lodged in the marrow of her bones like an insidious leukemia; rather, the wife for a fleeting ecstatic moment contemplated the luxury of not-hearing the husband's call for help, her excuse being that she was in a faraway room, or had turned on a faucet, or perhaps she was in the garage where *day-light* was not blinding. Just a moment, a precious moment of freedom, then—"Yes? What is it? Where are—" The wife hurried upstairs to a room where she discovered the husband standing on a chair barefoot, precariously balanced, gripping the claw hammer in one hand and with the other clinging to a window frame to prevent a fall, flushed face glaring and hair sharply receding from his forehead lifted in tufts of rage.

"Help me! For Christ's sake don't just stand there . . ."

Of course, the wife hurried to help the husband, steadying his tremulous legs (so thin! the muscles seemed to have atrophied) so there was less danger of falling as he resumed his task of nailing another blanket over another window; providing too a (thin, narrow) shoulder for the husband to lean heavily upon, as he stepped down from the chair.

"Thank you! What would I do without you, darling"—a remark of such jocose grimness, the wife could imagine the words uttered through the gritted teeth of a death's-head.

✦ ✦ ✦

The (happy) surprise was, each of them was discovering how yoked together they were in the aftermath of what is (commonly, promiscuously, banally) called *trauma.* Unavoidable in the intimacy of marriage?—each wondered.

"We have each other"—the wife dared to suggest, with a shiver of hope.

"We have each other"—the husband echoed, with a shiver of dread.

Nightgrief. No need to speak of it, as bog-creatures have no need to speak of the bog in which they dwell, companionably.

SOON IT WAS DISCOVERED that even in the shimmering Hell-light of summer an entire (new) life was possible, after dark.

In the (master) bedroom alone a galaxy of TV possibilities. Full range of cable channels including Spanish-speaking. Streaming films, DVDs. A new flat-screen TV seemingly floating in place, matte-black when turned off, sleek and handsome, larger than the flat-screen in the basement which they no longer watched, ever. At their fingertips on their laptop keyboards the ubiquitous Internet, "social media"—an infinity of distractions each of which demanded immediate intense attention.

✦ ✦ ✦

Insomniac hours. Eyes that fail to close. Brains that fail to shut off. Here were the (home) cures.

Meals in front of the TV replaced meals in the kitchen, dining room—rooms fraught with anxiety like bad, bog-smells. Meals delivered to the front door or defrosted in the microwave replaced meals (lovingly, tediously) prepared in the kitchen with "fresh" ingredients. (With astonishment and chagrin the wife recalled those years, that constituted at least one-third of her life. What on earth had been that charade? Had she been performing an arcane rite— *mother, provider-of-food? Household good sport, mediator of disputes, never failing to smile?* None of it had mattered in the slightest, as it turned out. She thought it bizarre, she hadn't guessed.)

Neither had much *appetite* any longer. Indeed, *appetite* had become a problematic issue. Once you've *lost your appetite* you have lost your comprehension of what *appetite* is, or was. (Yet, what could *lost* possibly mean, in this context? If *lost, lost* where? There can be no category of sheer *lostness*. And how could an instinct so rudimentary, yet so abstract, as *appetite*, become *lost?*) Yet, with or without *appetite* the couple discovered that the distractions of an animated screen made it possible to eat, if only mechanically, and certainly possible, in fact quite pleasurable to drink—white wine, whiskey. (The white wine wasn't invariably chilled, and the husband who'd favored scotch whiskey over ice cubes no longer troubled much about ice, for the walk downstairs to the kitchen and back upstairs was a bore.) A pleasurable sort of hypnosis in staring at fleeting images on screens, sudden swells and crescendos of "music" to signal meaning—no need to speak though sometimes by mutual consent, though wordless, one of them hastily switched a channel with the remote, or hastily pressed *mute*.

For even *nightgrief* must be protected. *Nightgrievers* cannot be too vigilant.

Of course each tried to read, in private. Recalling that some of the most intense experiences of their lives had been in (serious) reading. Yet each was discovering that books had become problematic since what had happened in the late winter of dripping eaves, thunderous skies. Requiring concentration, conscious involvement. It was disappointing—alarming—that neither the husband nor the wife was capable any longer of *reading*, except for short periods of time. No sooner was a sentence *read*, than its meaning was lost. Gamely the wife tried to (re)read one of the favorite books of her previous life, *Jane Eyre*. (The very paperback, with an introduction by her English professor at Bard, she'd read and diligently annotated in college.) But the paragraphs were too long, turgid; by the time she came to the end of a paragraph she was obliged to reread it;

if she was being honest, she could not allow herself to push forward but must read, reread, and (re)reread, the same numbing words. The husband found that he could not sit still long enough to *read* as he could recall *reading* in the past. He too had a cherished book to (re)read—John Rawls's *A Theory of Justice*, also in a paperback heavily annotated by the husband, a lifetime ago in law school in New Haven. But his skin itched violently, distracting him. His scalp itched, he scratched with his nails and drew blood. For *reading* involves a strict linear progression of thought, and an effort of memory; books involve pages that are meant to be turned, and pages contain lines of print that descend in a specific, immutable order, and "print" must be decoded in the brain, thus requiring a participatory sort of consciousness, the most exhausting sort of consciousness. In frustration the husband tore out pages of *A Theory of Justice*, crumpled them in his fist—"Fuck 'justice.' Fuck its guts." In another room, the wife stiffened in fright but did not hear.

The solace they craved was not to be found in *books*. True solace was a passive and narcotic activity of (semi)-consciousness that required no personal involvement—staring for hours at a glassy screen upon which images moved ceaselessly, music swelled, subsided, swelled ceaselessly whether a human consciousness was present or not.

＋ ＋ ＋

Venturing out after dark was another sort of adventure, risky and thrilling (at first). Guiding yourself by the headlights of a vehicle that are aimed straight ahead and do not waver. So that even if you are forced to drive along certain (familiar, terrible) streets and roadways, you will find that the terrain has altered simply because it is *night* and not *day-light* which was the condition in which you'd most frequently experienced these (familiar, terrible) streets and roadways.

For instance, instead of Northway Mall, a vast sinkhole they would never (again) approach, there was Southbridge Mall, a forty-minute drive along relatively unfamiliar roads. Parts of the mall remained open until midnight and so here was an oasis of festive lights, a floating island thrumming with a particular sort of after-dark suburban life: fast-food restaurants, "quality" restaurants with liquor licenses, a glittery CineMax boasting twelve theaters.

The promise of Southbridge Mall was that it could be experienced as "new"—even brand-name stores and franchises could appear legitimately "new" in the unfamiliar setting. A multi-tiered burbling fountain at its center, architecture that differed perceptibly from the architecture of the Northway Mall (though created by the identical architectural firm)—here was a new planet to be explored cautiously, its dangers not immediately apparent until, on their third visit, forced to wear tinted glasses in the fluorescent glare, thinking to see a film at the CineMax they chanced to discover on the lower mall level a row of garish fast-food restaurants adjacent to a video-game arcade swarming with teenaged boys from which, dazed and staggering, migraine-tears streaking their cheeks, they fled.

+ + +

Weeks, months. One hundred eighty-two days, one hundred eighty-three . . .

Without their having realized the (deadly) zenith of summer had passed. From now on days would be shorter, nights longer. From now on, the air would be easier to breathe.

Gravity was on their side now. Gravity would ease them down-ward.

A day when anything might happen. The wife might decide, for instance, to do the laundry. Run the dishwasher (crammed with plates, cutlery haphazardly rinsed). Clean the house. At least, parts of the house that were not, by mutual consent, off-limits. In the early hours of the morning, that's to say in the blackest hours of the night, tugging the vacuum cleaner from room to room, a bracing activity, caffeine-fueled. Stray thoughts were muffled by the reassuring roar and under cover of this roar the wife repeated the statement she'd given to authorities: "We had no idea." Clearing her throat, more calmly: "We had no idea. My husband and me . . ." Seeing with satisfaction how bits of dust and grime were sucked up into the vacuum bag. How easy housecleaning was, and how visibly dirt might vanish! That is, the sort of dirt detachable from a surface.

Stains were another matter. Stains in carpets might be left for another time.

The husband too might rouse himself from the TV screen that left him dazed and enervated to make minor repairs in the house with his screwdriver, pliers, claw hammer and handful of nails. One of the husband's happiest discoveries had been his toolbox, stored out in the garage. Sometimes, not invariably, the husband wore work-gloves. On his head, pulled low on his forehead, a carpenter's cap imprinted with white letters DUTCH BOY, he'd found in the garage. For in the aftermath of what had happened in the room at the top of the stairs, that had not been fully understood by either the husband or the wife, the house had begun to deteriorate in a sort of delayed shock as in the aftermath of an earthquake. Wall light switches failed to turn on lights, toilet tanks ran water incessantly. Dripping faucets, stuck doors. Loose tiles that had to be glued or hammered into place. Ill-fitting windows requiring caulking. Carpets infested with moth larvae, that had to be dragged out into the garage and sprayed. The husband became quickly winded having to squat, or kneel, or strain his arm and shoulder muscles, or his neck. The husband's spine ached, from his having dragged the heavy and resistant living room carpet across a floor. (How old was the husband now? Dimly recalled his last birthday, in his previous life, might've been—forty-five?—forty-nine? Like the wife, whose last birthday had been her forty-first, back in January, the husband did not expect to have another birthday.) Bits of grit fell into his eyes, that were yet reddened and swollen and failed to focus correctly. His heartbeat was erratic, whether with dread or a sort of ecstatic joy that the worst had happened, and so could not (again) happen. Yet there was pleasure in such elemental tasks of repair and renovation, that could be immediately seen, and appreciated by the other occupant of the (depleted) household. Especially tasks requiring the claw hammer, that had begun to fit the husband's hand with a mysterious elation.

Muffled by the hammer's pounding the husband repeated the statement he'd given to authorities in a voice of stunned wonder: "I had no idea . . ."

+ + +

Like nocturnal creatures they were becoming adjusted to *night*. By mid-autumn they might have found themselves blind in *day-light* like those poor mules who'd been worked for years in mines, discovered to be blind when at last they were brought back to *day-light*.

Now there was a distinct solace in the passage of time, that had been loathed before. Now, there was the promise of *night* expanding as autumn, then winter, advanced. Ever more, each day was eclipsed by *night*. The couple could, if they wished, leave the safety of the house earlier—on the darkest days, when the sky was a thick crust of shale-like clouds, steely-gray, canyons of rubble, as early as six P.M. though this was a risk for (possibly) they might see someone, an individual or individuals, or an entire category of individuals, they did not wish to see.

Discovering how certain stores were best patronized by night in any case. Safeway, Target, CVS, Home Depot, Walmart—cavernous spaces in which, in evening hours, there were no long lines at checkout counters, and rarely children. Only just adults like themselves somber-faced, pasty-skinned, pushing their carts and keeping their eyes to themselves.

Why, we are the walking wounded! Who would have known there are so many of us.

Sometimes in these mammoth bright-lit stores the wife might wear her stylish pinkish-gray sunglasses, for so many articles on six-foot shelves, so many competing and jangling colors, made her head ache. The husband might wear his ultra-dark glasses for his eyes were (still) reddened and swollen with a look now rather of anger and incredulity than *nightgrief.*

Reduced staff at checkout counters, especially as closing hour (eleven P.M.) approached. The wife found it uncanny how, observed at a little distance, certain of the clerks stood immobile and stiff as mannequins in their sexless store uniforms; only when you approached them and triggered a motion sensor did they "wake" to attention with friendly smiles and store greetings—*Hello! How are you this evening!*

As she'd disliked the largest of the stores in her former life so the wife retained a slight aversion for these in her present life, much preferring the smaller, more easily navigated Safeway which resembled in certain respects the grocery store in her own neighborhood where she'd shopped for fifteen years, yet differed enough from that store to erase, or to lessen, the wife's inclination to unease and anxiety in a public place; her sense of being, as she'd tried to explain to the husband, *unmoored, and drifting.*

(Often, when the wife spoke to the husband in a public place, in a quiet, confiding voice, the husband behaved as if he had not heard; indeed, as if there were no one close beside him murmuring into his ear. Enough times this had happened that the wife began to doubt her own existence, to a degree.)

(Or was the husband simply becoming hearing impaired? That morning in late March when the wife had screamed to him from the room at the top of the stairs, the husband had not seemed immediately to hear.)

One problem with late-night grocery shopping was that "fresh produce" was likely to be wilted and picked-over. "Fresh-caught fish" lay dispiritedly on melted ice, meats had turned gray. Even canned soups, a staple of the couple's meals in front of the TV screen, were often depleted on shelves and baguettes, the husband's favorite bread, were frankly stale. When you wanted to ask a store employee a question, there was no one in sight.

Yet the wife rejoiced that no children rushed about at this hour. No young adolescents were to be seen. Adult shoppers appeared harried, distracted, poorly groomed and no one to be envied.

Blessed quiet!—the wife drew a deep breath. No need to steel herself against a rude intrusion.

Except, a minor incident, pushing her cart down the aisle of cereals between shelves of cheerily colored cereal boxes, predominantly bright-yellow, reassured that the husband, often sulky and disoriented prowling the Safeway aisles for his own particular foods which he could not trust the wife to choose, was nowhere near, the wife stumbled seeing, or imagining that she saw, a slender fugitive figure in T-shirt and jeans just ahead, slyly disappearing around a corner—"Oh! Wait! Don't leave me—" the wife heard herself cry in the instant before all the blood drained out of her head, all the strength drained out of her legs, and the soft underside of her chin struck the cart handle, a good smack that woke her to the folly of her behavior.

Flushed and chagrined, jaw hurting like hell, but grateful that the husband had not been a witness.

Of course there was no slender shimmering-transparent figure in the next aisle, or anywhere in sight. The wife recovered at once, sensibly.

Impressive, the way in which a rapidly accelerated heart on the very cusp of tachycardia begins to slow, informed by a signal from the brain, sensibly.

Why didn't you have two of them for Christ's sake. If one is lost, the other will take his place, couldn't have been that difficult to figure it out, right? Weren't you always supposed to be smart?

Grateful the husband hadn't seen, would never know. Grateful.

+ + +

But then, worse, despite the warning, recklessly the wife insisted upon returning to the Safeway because it was convenient, because the husband complained less bitterly about the selection of his particular foods in the Safeway, near the end of October on a very dark starless night when the air smelled mildly of sulphur, and the electricity in the grocery store shivered and shuddered as if it were about to go out, once again the wife was pushing her cart alone, once again grateful that the (sulky) husband was elsewhere searching for his longtime favorite brand of pickles, the wife turned a corner out of the canned soup aisle to see a lurid Hallowe'en display: stuffed scarecrow figure, carved pumpkin head grinning, baggy T-shirt, jeans, around its neck an eerily realistic noose—not a mere loop of clothesline but an actual hangman's noose comprised of a terrifying number of coils, at least ten, fixed in place by a perfect knot.

This time, the wife fell in a dead faint. No time to suck in her breath, cry out. Struck her head on the edge of a shelf, slid onto the floor, on her side, consciousness obliterated in an instant as a light switch is turned *off.*

Waking then, faces looming above her, the husband's sharp scolding voice—"That's my wife. I'll take care of her"—lifting her beneath the arms, shaking her awake, panic in the husband's reddened and swollen eyes only the wife might have discerned if she'd been able to see. No need for anyone to call 911, the husband insisted, no need for an ambulance, absolutely not, no emergency, he would take his wife home, walk her out of the store since by this time the wife was revived, or nearly; the wife was herself again, or nearly; embarrassed at having caused a scene, attracted the attention of several shoppers, Safeway employees, more witnesses than she'd have imagined possible at this hour. Wincing with pain, right temple, right arm, fingers on her right hand felt mangled where she'd fallen on them but really, truly—she was all right, she was *fine.*

Indeed the husband walked the wife out of the brightly lighted grocery store, firmly gripping her beneath her arms, holding her erect; he helped her into their car, returned to the store stony-faced and determined to retrieve the wife's cart nearly filled with groceries at the end of aisle nine, for the husband had no intention of aborting the shopping in such a way, abandoning both their carts, squandering forty minutes' effort, a bloody waste of time. Pushing the wife's cart and, awkwardly, his own cart, filled with fewer items, to the checkout counter. In a loud voice insisting that his wife was all right, his wife sometimes fainted, she was on blood thinners, or maybe it was low blood pressure, or both.

Certainly the husband had seen the scarecrow with the grinning pumpkin head, (expert) hangman's noose around its neck, he'd even counted the number of coils, ten coils, all in an instant, scarcely blinking he'd seen, he'd understood, took charge, wresting the narrative into his own control, where it belonged; as he'd taken control of the grocery carts, maneuvering them together to the checkout counter, completing the shopping on this Thursday night but it would be the last time at God-damned Safeway, that was certain.

IT BEGAN TO HAPPEN THEN, she hated him. The husband—*him*.

Ceased speaking his name, indeed ceased thinking his name as (she realized) he'd ceased speaking her name months ago. In any case *night* made "names" ridiculous. The redundant is by nature ridiculous. *Night* swallowed, enveloped, rendered redundant and ridiculous the preoccupations of *day-light*—distinctions of identity. Why did anyone care in the slightest who they were, or who anyone was? As the husband would say scornfully what did any of this matter? Only the drop matters.

The drop is all that matters. Too close to the floor, your neck isn't broken in an instant, instead you die a slow death by strangulation. Too far to the floor, the weight of your body can cause your head to be wrenched from your body, decapitated. Gushers of blood, to the ceiling and beyond.

(Such astonishing instructions, on the Internet! They'd discovered, or rather the forensic specialists had discovered.)

Hating him, a humid sort of hatred, as a seed falls through a crack in pavement but becomes germinated nonetheless, pushing up, upward, blind, eyeless, in a perverse *tropism*. Hating him, wandering in the night in the back lot of their property, grateful for a starless night, moonless night, groping her way. Smelling the dark wet earth beneath her bare feet, her heart leaps with something like hope— she is alive, that's to say *she is alive*; but the sensation soon fades for he will be calling to her pettishly, he will be seeking her out, his companion in *nightgrief,* he will not allow her to escape. He is one who never forgets a grudge, his hurts are boils and bunions upon which his (ungainly) feet insist upon walking. The wife is aghast to discover that the husband, a fastidious man in his former life, has let his toenails grow in this posthumous life, thick as horn, deformed, surely painful; she wonders if the (ingrown?) toenails might become infected, abscessed, and in that way the husband will begin to die; a lengthy, awkward, improvident and spiteful way of dying that was, in its way, a refutation of his former efficiency. As if declaring, sneering—*You would like me to kill myself more readily but I will take my time.*

But if you want to die, go ahead. No one is stopping you.

+ + +

But it is to be nothing like this. For the second time within a span of 237 days, the wife is astonished.

The room at the top of the stairs. The room never (again) to be opened.

After the last of the investigators had left. After everything to be removed from the room had been removed. A confused memory of the emergency medics who'd been the first to arrive, the first of the strangers, the first to intrude, shockingly young, balletic in their grace, shouted words, commands, descending the stairs with the slender broken figure on a stretcher, belted in place. There was something tender in such care, in such dispatch. But the wife remembers mostly the silence of the young medics for words are mere sounds even when shouted, and fade rapidly.

Pressing her ear against the door. For some reason lifting herself onto her toes, as if this might help her hear. How long she has been pressing her ear to the door, she could not have said.

Yes, she can hear—faint music on the farther side of the door, *his music.* Never before had she listened to *his music,* which had (vaguely) repelled her. Almost she can hear—is it breathing? Of all sounds the most miraculous.

From the foot of the stairs the husband calls to her. "What are you doing? What the hell are you doing?"—he is excitable, frightened. His words are slurred for he has been drinking whiskey. He has been taking more than his share of the barbiturates. His eyes burn red with rage and bafflement and so quickly she calls to him— "It was not your fault."

She sees how he recoils from her. She sees that his (male) grief is rapacious, never to be satisfied. In a quavering voice he mocks her— "No. It was not *your fault*."

Then climbing the stairs to stand beside her, panting. It has been forbidden to open the door, to enter the room, there has been no need to speak of it, each has understood, and indeed the wife has not even thought of opening the door and betraying the husband's trust. Only just pressing her ear against the door, holding the breath in her lungs, listening. At first the wife expects the panting trembling husband to strike her but instead the husband gropes for her hand. It is a shock to her, the husband no longer looms over her, a threat. In his stocking feet he is no longer a tall man. His back broken, he is no longer a tall man. His hand gripping hers, not in recent memory has his hand gripped hers, not since the late winter of the year, she'd have thought that the husband would want to break the mangled fingers of her hand but no, he only holds the fingers, there is gentleness, almost timidity in his hand closed about hers. And so, blameless they stand at the top of the stairs side by side, virtually of a height. Blameless they will forgive each other, she supposes. They have no one else to forgive.

FINAL INTERVIEW

1.

You have arrived alone at the Purple Onion Café. Not long after noon judging by the position of the sun in the sky.

No idea why, why here. Why heavy hiking boots which would make running difficult if you had to run. And this *ticking* in the air close about you like the quivering of insects' wings, so small the human eye can't detect them.

Seated at a table near the rear of the (busy, bustling) terrace.

Where the *ticking* has followed you. Louder.

No idea why, but has to be here. And why now?—after so many postponements, has to be *now*.

Waitress approaches to take your order. Young, shimmering-blond hair. Bare legs. Bare feet in sandals. Eyes slide onto you with an expression of surprise. Female disdain. That look you've seen so many times in your life almost it's reassuring—*You are in the right place. This is the right time.*

2.

"D'you mind if I record our conversation?"—X fidgets with his iPhone.

Why the hell would I mind. "Of course not. That's fine."

"Did you say—*why?*"

"What? No. I said *fine.*"

Making an effort to disguise your irritation. Making an effort to appear courteous.

(Fatuous question, an interviewer asking if an interviewee minds their conversation being recorded!)

"Some people do mind," X says defensively, as if you've spoken aloud, "—they object to being *recorded.*"

You let this remark pass. Seething anger, quick as a spurting artery. But *no.* An error to reveal your emotions to a professional journalist.

"In any case," X persists, with that wide wet smile like a disinfectant swab across your raw brain, "I am not in the habit of misquoting those with whom I speak whether I 'record' or take notes the old-fashioned way."

X speaks English as if translating from another language. The German-inflected accent is particularly grating since you know that X was born in the United States.

Again, you say nothing. Noting that it is (already) 12:34 P.M. Four minutes into the scheduled interview. You know that X was informed by your publisher that he could have only one hour for the interview, the excuse being that you have another appointment shortly afterward, and so must end your conversation with him promptly at 1:30 P.M.

This way you will not be considered rude. Only just a busy man, practical-minded, expedient. Despite your reputation as a reclusive individual of "poetic" erudite texts.

But now, X has thought of a new way of annoying you. A small mean light glimmers in his rodent eyes.

"I'd meant to ask you—is this the café where a suicide bombing took place?"

"'Suicide bombing!' No."

It's a quick retort, reflexive as a sneeze. Almost, you feel the instinct to reach into a pocket, rummage for a tissue to wad against your eyes.

"No? Really? It was an outdoor café, I think. Here in Santa Luce. With a name like—'Purple Onion' . . ."

Does this terrible person mean to torment you? As if there could be another restaurant in Santa Luce with a name *like* Purple Onion!

Since his (several-minutes-late) arrival X has been glancing about the bustling café terrace. As if, the fool, he might be in actual danger in such a banal place. (Most of the luncheon patrons are women. A tribe of well-to-do, very fit, streaked-blond "youthful" women whose laughter hurts your brain like the sound of crystal being shattered in manic repetition.)

Can't determine if X is serious about this concern or merely being comical. X's face—which is unusually long and droll, with a high dome of a forehead and thick tufts of eyebrows—is markedly expressive, like a mime's. Fatuous behavior can sometimes conceal genuine anxiety, as you know as a "keen observer" of human psychology, so you make an effort to be patient with X.

You acknowledge that yes, you'd heard that there were bomb threats made against the restaurant, some time ago. The proprietor, Nadia, the cheerful *zaftig* woman with the untidy horse's mane trailing down her back, who'd just shown X to the table, has been an activist in liberal causes for years—protesting, picketing, marching. Gay/lesbian rights, immigration rights, No Nukes, Clean Water. Possibly there'd been an attempted bombing at the Purple Onion, but—so far as you know, no actual bomb was detonated . . .

"Hmm! Are you sure? Because I—"

Tersely, calmly you say with a clenched set of jaws: "I live here, and I would know."

"Ah! I see. Of course."

X, who has traveled thousands of miles to interview you, does not wish to antagonize you. (At least until the interview is over.) Very easily X could consult his iPhone to determine who is correct, you or he, but he says only, in a conciliatory voice, that he'd heard "something vague" about a high school dropout in this part of California, near San Francisco, who'd assembled a bomb following directions he'd gotten on the Internet from an ISIS site . . . But whether it was actually detonated, X doesn't know.

"This sort of 'terrorist' news is usually exaggerated"—you laugh softly, a sort of hissing-laugh, the laughter of contempt and indifference, finality.

At the time of the (alleged) bombing you'd been in residence at the American Academy in Rome. Or maybe it was the American Academy in Berlin. Focused on your work, no time for news of bombings, school shootings, mass murders in the United States, that seemed to be a near-daily basis.

Overhead, a high droning sound like a dentist's drill but you refrain from glancing skyward.

At last, a waitress approaches your table, takes your orders gravely, departs. X pushes the iPhone gently toward you. Bares his big teeth in a smile that appears lewd but might be only conspiratorial and says, with a wink: "Cut to the jugular, friend. Tell me what you've never told any other interviewer."

3.

Precisely 12:19 P.M. when you arrive at the Purple Onion Café for your interview with X which is scheduled to begin at 12:30 P.M.

For it is *your way* to arrive early for appointments. Particularly those appointments you dread.

X, the internationally renowned interviewer, is known to be a disagreeable person. X will flatter you in conversation, then eviscerate you in prose. You know, though you must pretend otherwise.

X has a name but you decline to supply the name. In fact, you will never address X by his name.

You were away in Europe when the Purple Onion was closed for repairs for nine months. Just recently reopened, much fanfare in local media. You see that the exterior of the restaurant has been repainted—the shingled roof looks new—a new flagstone terrace, new tables and chairs. A low evergreen hedge, some of it partially damaged, running the length of the terrace. You have no interest in going inside the restaurant, you suffer from a mild claustrophobia and recall that the interior of the Purple Onion is crowded with tables, and loud. The voices and laughter of your species do not suffuse your heart with joy. And close quarters, in the company of X, would be particularly disagreeable.

Hello, sir!

You try not to cringe as you are greeted, a little too exuberantly, by the proprietor/owner of the Purple Onion, Nadia with her brave smile, ankle-length peasant skirt, knitted vest, and Navajo jewelry. Nadia is a stout, hearty, big-boned girl of fifty with graying hair falling loose over her shoulders and skin that glows with incandescent light except for the net of fine white scars across her forehead. One of those well-intentioned but exasperating locals who murmurs slyly in your ear—*Mr. ___, I have read all your books!*

Also—*It's an honor, sir. Thank you, sir.* Air of excited girlish embarrassment that makes you wince.

Nadia seats you at the table you've requested which is your usual
at the Purple Onion—farthest corner on the terrace, beside a wall
of wisteria just beginning to bloom. You will take some small solace from the fragrance of the wisteria. Often in this (late) phase of
your life your eyes glance skyward, astonished at the heartbreaking
beauty of clouds that look sculpted in white marble, sometimes a
faint daytime moon, blue sky beyond like washed glass. That beauty
that is (literally) *out of your reach.*

You are not a person who is comfortable *being seen*; it has always
been your strategy to be the individual who *sees.* Not to be the center of attention is, to you, the goal of your relationships with others
for you are not unlike a thief, a thief who steals whenever he can,
and from whom he can, often randomly, with no plan, as a matter
of survival.

Yet, you are acclaimed as a "master" of some sort: the criminal
hiding in plain sight.

From your strategic table you can peruse the terrace as it fills up
with a chattering lunchtime crowd of mostly women. (Some of these
women you know socially, but would be pressed to say their names;
if they glance in your direction smilingly, you quickly look away.)
From this vantage point you take pleasure in observing, through
charmingly gnarled wisteria vines, figures approaching the café entrance on the walkway; if you lean forward you can see a corner of
the parking lot, and observe them even earlier.

Is there something unreal about the scene? You feel uneasy, un-
settled.

A prematurely warm April day. But—which year?

As in dreams we often have no idea how old we are, and what
exactly we look like, so you are thinking that this place has become

strange to you, though in all (evident) respects it is (dully) familiar to you.

The sky has become overcast, the hue of watery skim milk. Weather at this time of year can be mercurial in northern California near the coast. Sudden wind from the Pacific Ocean twenty miles to the west, darkening sky, within minutes a violent thunderstorm. Or, wind from the east, dry-desert wind, the sky bursts into pieces of sunshine like shards of broken glass raining down onto your head.

Laughter at nearby tables. Evidence suggests that humankind seems to have decided it is wiser to laugh than to cry.

4.

Waiting for X to appear. Reluctant to admit, you are fearful of X. Fearful that X can peer into your very soul as it has been (ludicrously) claimed of X by previous interview subjects whom you respect— Rushdie, McEwan, Oz, Ondaatje.

Glancing nervously at your watch. Already—12:26 P.M. You feel a pang of loss as the minutes pass.

Almost, you can hear time *ticking*.

The (notorious) interviewer, based in Berlin, was scheduled to fly to San Francisco via Chicago; from San Francisco, to be driven by hired car to Santa Luce, twenty miles to the east and south, where you have lived an (inexplicable) suburban existence for more than three decades.

X will surely comment upon that fact. *Withdrawn, reclusive, near-anonymous, innocuous. A bourgeois existence—shameful?*

In bed this morning you felt oppressed as by a heavy object, a body, lying upon you—hot-skinned demonic face pressed against yours. Bulging eyes pressed against yours.

An effort to open your eyes, force yourself out of bed.

Wanting badly that X disappear. Midair?

You have acquired a reputation for being cantankerous, unpredictable. Though to anyone who knows you well you are totally predictable.

"Just one hour with *Der Spiegel*. Is that too much to ask? What can go wrong?"—your editor in New York City pleaded.

Your publisher is eager for the interview to take place. Publicity for your books, which enjoy a degree of critical acclaim but which have never been commercial. The interview will appear in *Der Spiegel* on the occasion of your receiving a distinguished international literary prize, to be presented in Berlin later in the year but until that time, confidential.

This new award is a source of pride to you, and unease. *Lifetime achievement*. Will you then become posthumous?

Idly you think, the interview will be published as an obituary.

Unless X doesn't appear? Then, all remains unaltered.

Often in recent years, most markedly this past year, you find yourself hoping that whoever you are waiting for will fail to appear. Even appointments which are crucial to your well-being, like medical appointments—secretly you hope they will be canceled.

Waking early this morning, hours ago, with a jolt. Unwilling to open your eyes—*God, let today be canceled*.

But now your eyes lift, startled: you are in a bustling public place and a tall lanky man looms above you. Tight-fitting suede jacket, black T-shirt, jeans. Big-buckled leather belt. Ridiculous!—X, a citizen of Berlin, has costumed himself for the American West like a character in a film by Werner Herzog.

Somehow, this person managed to slip past your scrutiny on the walkway. Identified himself to the *zaftig* proprietor of the Purple Onion who led him at once, proud as the prow of a Viking ship, to your table. Bursting your precious solitude as a balloon might be burst between big-knuckled hairy-backed hands.

"Hel-*lo*! Sorry I'm late, man."

5.

Alone and breathless on the outdoor terrace at the Purple Onion Café. Never came to such a place before by yourself. Everyone here is an adult—*old*.

Just the place your mom might be. Drinking wine with her women friends. Last person she'd expect to see here—*How-ie? What on earth?*

That look in the woman's eyes. Sick, sinking. For though she couldn't possibly know, she would *know*.

The pupils of her eyes would shrink to pinpricks and her mouth contort to a perfect O of a scream.

But no, you don't see your mom. Anyway not yet. Blindly making your way onto the terrace without waiting for the hostess to seat you because (let's face it) you don't know any better, or have forgotten that's how it is done in restaurants like the Purple Onion where the clientele is adult and has money.

Stumbling to an empty table in the farther corner. Weeks, months of fantasizing the scene yet somehow you'd failed to factor in the presence of other people. The possibility there would be no empty tables and you'd be turned away, ticking tote bag and all.

Panting, sweating. Though also shivering inside the hoodie. Christ!—just to get here, twenty-minute walk from your home on Cargot Street, has been exhausting like climbing a rocky landscape uphill.

The hostess is a broad-hipped woman your mom's age with

straggly hippie-hair, jangling Navajo jewelry, frowning mouth. This female isn't happy with a pimply kid like you in a khaki hoodie, baseball cap, mud-crusted hiking boots daring to take a seat (by himself, no adult) on the terrace café at this busy time.

Still, she signals it's O.K., she will send a waitress over.

Because they're basically pushovers, females like this. Droopy Mom-breasts, bovine faces. This one doesn't recognize you as your mother's son, it seems.

Relief!

1:11 P.M. when a cheerful waitress approaches your table with a menu.

You calculate: Should you order something to eat, or will that be a waste of money? There isn't much time. The detonation is set for 1:30 P.M. Still, you have not eaten since the previous night. You'd meant to eat this morning but were distracted. And even the night before, you'd choked and gagged on whatever it was your mom had prepared, well-meaning mom, always well-meaning. You, puking into the toilet locked upstairs in the bathroom.

The waitress is a girl with long silky blond hair, your age. You are panicked to think that maybe, just maybe, you'd been in high school together—but no, she doesn't seem to recognize you.

Loser. Nobody.

Hot bitch the guys would call this one. Not your friends, you don't have friends, but *hot bitch* is what they'd call her, your guy-friends. If you had them.

In high school, you had a friend. At least one friend. For a while.

Fag. Fags not wanted.

Fuck fags.

Inside your caved-in chest there's something beating and fluttering like a bat. You'd read online, lots of bats are rabid right now in the dusty foothills of California.

Or, bats are dying from a weird kind of lice. Fungus?

How nature fucks itself up. Almost, you'd think it was on purpose.

Warm day but you're wearing your khaki hoodie. Boyz in the hood. Good to hide your bumpy shaved head that looks like shit, grimy *Giants* cap pulled down tight over your forehead pinching your ears flat.

Hiking boots laced tight: paramilitary. Thick soles, rubber treads. Proper hiking socks, wool. (Stiff with dirt. Old dirt. Bunched up at the back of the sock drawer.) In another lifetime you'd have been a hiker, mountain climber. Rock-face climber. That mountain in Yosemite—El Capitan. Breaking the world record. If your dad hadn't left your mom and you. If your dad had taught you to climb. But then, your dad wouldn't have been *your fucking dad* if he had.

Too big, too heavy for the backpack. In your mom's Whole Foods tote bag you set beneath the table at your feet. What's inside is damn heavy, *dense.*

Sweat like cold oil oozes from your face drawn tight as a plaster of Paris mask. Brush away those tiny insects—gnats—you can't see but hear.

Ticking.

6.

You tell Nadia that the "new" Purple Onion is looking very good.

The exterior has been renovated, repainted—old weatherworn blue replaced by pale cream, covered in purple vines and tendrils in a hippie-LSD feverish pattern that undulates up onto the roof.

Wisteria just beginning to bloom, red geraniums in clay pots, petunias in hanging baskets—glass-topped tables, woven-hemp chairs on a flagstone terrace that looks impressively smooth.

(Possibly, this flagstone is synthetic—not "stone" at all. The old flagstone was discolored, cracked.)

Many customers. Midday din! Nearly every terrace table filled. Clever idea to meet an interviewer here, he'll have to work for his interview.

Definitely, you'd wanted to sit outdoors. You'd wanted a place with no liquor license. You'd wanted a place not far from your residence on Cargot Street, no driving required.

True, you have become (increasingly) eccentric in late middle age. And now, you are beyond late middle age. An individual of certain fixed habits, routines. At first you'd experimented with making demands of others, then you saw how they capitulated to the demands, how easily it was accomplished. Your shyer self was abashed, that a bully could elbow him aside so readily; that a bully could be mistaken for *you*.

Especially, women will allow this. How far a bully can push a woman, so long as he oscillates with a "reasonable" man, before she breaks, flees.

And now, you are boxed in by your habits. Can't remember your life before your habits. Can't remember *you*.

It is 12:32 P.M. A minute before, 12:31 P.M.

A minute later, 12:32 P.M.

(Has no one realized this, before you? Your eyes stare glazed, hypnotized.)

You are reasoning that, if X has been eager to interview you for months he should have made it a point to arrive earlier than you did, out of politeness.

Accident, plane crash . . . Never arrived at the airport.

Blasted out of the sky, all passengers and crew perished.

Midair, thirty thousand feet, utterly—vanished . . .

You smile. You shudder. It can happen that quickly, you suppose—annihilation.

Tick tick ticking. Blood-pulse in your inner ear.

7.

Cut to the jugular, friend. Tell me what you've never told any other interviewer.

Indeed, this is a challenge. Your mind has gone blank like power-washed pavement.

Seeing that he has surprised you X continues, almost self-effacingly, a young pedant advancing a theory: "My definition of a serious artist is a 'buoyant imagination' attached to an individual, as a balloon might be attached to an individual, floating above him, string tied around a finger. Yes?"

Vaguely you indicate *yes.* But your manner is noncommittal.

"In the true artist the imagination is always stronger than the individual. That's to say, the individual's personal life. The imagination is, in a sense, impersonal. It is transcendent, it is all-consuming. If in a duel with the personal life, the imagination wins."

You suppose this is so. It is—almost—too accurate for your comfort. But you don't give the interviewer the satisfaction of agreeing. Instead you merely smile in that (maddening) way observers have described as *inscrutable, enigmatic.*

"So, the challenge for the interviewer is to penetrate the 'personal self'—the *persona*—in order to speak with the artist's deepest and truest self which has nothing to do, as we know, with the outer being."

Outer being. You are thinking, what a curious phrase.

Outer being. You feel the impulse to scratch at your arms, the backs of your hands—to see if you can bleed.

Fortunately an attractive young waitress with long silky blond hair and a fetus-blank face comes to your table to take your orders. X fumbles to *pause* the iPhone, cursing under his breath.

Self-consciously and gravely, like a schoolgirl reciting poetry she doesn't understand, the waitress recites the specials of the day: kale / almond soup, kale / cranberry salad, kale / radicchio smoothie, "Green Rush . . ." X is visibly amused by the solemnity, cocking his head in a pretense of attention; when the waitress has finished the litany, X asks her please to repeat.

This makes you furious. Exasperated. Grinding your back teeth.

Nor do you like the way X engages the waitress in supercilious banter while undressing her with his eyes, glancing at you sidelong, inviting complicity.

Ignore X, of course. You have hardly looked at X fully since he'd arrived.

Sharing a meal with an interviewer is like sharing a meal with your executioner. An awkward ritual.

Briefly you examine the Purple Onion menu, oversized, pretentious, sheets of parchment paper stapled to a purple hemp board, fodder for the malicious journalist to note in his snarky prose—*vegetarian, vegan, organic, locally grown, dairy-free, gluten-free.* X will mock you, by mocking the menu, unavoidably; yet you tell the waitress with a beaming smile that you will have the *soup du jour.* And with a wink X says—*Eh bien, moi aussi!*

X is less amused having discovered that the café has no liquor license. No wine, not even beer. A very strange sort of café!

No meat on the menu either, not even seafood. Not even oysters. And X has come so far. . . . For a moment, a genuine expression comes over X's face, of childish disappointment.

Restarting the iPhone, continuing the interview. Extending the iPhone aggressively in your direction.

"You were saying, my friend?—when we were interrupted?"

8.

You must know, I am not your friend.

Explaining to X as you have explained countless times: You were not in Santa Luce at the time of the "event." You were not married to that woman at the time.

You were not an *absent dad.* You insist, you have never been any-one's *dad.*

Whoever wishes to blame you, take a good look in the mirror.

As Jesus said, he who casts the first stone had better be without sin.

Yes it's curious, why you chose to live in Santa Luce. Why, when you might have lived in any of the great cities of the world, you came to Santa Luce where nothing happens, repeatedly.

Curious, eccentric. Yes. But not reprehensible.

When you can't prevail, retreat. Eventually the world will come to *you.*

In Santa Luce there is "local news"—but not "news" that will travel more than a few miles beyond the perimeter of Santa Luce. The police department here is comprised of fewer than a dozen offi-cers. The department is housed in a single-story municipal building that also contains the public library and the township office. At the time of the (alleged) *Purple Onion bombing,* which was also known as the (alleged) *suicide bombing,* there were only four full-time of-ficers on duty. The police chief Dave Ruggles, fifty-eight, a thirty-year veteran in law enforcement, was slated for early retirement in another month.

No one was more surprised than the residents of the upscale community. No one was more shocked. You knew (of course) of "suicide bombers"—Islamist fanatics who dwelled in faraway places with unpronounceable names. You were filled with pity seeing smoking rubble, carnage, lifeless bodies on your flat-screen TVs.

You hesitated to switch channels for you knew that you should bear witness to the world's suffering. But such suffering soon becomes repetitious on flat-screen TVs.

You were not in Santa Luce at the time. You are certain.

Not clear that such an act of violence could occur *here*. The midday terrace of the Purple Onion is the most innocuous of privileged places.

What was the motive for the (alleged) bombing? The delusional bomber himself hadn't known.

Posted in his Facebook account—*I am not politicle, I did this for mysef*

Inexpert, fumbling-fingered, the *suicide bomber* blew himself up with his (partial) bomb. Three other persons died in the blast, it was claimed. Seven persons injured including the café proprietor who was seen helping the wounded though she was herself bleeding badly from a head wound.

Parts of bodies, hair, food mixed as in a crude low-speed blender. Shattered glass, metal fragments, teeth, toes. Pieces of skull, brain. Remains of a wild staring eyeball. Fingers, no nails. Brain matter, pulpy and suety, laced with shreds of kale flung across bloodstained flagstones.

Most lurid photos not shown in local media but, within minutes, widely disseminated online and in weeks, months, years to come.

Santa Luce Police Chief Ruggles collapsed at the bloody scene. Near-fatal cardiac episode. Treated by EMTs at the site with other casualties.

No, that is not funny. Not as it was replicated on social media. Viral on Twitter. Cruelty of the young.

At the time of the explosion we can imagine chaos, pandemonium. Sirens. Emergency vehicles, barricaded streets. Police helicopters from adjoining townships.

The (alleged) *suicide bomber* was nineteen years old, a dropout from Santa Luce High School two years before. Son of a single, divorced woman who lived less than a mile away from the Purple Onion on (coincidentally: for this is your street too) Cargot Street.

While still in high school the (alleged) *suicide bomber* had been suspected of having made prank calls to local schools, libraries, theaters, and other public places threatening bombs, shootings. Online he'd posted mysterious references to ARMAGEDDON.

Possibly, it hadn't happened quite as it was reported. Possibly, the young *suicide bomber* had only "threatened" to detonate a bomb. Acting on a tip, local police officers discovered, in the house the boy shared with his mother, materials for making bombs, as well as a "small arsenal" of guns. Much was made in the media of the fact that the boy's mother had long been a gun control activist who'd (evidently) failed to notice that her son was hoarding rifles, ammunition, and explosive materials beneath her very roof.

Rarely do you watch TV. Yet more rarely, what is bruited as "breaking news." Yet you recall having seen the distraught mother of the (alleged) *suicide bomber* interviewed on local TV: once-attractive, now ravaged face, eyes bloodshot and voice hoarse from weeping, defending herself to the camera: *If you have a nineteen-year-old son who dropped out of high school without graduating, unemployed, living at home, locks himself in his room playing video games, won't let you in his room even to clean it, won't talk to you when he sees you, won't look you in the face, you wouldn't need to ask these questions, you would understand.*

Bursting into tears. Painful to watch. Quickly you switched channels.

You admired the woman's courage even as you pitied her. Baring her tattered soul on TV. Every pore of her aging skin, every burst capillary in her eyes, every crease and dent in her face—exposed to the ravenous eyes of strangers. If you had half such courage, such audacity, such heedlessness you would not have required the circuitous route of *artist* to confront the world but would have confronted it without subterfuge, head-on.

You consider confessing this to X—but no. Better not. Such a sincere remark would only return to haunt you.

". . . an artist is one who detaches himself from his surroundings. If indeed the artist perceives his surroundings it is as *material*. Not as *surroundings*."

Damned voice overloud in your ear. Or, X is leaning closer to you than you would wish.

In panic you think—*Is this someone who knows me? Someone I should know?*

You have always feared interviews. Often you fear that an interviewer is someone who knew you in another lifetime, whom you fail now to recognize.

Someone who knew you when you were not yet yourself but *no one*. And no one who has been *no one* is ever *not-no one* in the memory of those who knew him at that time.

". . . like a dirigible, your imagination—your soul; floating and roaming the sky while your body, and these other bodies, are left behind here below."

To these soaring yet somehow accusatory words you can think of no reply. You dread to feel that you have been *found out*.

Acknowledging that yes, there may be some truth in that observation, but you have always been a practical person as well as an artist.

Calmly you tell X that it's a common mistake, to overemphasize the "romance" of the artist. In truth, most artists are bourgeois individuals who care about their comfort, their routines, their safety, the next meal, social status, finances . . . The implication being, *you are not among the bourgeois.*

X hasn't been listening. X has been frowning at his iPhone. Peering at the little screen. Fussing. You feel a flash of sheer rage as X mutters, "Sorry! Excuse me, I think something is seriously fucked up here . . ."

As if it were not X's fault but the fault of the device.

X dares to insist, please would you repeat what you've been saying?—"In the identical words if you can."

Identical words! You've totally forgotten what you were saying.

"Man, I am sorry! I can see that you're annoyed as hell. I don't blame you in the slightest. You are a famous person, and a very busy person, and this interview with me is a terrible imposition . . ."

X is vehement, contrite. Forcing you to protest—"No. Not at all. I'm not—annoyed . . ."

Smugly X is saying: "We all know people who *fantasize.* It's a child's first strategy of defense. In the artist, *fantasizing* is compulsive. It might seem voluntary to the artist, but in fact it's involuntary. It's a retreat, but an aggressive retreat. People engage with you, you appear to be engaging with them, but you are not involved in the slightest—are you?"

X laughs offensively. Though you are annoyed as hell you insist yes, of course you are involved; you are involved in the conversation.

"Well, you appear to be. With me. Right now. But we both know that you are not—really—*here.*"

Again, you insist, *foolishly:* "I—I am here. I am here."

Even as X peers impudently at you, leaning forward on his elbows. To your additional annoyance, he has caused the glass-topped table to tilt.

The more you smile, the more you insist, the more reasonable and amicable you are, the more *insistently* you stare into his eyes, the less you are here, with X.

Observing the two of you from an aerial perspective. Twelve feet above the Purple Onion terrace. Your head is inclined forward, you give every sign of listening to your companion who is also leaning forward, shoulders hunched.

From above, the two heads are scarcely distinguishable. On both, hair thinning at the crown, dark streaked with gray. Almost, your heads could be brought forcibly together, joined at the forehead.

And then, abruptly the scene fades. Bursts to white. A deafening flash like a nova and yet—soundless.

9.

Where is your mind?—no one has ever thought to ask.

Already in the cradle. In the crib. In the mommy's arms. At the mommy's breasts. In the arms of the daddy.

Drifting, detached. Resisting capture.

In school, in a row of desks. In church, in a hardwood pew.

Leaping ahead to the solution of the problem. Impatient with "steps." As others spoke slowly enunciating each syllable of each word like a tightrope walker buffeted by wind.

Though you sat very still at your desk with your hands clasped and beneath the desk your feet side by side like roots secure in the earth.

But your brain was buzzing. In flight.

Blizzard. Swirling, spiraling wet-white-blossom snow.

You have slipped away. Sleek and sinuous as an eel forcing your way to freedom.

In fact, you are yourself, but a child. That old-young child. Making your way along a road. An unpaved road, in a forest. The trail splits in two, each equally faint, trampled grass and damp earth. You take the left trail but then, when the trail splits again, this time you take the right trail. Is there any reason? Any reason of which you know?

Something tugging me forward. A kind of gravity.

10.

Dyslexic was the label. The way your eyes scramble letters front to back, upside-down. Fuck words!

Your mind turns off, detaches. Whoever is speaking you hardly listen to, though it's your "self."

Might be a stranger or might be you.

If you blow yourself up which you don't think (seriously!) you will do, or if you do it's something you can erase or delete or repeat, reboot, it will be mostly an experiment to see how many brain neurons retain the memory of who you are, what the fuck you thought you were doing, and what your guy-friends will think when they see the footage online, on their iPhones, if you had guy-friends. Or on TV. Every cable channel. Any scene in your life, plucked out of your memory, you only see yourself at a distance of about five, six feet. Was that who I was? No.

Not that you hate yourself. Not that you love yourself. Mostly, you stare at whoever he is, a brain inside a skull inside a head with "hair" on top and "face" at the front and you marvel at how such a creature came into existence.

Well, the "hair" and "face" can be peeled away. Fast!

Not just you, it's the human part of it that is hard to understand.

Wonder if you have already died and some part of you has remained behind, like vapor. Or a strong rotted-rancid smell.

Making your way along a path cut jaggedly through underbrush. Many paths through the underbrush but this is your path. Glance down—you are wearing your hiking boots. The kind that protect your ankles when you're climbing in a rocky terrain.

You'd tried, alone. Not much fun alone. Not good to be alone in a remote rocky place.

Dad! Hey, God damn. . . . Where'd the bastard go?

Never planned to grow up to be the (alleged) suicide bomber. Never planned to grow up at all.

11.

For the record: you weren't in Santa Luce at the time of the (alleged) bombing. You weren't in California. You weren't in North America. You are not sure of the details, even if it took place, or what it was that took place. And it isn't clear that it did take place. For what an extraordinary act of courage, if it had! *You* doubt that you are capable of it.

Though you are beginning to see, the Purple Onion has been repainted. Rebuilt. Can't remember what color the walls used to be but the cream color is new. Flagstones also look new, synthetic.

But the wisteria vines are mature, gnarled. The wisteria vines are not new.

If there was a detonation it looks as if only a part of the terrace was destroyed. A corner of the restaurant. (You seem to have read this somewhere. Or heard it somewhere—a rumor?) You were not here in Santa Luce at the time and you are not an individual who *doomscrolls* the Internet in pursuit of the most stomach-churning news.

You didn't know the (alleged) *suicide bomber*. You didn't know his (alleged) father who'd moved away from Santa Luce years ago, a research biologist. Yes, you knew the mother. You know the mother.

You are not the father. *You* are not to blame.

Single mother, divorcee. Grim bright brave *civic-minded, activist*. The kind who takes Pilates classes. Yoga. She's a vegetarian, not a vegan but she believes passionately in organic foods. Shelf of vitamin pills—A (anise seed) to Z (zinc). One of the smaller houses on Cargot Street. You've passed that house countless times without knowing who lives there. The (alleged) *suicide bomber* had an ordinary name—Howard, Howie. He'd been a child like any other child. Baby like any other baby. Soft-boned head like any infant's. Years were required to shape him into the (alleged) *suicide bomber*. Pimply face, pimply back. On his back, reddened pimples like boils. Topology of pimples, pustules, boils. Scratches with his nails. Draws blood. Homely face, eyes too small. Nose too long. *Homely* rhymes with *lonely*. You'd heard them quarreling all your young life. Behind shut doors, drone of adult voices. *Why'd you marry me then, if you hate me. Why'd we have a child. Now—it's too late.*

Your dad moved out, you were just a kid. Ten, eleven. Scrawny little guy. Trying to figure—How's it your fault? Knew it was your fault. Cried and cried.

Learn young that crying will bring you nothing except a runny nose, headache, sick sensation in the guts. So badly you wanted your dad to return you'd remained upstairs hiding when he did return for a visit. *Howie, come down—your father is here.* . . . Your mom calling up the stairs excited, drunk-sounding.

Fuck you, Dad. Thanks and fuck you.

Love you son, you know that don't you.

Yes I know that Dad, fuck you very much.

Fuck you too, son.

Fuck you Dad!

Laughing. From inside the room you'd barricaded the door.

Angry at you, like hell your dad is going to climb the stairs and knock on your door. God damn spoiled kid.

Years later, still hear these words through the floorboards.

Years later, no one would dare knock on your door for you've posted warning signs: NO ENTRY. NO TRESPASSING. VERBOTEN.

A smaller sign, female figure, *X* drawn through it in black.

You were never a Nazi. Whatever they said of you, assholes got it wrong at school. Sure, you'd inked stuff on your arms. One of the tattoos meant to be a four-leaf clover but the swastika is tricky. Hammer and sickle? You wore long sleeves. You picked at the scabs. Some of the cuts became infected. Fuck!—a hurtful kind of pleasure scratching and *scratching.*

Disappointment you saw in adult faces. Teachers, your mom.

(Your dad too for sure. Except you never saw your dad any longer.)

Think that I am a disappointment? I will give you something to be disappointed about.

Think that I am fucked up? I will give you fuck-up.

Mesmerized by the Internet. Hours, nights. Years. Age thirteen to whatever you are now—nineteen? Waking with an aching neck, head on your desk like it'd fallen off your shoulders. Cheek on the desk-top. Eyeball pressed flat. Faint hum of the Internet like your own fetid breath. Had the idea since sixth grade. Researching for years. For months actively working on the Device.

Never thought of it as a bomb. Technical term—*explosive device.*

Not a fucking terrorist. Middle East, towelhead ISIS. Not an asshole Nazi either.

Thing is, you are unique. You are not a herd animal. ISIS, Nazis are herd animals.

To yourself you call it the Device. (Not once do you utter the word *bomb*.) Shave your head like a monk.

Howie? Honey? Why on earth did you shave your—

You'd yanked the cap down over your ears. Tight over your forehead. Stiff-backed walked away from your mom. None of your business, Mom, fuck you.

Beginning to lose your hair, like your dad. Male pattern baldness. Already combing your hair, hairs came out in the comb. Fucking shit, only nineteen.

Trying to decide, *where*. The Device is only as effective as its location.

First target you'd planned was Santa Luce High. Assholes who'd made your life miserable, those years. But fact is, they've all graduated. They are all gone. Away at fucking college, and would not even remember you.

Who? Him? That loser?

The café with the weird name—Purple Onion. Yes.

Crazy coincidence if your mom is there. No doubt, some of your mom's friends will be.

Preparing the Device requires months. The most painstaking work of your life, nobody to observe and admire. You'd flunked junior year chemistry. If Mr. Alonso could see you now he'd be Goddamned impressed.

Your first time in the Purple Onion Café. Though you've passed the place many times. Kind of run-down, back terrace with tables and hanging plants. Painted a dull blue, starting to peel. Kind of place old hippies used to hang out at, now more upscale.

Carefully choosing clothes. Khaki hoodie, T-shirt. Jeans, hiking boots, *Giants* cap. Dark glasses. Mom's Whole Foods tote bag hanging from a doorknob with a half-dozen other useless tote bags.

The sort of precision device you set beforehand. Not the kind of device you trigger at the site and not a belt you strap around your middle like some asshole on TV.

Many hours are required to calibrate the Device, attached to a clock. Old windup clock you'd found in the house but it seems to be working. Reliable. Loud-ticking.

Sweating as you calculate: If you set the detonation for → 1:20 does this leave enough time? But you don't want an excess of time, either. Your fingers are icy, numb. You are disbelieving—*Is this really happening?* Laughing at yourself, what kind of bullshit is this, you fuck up everything you do, flunked out of chemistry, never showed up for exams, some kind of joke you'd actually *build a bomb.* Wild!

At the Purple Onion making your way to the back terrace, trying not to be distracted by so many people, women's voices, laughter like breaking glass. Usually no one looks at you but now, they are. In your imagination the scene has been silent, dreamlike. Not so many other people and the figures were filmy, imprecise. Now, you can see they are *real.*

Trying not to panic you sight an empty table. Make your way to the empty table gripping the tote bag tight with sweaty hands. All you can see is what's ahead of you, so sharp-focused it hurts. Your peripheral vision seems to be faded.

Realizing belatedly you'd forgotten to wait for the hostess. That's the way it's done in a restaurant like this—you wait for the hostess. Wait to *be seated.*

Anyway, you're sitting down. Buzzing in your head like locusts. It seems to be OK, nobody is asking you to leave. Can't see very well. Eyeballs feel dry. Interior of mouth very dry. Busy café, servers carrying trays, shimmering-blond waitress approaches you as if she's hesitant to give you a menu, you fumble taking it from her, dry lips mutter *Thanks.*

Staring at the menu. Can't make out the words. Some of the menu is handwritten in purple ink.

Ticking sensation inside your head. Clock-ticking, beneath the table.

Really you don't believe that anything will happen. That *it will happen*.

Your mind just bypasses it like water rushing around a rock. Could be an old boot tossed in a stream, water rushes around it indifferently. Though you are sweating pretty badly, and your heart is beating like crazed wings inside your rib cage, and there's a two-inch scared smile on your face. In a movie, light breaking onto your face like wonder.

Glancing about, curious to see who is close by, who will die with you in—how many minutes? Twenty-two? No, twelve.

Of course, you can leave the tote bag beneath the table. You can walk away. No one is stopping you. No one knows where you are. No one is waiting for you. You have no "associates": you are a "lone wolf." Act as if you're going into the café to use the restroom, instead keep going out onto the street. At the street, walk fast. Don't run, walk fast. A block away when the device detonates, nobody will know it's you. No trace, you are sure.

But your legs are leaden. Feet heavy as hooves in the hiking boots. Heartbeat so hard, blood is draining from your head and there's the risk you might faint if you tried to stand up. So better sit still. You are here, you are not leaving. Why'd you go to such an effort if you leave now. You are making a profound statement. First project you've actually finished since seventh grade. You are rejecting the rejectors. You are sneering at the sneerers. Your mouth is dry as sand, like a convulsion the way you are swallowing. Imagine breaking news on CNN. Santa Luce, the place where nothing happens. Rarely on TV. Bond issues, school board elections, sewer repair, library referendum but now, this evening—*breaking news. Santa Luce, California, rocked by ingenious explosive device . . .*

You are actually becoming calmer. Draw a deep breath. Dad will be seeing this. You'd remembered to take three of your mom's "nerve" pills. To your left, a table of chattering women. To your right, a table occupied by just two men.

One of the men seems to be interviewing the other. Fake foreign accent, annoying as hell. IPhone on the table.

In a sudden rage you think—*Who the fuck cares about what either of you think? What any of you think?*

That's when you realize—*It will happen!* You feel a rush of relief as if a burden is being lifted from your shoulders. Time ticking away means time running out and time running out means all choices running out.

Peering at your watch inside the khaki sleeve—1:19 P.M.

12.

You have arrived alone at the Purple Onion Café. Not long after noon judging by the position of the sun in the sky.

No idea why, why here. "D'you mind if I record our conversation?"— a stranger, who looks familiar, positions his iPhone between you and himself.

THE UNEXPECTED

T hank you for the honor. I am very—honored."

A solemn moment. If like most solemn moments, tinged with an element of the absurd.

You have been instructed to remove the clumsy black mortarboard from your head, at this point in the commencement ceremony. Now inclining your head, that a red ribbon bearing a brass medallion inscribed with the Latin phrase VINCIT OMNIA VERITAS can be looped around your neck.

Then, a royal-blue velvet doctoral hood with white satin trim is also lowered over your head, and secured in place around your shoulders with a snap.

A rotund little man identified as the president of the college congratulates you, shakes your hand vigorously. You are left alone at the podium, smiling foolishly.

Applause. Not a thunderous applause but polite, even warm—you choose to think. You are made to feel encouraged—empowered.

You adjust the medallion, that falls heavily onto your breastbone. You stare out into the audience of expectant young faces pale and translucent as sea anemones, that, like sea anemones, appear to be slightly swaying.

". . . an honor, and a pleasure . . . this celebratory occasion . . ."

You have not died. You have been invited to receive an honorary doctorate of humane letters from the community college near your old hometown in upstate New York. In exchange, you are obliged to deliver the commencement address to several hundred black-robed graduates seated on bleachers on a playing field rain-soaked from recent showers.

It is a chill pale day of cirrus clouds, a capricious wind borne southward from Lake Ontario. High overhead, with ominous frequency, fighter jets pass in formation. You make a joke about the planes, you express gratitude that the planes are *on our side* but the joke, if that's what it is, falls flat, or is muffled by the jets' roaring; on the commencement stage behind you there is a polite sort of laughter from your hosts but few among the graduates join in. No doubt they have grown so accustomed to fighter jets in the sky above the college—and their homes—that they no longer hear them. The graduates are a practical lot who have earned degrees in such subjects as education, hotel management, nursing, business administration, engineering, communication arts, forestry, animal husbandry.

You are obliged to speak louder, to be heard over the dull roar of the jets. You confide in the graduates that you have not been invited to the region of your birth to receive a degree, to give a lecture, to read from a new book or even to sign books, since you left thirty-six years ago. And so, this commencement ceremony is indeed a significant event in your life. Wittily you say to your audience: "I am very grateful to my hosts for inviting me, after thirty-six years! I hope that, in another thirty-six years, they will invite me back again."

But this remark too falls flat. Your audience stares at you with baffled smiles.

You are joking, are you?—or, you are not joking?

Very likely, the young graduates don't expect *humor* on this occasion. Certainly not humor from the (female) recipient of an honorary doctorate in humane letters.

Chagrined, you return to your written speech. Laboriously you'd written it in longhand, in a script large enough for you to read easily, for you feel most comfortable with handwritten material on such occasions; but the pages are fluttering in the wind, and it's difficult to read them.

A page is loosened from your fingers, and blows from the podium— desperately you lunge for it, but it blows across the stage, past pairs of feet, until it is retrieved by a gentleman in a black cap and gown, one of the college dignitaries, who returns it to you with a smile.

So embarrassing! By this time you've lost your place in the speech— can't remember what you've been saying.

And so, you address your audience directly. *From the heart.*

At first you stutter, stammer. Speaking without a text is not unlike diving from a high board, in front of spectators—striding to the end of a high diving board, as the crowd gapes up at you. Once you've made your way to the end of the diving board, you cannot retreat.

You are short of breath. You are suffused with adrenaline. After your initial stumbling you begin to speak more fluently. Then, passionately. You have no idea what you are saying—what you will say. Your audience has become riveted, aroused.

In the bleachers directly before you are the graduates of the college in their somber dark robes and mortarboards; behind them, and flanking them, are rows of guests—families, friends, visitors from the community. All of these gaze at you in silence as if startled by genuine emotion amid prepared speeches by college administrators, trustees, a local congressman or two. You had intended to speak in abstract terms of the value of a college education but instead you speak of your childhood in the small city of Yewville nine miles away. You speak of the gratitude you feel for your teachers, some of whom are still living in the vicinity, though long retired. You speak of your family, most of whom are deceased. You speak of the beautiful rolling hills of western New York State, the stark glacial formations, the prevailing winds of this harsh landscape south of Lake Ontario. You speak of the public library in Yewville where you'd spent so many hours as a young person.

Our gratitude for those persons who helped to shape our lives. Those persons to whom we owe our lives.

You are wiping at your eyes. You feel as if you might burst into tears. The audience has become very quiet. Uncomfortable at witnessing such unfeigned emotion, in such circumstances. Nor are you comfortable out of your role, for you are the most *calibrated* of persons.

Soon then, you conclude your speech. Your voice cracks, you feel you must apologize.

There is a moment's silence—an awkward silence. Then, an outburst of applause.

Especially, the response from the graduates is warm, enthusiastic. Here and there individuals rise to their feet, applauding. For a dazed moment you think—*Do I know them? Are these my friends?* But it is decades later, these are not your classmates.

Parts of rows, entire rows on their feet—waves of emotion rush at you like the waves of Lake Ontario roiled by wind, rushing at you on the beach years ago.

Moved by gratitude you think—*Am I home, at last? Is this where I belong?*

+ + +

"Oh. My God. *No.*"

Beneath your academic gown you are—part-naked?

You make the discovery after the ceremony has ended. After you have marched offstage with others in the presidential party to the heartening rhythms of "Pomp and Circumstance."

Disrobing in a field house nearby, preparing to hang your gown on a rack with others, you realize to your horror that you aren't fully clothed beneath the gown—not naked, of course, yet not fully clothed . . . How is this possible? Had you prepared for the ceremony so carelessly, stepping into the robe provided by the college without realizing you weren't dressed beneath? You'd been alone in your hotel room, distracted by thoughts of your upcoming speech. No one to examine you before you left the room for the ceremony at the college.

Perils of a lonely existence. You might die alone, and you might make a fool of yourself, alone.

And so you'd gone out half-naked, inside the academic gown.

Surely the wind had lifted the hem of the gown exposing your bare white legs on the commencement stage, and God knows what else . . . No wonder the young graduates were riveted by your performance. No wonder they could not look away. Trying not to laugh at you, taking pity on you, no wonder they clapped so boisterously when the excruciating performance came to an end.

+ + +

After the commencement luncheon you are brought in a hired car to the small city of your birth nine miles away. What a relief, to escape! The humiliation will smolder forever in your heart, you think.

At the luncheon you'd accepted the congratulations of college officials who claimed that they had never experienced graduates reacting so enthusiastically to any commencement speaker before. *Wonderful how you connected with our graduates! Born here, went to school here, evoked the time and the place so we all had tears in our eyes* . . .

Seated behind you on the speakers' platform they hadn't seen your gown lifted in the wind. Hadn't glimpsed your stark white body beneath. Probably they'd only half-heard your faltering "genuine" words. Their gratitude to you seems sincere. *You* are the one who feels like a fraud.

Yet, as soon as you are alone in the rear of the hired car, headed for Yewville, you begin to forget the humiliation, and the triumph. As the familiar landscape of your past drifts by silent as a dream you find yourself transfixed with longing.

You'd intended to work on the drive. Such spare moments are valuable to you, you dare not waste them. In your lap your notebook lies untouched except for a single sentence which you will discover after you return home from Yewville, without remembering that you'd written it.

So little has changed, her temptation is to believe that she herself has not changed.

Farmland, rolling hills to the horizon. Glacial formations: drumlins, trough-like ridges in the soil, small mountains covered in deciduous trees. The roughened landscape looks as if it has been scraped with a great trowel; mirrored by similarly roughened clouds overhead, now covering most of the sky. There is a heightened wind from Lake Ontario, only just visible, a faint hazy blue, in the distance.

Then, a long descent. Ahead is the Yewville River narrow and scintillant in the sun as a snake's scales. Ahead is the Yewville Valley, famous for its thousands of acres of fruit orchards: peaches, pears, apples. A two-lane wrought-iron bridge, scarcely changed since you saw it last. A blacktop state highway formerly two lanes, now three. Farmhouses, orchards. Grazing pastures: Holsteins, horses. Names of roads you haven't recalled in decades that stir your heart like fragments of dreams.

When you were a child you couldn't have guessed that the names of these country roads were only just the names of individuals who'd purchased land here in a bygone century. Adams Road, Eimer Road, Skedd Road, McDermitt, Cadden, Dunway . . . No one now living remembers these landowners for whom the roads were named and surely children in the Yewville Valley grow up exactly as you did, unquestioning.

Entering Yewville on the blacktop highway you see the old water tower silhouetted above the city. Now too it has been defaced with graffiti, savage red initials, cryptic signs, familiar boasts—*Class of 2018* overwriting *Class of 2017*. Graduating seniors from Yewville High have had a tradition of climbing the tower on the serpentine ladder, ignoring warning signs, DANGER DO NOT CLIMB, boldly spray-painting their names, initials, class years on the metallic side of the tower. Every several years the water tower is power-cleaned of old fading graffiti and a new generation climbs the serpentine ladder to make its claim.

Class of 2018! You don't want to recall the year you'd graduated from high school. Long ago in the previous century . . .

In the year you'd graduated, one of the (drunken) senior boys who'd climbed the water tower had fallen, to his death. Not a friend of yours—though his name is indelibly imprinted in your memory: Jamie Haas.

Useless memories, yet precious. Virtually every name of every classmate of yours from elementary school through graduation is imprinted in your brain.

You don't want to speculate how many of your classmates have vanished. How few probably remain in Yewville and of these, how few will remember you, and come to your presentation at the library this afternoon.

There you will be honored for the second time today, as Yewville's "most distinguished literary figure." So far as you know there has never been any other writer from Yewville, literary or otherwise.

Driving along Main Street you are stirred by memories of shopping in these stores with your mother and your grandmother when you'd been a young girl. Repetitive activities must imprint themselves most deeply in a child's brain and shopping was the most repetitive of all activities in your family life. Food shopping, once a week at a store called Loblaw's. Shopping for clothes, shoes. Accompanying your mother, sometimes your grandmother, occasionally both your mother and your grandmother along the street. The adventure of store windows! (You were fascinated by the double vision in a store window: inside, merchandise; reflected in the plate glass, a luminous view of the street beyond a shadowy image of your own face.) Led along the aisles of Yewville's premier department store, Schuyler Brothers. The feel of a warm firm adult hand gripping yours.

Never let me go! Never.

Disappointed to see that Schuyler Brothers with its shiny onyx-black facade has vanished and in its place is an office building with a dull stucco facade. What a loss! Vividly you recall the interior of the grand old store: high, hammered tin ceilings, brass lighting fixtures, floor tiles of a dark, dusty rose marble . . . With mounting excitement you remember strings of glittering Christmas lights, evergreen boughs, bright red berries, an almost unbearable excitement in the very atmosphere that seemed to promise *Something important is happening here. You are important, because you are here.*

Farther along Main Street you see that Sears, Roebuck has vanished as well. Flanagan's Shoes is gone, replaced by a nail salon. Where Brewer's restaurant was once, there is Main Street Grill. Where South Main Books was once, a vacated space with FOR RENT / FOR SALE signs in the dusty front window. But the Palace Theater remains, if somewhat shabby, and with a marquee advertising a local fire sale. The Empire Building, a dour twelve-floor office building invariably smelling inside of something sickish-sweet like ether, where you'd endured years of dentist and doctor appointments, remains at the farther end of the street like a totem of a bygone era.

The white-coated men whom you'd feared even as you'd hoped to placate—all vanished now. Harmless.

The Mohigan Street bridge. And beneath the bridge, a pedestrian walkway along the river that was no longer maintained by the city and allowed to crack, crumble. Rusted girders, broken concrete in vacant lots. The girl—so small, frightened—what was her name?—in sixth grade—poorly dressed, snarled hair, hounded by boys, screaming for them to let her alone. A girl with tight-kinky hair, wet dark eyes, a girl with whom you'd sometimes walked to school but you have forgotten her name . . .

Olive? Olivia? An unusual name . . . But no, you have forgotten. So much to forget, in Yewville.

But you are recalling how, fewer than twelve miles from Niagara Falls, Yewville was discovered to have been contaminated, to a degree, by hazardous waste materials in that stricken city, by the time you were in high school. Headlines in the local paper. Downwind from Niagara Falls, Yewville was vulnerable to airborne toxins as well as seepage into the local water supply. Incidents of lead poisoning in very young children, an unnatural number of cancers, including leukemia, in the general population. You recall how officials of both cities as well as expert witnesses—scientists, professors—testified on behalf of the (notorious) chemical companies at the Falls that most common cancers were likely to be caused by smoking, secondary smoke inhalation, watching TV, and living in a "power grid" neighborhood.

In recent years federal regulatory agencies have been weakened, their budgets reduced by a conservative Congress. No doubt the chemical plants in Niagara Falls are required to be less cautious in cleaning up waste. Soon the old pollutants will return to this part of upstate New York, that has never entirely recovered from the initial poisoning.

Yet, you recall happy times. Something stubbornly resilient about the child-brain, that insists upon happiness.

Sunday drives along the cliff above Lake Ontario, picnics on the rough-pebbled beach with your family. (Your parents, long deceased, were young then! Younger than you are now.) Visiting your grandmother after school in her house on Amsterdam Street, Yewville. Butternut cookies, pumpkin pie with whipped cream. In winter, hot chocolate with melted marshmallows. Library books in crisp plastic covers, which your grandmother was reading and into which you looked, curious, enthralled—*What does an adult read?* Yet, you don't recall. As in a dream in which the eyes refuse to process print, you don't recall a single title except—was it *Anna Karenina*? Life seemed to have unfolded in Yewville without incident like a Möbius strip that turns with almost imperceptible slowness, the long summers stretching to the very horizon.

Now, your life passes with alarming rapidity. Each year is an acceleration.

The future: a mirror in which you see no reflection.

Impulsively you ask your driver to take a brief detour, past your old middle school—DeWitt Clinton. (You'd never even known who DeWitt Clinton was, as a child. A New York State politician responsible for the construction of the Erie Barge Canal.) On Amsterdam, a few blocks from where your grandmother lived—where she'd rented the upper half of a gray-shingled wood-frame house to be near the school for the three years you'd attended it. Passing the house in which your grandmother lived decades ago you feel a sensation of profound loss, yet also elation—for you'd been loved once, cherished.

The only love that matters is the absolute unreasonable unqualified and unearned love—the love you'd absorbed into the very pores of your being as a child, scarcely aware of your good fortune.

Imagining now how you might ask the driver to park at the curb. Run to knock on the door, hurry up the stairs as Grandma calls to you—*Darling, I didn't expect you. What a wonderful surprise . . .*

The old school has been renovated. Beige brick, stucco. Except for a wide expanse of patchy lawn in front it resembles a small-parts factory. You wait to feel something but can't even remember which door you'd entered—who were your closest friends, with whom you walked to school. Abigail?

Lorraine? Not Olive—or was it Olivia . . .

Back on Main Street the driver is again required to detour, routed around a pedestrian mall. Here is an innovation for Yewville—a street without vehicles. Stunted trees, evergreen shrubs in pots, pastel-colored benches, a small (dry) fountain. The mall is only a block long and resembles a stage set composed of cheap materials. Several stores appear to be shuttered. FOR RENT signs in windows. Not many shoppers—not many pedestrians. Are those homeless persons? A truculent-looking woman in an oversized coat, knit cap pulled down over a bald scalp, beside a grocery store cart heaped with her possessions. You feel a twinge of panic—is this woman someone you know, or who knows you? A former classmate, a neighbor?

A relative?

But no. Most of your relatives are gone. It is a curious thing to realize that you are not *relative* to anyone any longer.

The driver of the hired car has been surreptitiously turning up the radio volume. Raucous hip-hop music is just audible, breaking your concentration on the drive. You would ask the driver to turn down the radio, or better yet turn it off, but hesitate to offend him; at least until you are safely on your way back to the airport at Buffalo.

It is the stately old Yewville Public Library to which you have been brought, to give a presentation and book signing. The head librarian, with whom you have been in correspondence, has spoken warmly to you of *your many Yewville fans.*

But as you climb out of the limousine you are overcome by a sensation of dismay, despair powerful as vertigo. Yes, the Yewville library is virtually unchanged—a dignified sandstone building in the Greek Revival style of a bygone era. For what does Yewville mean to you without your mother, your father, your grandmother? It is true that their spirits seem to dwell here—in the very air, heavy with moisture—yet there is no denying the blunt crude fact that they are *gone.* And what does Yewville mean without your closest friends Abigail, Lorraine, Beth? The boy you'd (secretly) liked, a particular friend of yours in math class, what was his name—Roland Kidd? You'd heard a decade ago that Roland had been stricken with a terrible neurological disease that had paralyzed his legs. You'd heard that he had died . . . Or was this another boy, Peter Amo who'd been too shy to call you on the phone, in high school—with his acne-riddled face, too (maddeningly) shy to have called any girl.

You give instructions to the driver: you will be inside the library approximately one hour. Then you will rejoin him, and he will drive you to the Buffalo airport as planned. Your single suitcase is in the trunk of the car. Your flight departs at 6:46 P.M. and you do not intend to miss it.

A second night in this place!—no.

Addressing the driver with a smile, always remember to smile, a rictus of a smile for it is your defense, the smile of terror, with which you have learned to confront the world all the while thinking— now—of how so many people are gone from your life. And espe- cially here in Yewville where (contrary to your wishful thinking) time has not ceased but moves at the same accelerating pace as else- where. No idea what the lives were of those whom you'd known here. No idea what has become of them. Where they have vanished. The teachers who'd praised you and imagined great things for you as if (wistfully, grandiloquently) speaking of themselves. Bearing you aloft on their wounded, faltering wings. Lighting a roadway for you with the uplifted torches of their hope, now gone; and the torches long gone, dropped by the wayside. All those lives, those particular persons, their mannerisms, habits of speaking, smiling, all vanished; erased; unreal, and lacking immediacy. What is im- mediate is the corrugated tin-colored sky that hurts your eyes, and a V-formation of planes passing high overhead, the grating radio music to which your driver will listen as soon as you leave him. What is immediate is your hand being shaken by a stranger—so often these days, a stranger—and your courteous robot-response: "Oh yes. Thank you! I am honored to be here, too . . ."

But there has been a change in plans, you are informed. In fact, your presentation at the Yewville library has been canceled.

Indeed, a yellow band with rude black letters CANCELED has been taped over a poster announcing your visit, displayed at the front entrance of the library. The *N* obliterates your face in a grainy pho- tograph of years ago.

You are too surprised to be indignant, hurt, or even relieved. You ask why?—why has your presentation been canceled?—even as you suppose it would be better not to ask. Better not to know.

It seems that the library felt obliged to cancel your event because more people were expected than the library could accommodate safely. The terms *fire code, fire marshal* are uttered with an air of finality. You listen in disbelief. Too many people?—in Yewville, of all places?

The head librarian who'd written such gracious letters to you is not here to explain. Instead, an assistant librarian has taken her place. With a look of mild vexation the woman informs you that a few people have showed up after all to meet you, so you can sign books for them in a back room—"If you are up to it. We understand, you are probably exhausted after your travels."

You protest, you are not exhausted at all! You have traveled only nine miles that day. You have come to Yewville instead of returning home immediately after the commencement because you'd looked forward to the visit, and had been assured that there were readers of your books here, who are eager to meet you.

How petulant you sound, like a hurt child! And how nasal your voice in your ears, as if in mimicry of the western New York State accent you have been hearing since your arrival the previous day.

The assistant librarian listens to you politely. She introduces herself as "Marian Beattie"—as if this were a name that might mean something to you. The woman is middle-aged, stout, somewhat disheveled, with a doughy, oddly familiar face. Her bulky pants suit is a wry cranberry color, in a fabric synthetic as vinyl; her feet appear to be swollen, in bandage-like socks worn with open-toed sandals. Behind bifocals her eyes are blurry with moisture and a kind of malicious merriment. She exudes an air of ashy, unlaundered clothes, stained underarms.

How disappointed you are! You realize that you must have been anticipating this visit to Yewville with something like—*hope*? For it was here, long ago, that the elusive emotion was first kindled in your soul.

Soon short of breath, panting and puffing, and walking with difficulty on her bandaged feet, Marian Beattie leads you into the interior of the library. You see that it has been altered considerably since your girlhood, with an eye for the practical and utilitarian. The ceilings are no longer so magisterially high. The floor is obviously not marble but inexpensive tile meant to resemble marble. The chandeliered lights you recall have been replaced by tubes of ugly fluorescent lights that flicker as if on the verge of extinction.

"We're particularly proud of our computer reference room"— Marian Beattie tells you.

What had been the Reading Room, one of the happy places of your life, has been transformed into a hall for computers. Three long tables, six computers at each table, rapidly you calculate—eighteen computers for the relatively small Yewville library. At these are a few adults, mostly older men with sad, slack faces, and long-limbed teenagers scrolling through websites. No one glances at you in the doorway.

You recall how in this room on shelves reaching to the ceiling were books designated as *Classics*—tall, illustrated books which did not circulate like most library books, but were required to be read in the library, at one of the long polished tables, or in one of the leather chairs in a corner of the room. Naively, as a girl you'd tried to read Dante's *Divine Comedy*, Homer's *Iliad* and *Odyssey*, even Plato's *Republic*. Even Plato's *Great Dialogues*. You smile to think of how little you must have grasped of these great works, like a child trying to climb a stone wall by the desperate effort of her small fingers, her weak muscles. Now, the shelves of *Classics* have vanished, presumably into another region of the library.

With a condescending smile Miss Beattie leads you to the small room at the rear of the library where "fans" have gathered—fewer than a dozen people seated on folding chairs that look as if they have been hastily set up. Most of these are older individuals and one is in a wheelchair, formally attired in a tweed jacket, head crooked to one side with an expression of acute interest. Many are carrying books, presumably yours. In the front row is a middle-aged frizz-haired woman leaning far forward on her knees staring at you so intensely, her face is furrowed with fine white lines.

In a bemused nasal voice Miss Beattie introduces you by saying that you need no introduction. There is a smattering of applause.

No podium here, no place to stand except awkwardly at the front of the room. You are far more uneasy here than you'd been at the commencement that morning, on a stage facing hundreds of people.

Hesitantly, you greet your audience. Your modesty is not feigned. You are very, very self-conscious. You cannot not see eyes fastened upon you or, worse yet, drifting downward to your feet, rising to your face, as you stammer that you are "very honored"—"very excited"—to be back in your hometown after thirty-six years.

You decide not to explain why you are in the vicinity of Yewville. Calling attention to the fact that you'd received an honorary doctorate in humane letters from the community college would seem at once boastful and pathetic and there would be the bewilderment— what are *humane letters*?

A poster in the corridor claims that the Yewville Public Library was to have hosted a "conversation with Yewville's best-selling author"—(not "most distinguished literary figure" after all)—this afternoon; and so at once several hands are raised in the audience. You are asked where you get your ideas, and how old were you when you published your first story. Do you make an outline for a novel beforehand, or "just start writing." You are asked if you type directly onto a computer or do you write by hand. You are asked if you revise. You are asked how you know when you are finished with your revisions. What advice do you have for beginning writers. What advice do you have about getting an agent. What was the best advice anyone ever gave you. What is your morning schedule. Do you ever suffer from "writer's block." What is your remedy for "writer's block." Do you have children. Are you sorry that you don't have children.

A heavyset woman in a sleeveless, tent-like dress who has come late sits in a chair by the door, panting. She lifts an arm from which slack flesh hangs in a tremulous web to inquire of you what tips you have for poets "just starting out"—and "do you have children?"

When you tell her that you don't have children she smiles pityingly at you, as the others have done. "Ohhh! That's too bad. Are you sorry?"

Politely you explain that it would depend upon the children you might have had, whether you are sorry never to have had them; but, since you don't know who they might have been, it is impossible to answer the question.

A shrewd reply, you think. Yet your little audience looks baffled, dissatisfied.

"None of us knew what our children would be like, before we had them," the heavyset woman points out sensibly. "But we had them anyway. And now we have grandchildren."

This meets with murmured approval. "Yes! Now we have grandchildren."

A bushy-bearded man who has been smiling at you declares that he has a bag of books for you to sign—"For next Christmas." The bag is made of burlap, oil-stained. Covers on the books don't look familiar. Several books are very old, smelling of mold.

The youngest person in the room is a teenager with a grimly

earnest oblong face. She has been sitting with a pen poised above a notebook but hasn't yet written a word. Now she raises a hand to ask how to "break into publishing" but scowls at your answer as if she suspects you don't know the answer.

"Yes, but what about an agent? How d'you get a good agent?"

Your lips move numbly. You hear your voice echoing from a corner of the room mingled with the retreating roar of jet planes in the sky.

"Yes, but I mean a *good agent*. Not just anyone."

Soon then, the skeptical teenager shuts up her notebook, exits the room.

A person with a wizened face asks brightly: "Do you think your life was worth it? All those books!"

Now you realize, everyone in the room is older—*old*. Most—all?—are (former) classmates of yours whose names you should know, but have forgotten.

Not high school but earlier—middle school, grade school. Their faces are blurred with time. Several faces look as if they have begun to melt, decompose. The very air in the small space is sepia-toned, gluey. Yet eyes are alight, alert.

"Are you proud of yourself, exploiting your past here in Yewville?"

"Are you ashamed of yourself, exploiting your past here in Yewville?"

"Do you consider yourself underrated?"

"Do you consider yourself overrated?"

"You would not do it again, would you?"

"You *could* not do it again, could you?"

These bold remarks meet with muffled laughter, titters. Marian Beattie laughs heartily.

A woman with a smooth bald face, paisley kerchief tied about her hairless head, belligerently introduces herself as "Lizzie Heardon"—

(once a friend of yours? seventh grade?—you are remembering, vaguely)—proud to have been a kindergarten teacher for her entire life. Never wrote a word—never published a book—but—took great joy in her career, and never regretted a moment.

Another woman—(is this Abigail?—so changed, you don't want to acknowledge her)—speaks of being married, having children, working hard as wife, mother, homemaker, caretaker for the elderly and the infirm in her family and in her husband's family, working very hard, working damned hard, never wrote a word, never published a book, never had time to read a damned book, worked harder, grew older, grew old, died (in 1999). She has grandchildren, however. She is not (yet) *forgotten*.

And there is Olive. Olivia? One of the shrunken females, hardly more than child-sized. She too is hairless, but wears a perky knitted cap. Hesitantly you smile at her. Hesitantly you ask—"Did you ever forgive me?"

You'd run away and abandoned her by the river. Of course—she was the girl. The howling boys, peals of jeering laughter.

Someone had been throwing chunks of concrete. A rusted rod. *You* did run—panicked, in terror.

But Olive, or Olivia, is saying now, laughing—"Ohhh no that wasn't me. You're remembering wrong. In everything you write, you *remember wrong.* You were the one the boys chased, and caught—you were the one who cried, and tried to crawl away, and they laughed at you."

"I—I was not . . ."

"Of course you were. *You* were. That's why you write such lies—to change the way things were, when you couldn't change them any other way."

"That is—not true. It is—just—certainly—not true . . ."

You are speechless, indignant. You are furious. Your eyes fill with tears. Olive, or Olivia, is rocking in her chair, laughing. She is maddeningly complacent, smug. *You. You. You. You.*

Fortunately the others are distracted by photographs of grand-children being passed around. Exclamations of delight, pride. No one thinks to include *you.*

Vastly amused, Miss Beattie wipes her eyes. Tears of laughter have gathered in the fatty creases of her face. She asks a "favor" of you—to inscribe books for the library "for our special collection." But she has only five of your numerous books, published long ago in the previous century.

"Is this all you have?"—you ask, surprised.

"*All?* How many novels did Jane Austen write? Only five or six, yes? And she is immortal." Miss Beattie speaks snidely to you.

To prove her point she brings a card catalogue drawer to show you—"You see? There are only five books under your name. Here are the cards." You examine the dog-eared cards that give the correct birth date for you but also a death date—1979. You protest, this is a mistake. You are *not dead.*

Miss Beattie laughs. A clerical error, obviously!

You are hurt. You are incensed. You would wrest the drawer from Miss Beattie, and cross out the ridiculous death date, but Miss Beattie returns the drawer to the card catalogue. (This antique feature of the old library, long superannuated by the online catalogue, has been moved to the rear of the library.)

With an impish expression Miss Beattie says, "By now you should have begun to recognize me. Are you really pretending you don't know who I am?"

"Who you—*are*?"

"Yes! Indeed."

"I—I do not . . ."

Marian Beattie regards you at close range with a skeptical smirk. It is plain that this annoying woman does not respect you—considers you deceptive, dishonest—you have no idea why. Your nostrils pinch with her distinctive scent, the intimate smell of her fleshy body, soiled clothing, oily hair. Not an altogether disagreeable scent, and somewhat familiar, like the interior of your laundry hamper.

"Look! Look closely." Miss Beattie thrusts her face toward yours.

Badly you want to push away from the strong-willed woman, who treats you with such familiarity. She is just slightly shorter than you, at about five feet six inches, but heavier by as many as seventy pounds; she holds you in a kind of hypnosis, gazing ironically into your eyes.

The person you were meant to be, who'd never left Yewville.

Is Marian Beattie—somehow—you?

You want to protest: you look nothing like Marian Beattie!

The woman is saying, still with an attempt at lightness, levity, though now you sense the bitterness beneath, how *she* had not left Yewville on a *fancy scholarship* as you did—"I didn't abandon my family who needed me. I got a degree in library science at the state university at Elmira and came right back. That was good enough for me!"

How to respond to this?—an accusation buried inside a boast.

It is true, you'd once thought you might be a librarian, and remain in Yewville. Or a teacher. And it is true, you were the recipient of a *fancy scholarship* that bore you away as if on wide, extended wings—the *leathery wings* of Milton's Lucifer, you've thought.

"But—I am not you. You are not—*you are not me.*"

Your rejoinder to Marian Beattie is feeble, near-inaudible. For you have no idea how to respond to her.

You are happy for Marian Beattie, that she is, or seems to be, so satisfied with her life in Yewville, yet you understand that you are being blamed, somehow, for not having stayed. She is accusing— *You are me, as I was meant to be. You have destroyed me.* Bitterly she tells you of those many classmates of yours who have passed away prematurely: individuals who died in car crashes and other accidents, of cirrhosis of the liver, of opioid overdoses, emphysema, strokes, heart attacks, cancer—"every kind of cancer"—as well as suicide—"every kind of suicide."

You are overcome with remorse. Sympathy. Yes, and guilt. But you have no idea what to say.

If you'd failed to leave Yewville, if you'd failed utterly as a writer, and if you were living now in Yewville, how would that have altered the lives of Marian Beattie and the others? You would like to explain this, but Marian Beattie isn't in a mood to listen to you. Now she is indignant: "But we don't complain. Not hardly. We are patriotic. We are not treasonous, we don't question our government. We don't write fancy books that no one reads. We don't look down our noses at the 'common folk.'"

You would apologize, but Marian Beattie isn't interested in an apology from you. Huffily she leads you to a "reception" in your honor: on a card table, a punch bowl filled with gasoline-colored liquid, paper cups, platters of orange cheese and Ritz crackers, scattered bowls of peanuts. "Mingle with your fans, please. Some of them have journeyed a long way."

Grateful for something useful to do, you occupy yourself with signing books. Most of your audience has departed but a few diehards remain, grinning at you. Pictures are taken with iPhones. You note that most of these books are years old, paperbacks with torn covers. No one seems to have purchased a hardcover copy of your most recent novel and so you come to wonder if indeed it has been published yet, or even written. You recall how difficult this novel had been to write, how *harrowed* you'd felt . . . as if you could not bear to endure such an ordeal another time, but would rather cease to exist.

If I am a card catalogue, how easy to remove!

Signing books on the title page with a flourish. Even your signature begins to be unrecognizable. Still you are being plied with a few final questions that buzz about your head like gnats. When did you know you wanted to be a writer. What do you regret most about your life. Which is your favorite book of your own. Which is your least-favorite. Would you do it all over again, if you had the choice. Or would you choose another life.

Would you remain in Yewville instead of leaving as you did at the age of eighteen. In which case—where would you be at this very moment?

Wordlessly you shake your head at this last question. Indeed, this is a riddle!

For surely you would not be *here*, signing books. Yet, you might well be *here*, visiting the Yewville library as a longtime patron.

"Excuse me, please . . ."

Edging out the others, the gentleman in the wheelchair rolls himself forward to meet you.

It appears that he is misshapen, or disfigured: his spine twisted, one shoulder higher than the other, neck and head forced forward at an angle.

In his lap, on his wasted thighs, is a large duffel bag filled with books heavy and bulky as rocks.

You see with relief that this man, though severely handicapped, is relatively youthful-looking, with a head of thick gray-white hair, a ruddy complexion, earnest pale eyes. He is clean-shaven, well-groomed. His clothes are of high quality, if somewhat worn. Tenderly he confronts you: "D'you remember me? Rollo."

Rollo? *Roland?*

Of course you remember: Roland Kidd. Your friend from math class. Eighth, ninth grades. A tall soft-bodied boy with an unexpectedly sweet smile, a (left) eye with a slight cast. Roland, or Rollo, is telling you how he has read virtually everything you've written, he has followed your career for decades. In the duffel bag are a small fraction of your books, he has brought from his library. "You know, I never married. I almost did—I was engaged more than once—but truth is, I never felt for any girl or woman the way I've felt for you. Many times over the years I wanted to write to you, to explain how important you are to me, how avidly I read everything you write . . . I admit, I am searching for myself in your fiction, and a few times I think I've found portraits of myself, not altogether flattering, but— well, it is flattering to be made 'immortal' in prose. At least, I've discovered enough of myself in your fiction to keep reading, and to keep hoping."

You are astonished, hearing these extravagant words. You would recoil in disbelief except Rollo Kidd speaks with enormous sincerity in a deep baritone voice like a radio broadcaster. So charismatic is he, the bullying Marian Beattie shrinks away abashed, the smirk fading from her face.

You want to ask Rollo Kidd what he can possibly mean— "searching for myself" in your fiction. You dare not ask Rollo Kidd what he can possibly mean—"never felt for any girl or woman the way I felt for you."

Rollo is intent upon telling you about his house on Ridgemont Avenue with its walls of books in nearly every room, to the ceiling— "Many of them your books, dear. Both hardcover and paperback. I collect other contemporary American writers as well but you are the center of my collection. Will you do me the honor of signing just a few books, inscribed to me? And dated? Thank you!"

Remarkably, Rollo has brought seventeen of your books to be

signed—all hardcover. You are thrilled, a bit dazzled, as if a blinding light were shining in your face, out of a pit of darkness.

Signing books in the midst of chaos has been a kind of solace for you, like scrubbing a floor on your knees—in a way a pointless activity, except that the activity *is* the point. And now, signing Rollo Kidd's books, so meticulously encased in plastic covers, you feel relief mounting to actual pleasure.

As you sign his books Rollo waits close by in his wheelchair. He speaks of his "fidelity"—his "longtime commitment"—to you; the only one of his classmates whom he'd respected, and one of the very few to leave Yewville. He confesses that, several times, he did write to you, in care of your publisher; but he never had a reply, which he attributed to your publisher not forwarding his letters.

Can this be true? You receive very few letters from readers, fewer in recent years than in the past, but had never given it much thought; from time to time people have complained to you that their letters to you hadn't been forwarded. Possibly, Rollo Kidd's letters had disappeared into that abyss. You feel a pang of regret, for (possibly) you would have answered Rollo's letters. Even before the days of email, you sometimes replied to letters from strangers, in handwritten outbursts of sincerity.

Rollo profusely thanks you for signing his books. His eyes brim with tears, he is deeply moved. (You see, yes—Rollo's left eye is indeed slightly out of focus. But both Rollo's eyes are thick-lashed, rather beautiful. You have to wonder if you'd dared to notice years ago, when you were a girl.)

"Now I am hoping, my dear, that you might visit my house? Where I have a complete collection of your work? Not just hardcover books but paperbacks and other reprints, and many—many hundreds—of magazines and literary journals, and anthologies, in which your fiction has appeared. I would doubt that you own a complete set, yourself. I think—my dear—you might see yourself in my collection, in my house—as you've never quite seen yourself."

My dear. These words too are caressing, hypnotic. No one has called you *my dear* in a very long time.

"It's only a short walk back to my house. Ten, fifteen minutes. I would be so honored! The culmination of my life, actually—to see *you* standing before shelves of your books—in my house . . . Of course, you are welcome to spend the night here, instead of in the fancy hotel your hosts at the college have surely arranged. My house is at the farthest end of Ridgemont, overlooking the ravine, and the river. D'you remember those old cobblestone houses we all admired when we were children? Like fairy-tale houses, with turrets, towers, slate roofs, wrought-iron fences? Built in the early years of the twentieth century? *You* remember."

You do remember. Vaguely at first, then more vividly. Ridgemont was one of the few prestigious streets in Yewville, adjacent to Ridgemont Park. In the loneliness of your life in exile from Yewville you have often performed an eidetic exercise: making your way, on foot, along Ridgemont, seeing in your mind's eye each of the distinctive old houses. Now, you realize that the houses were small mansions built in imitation of English architectural styles—predominantly English Tudor. But there were other styles as well, one of them the large foursquare cobblestone house set back amid a lawn of tall elms—probably, this is the house Rollo Kidd lives in. You wonder how on earth he came to acquire it. For, if you recall correctly, the Kidd family was no more affluent than your family.

"I have to admit, I purchased the house because of its numerous bookshelves—because I hoped to accommodate *you*. I became a local businessman—dabbled in real estate—expressly to make a little money, and buy a house on Ridgemont Avenue. For I hoped, one day, if you ever returned to Yewville, you would come to visit me, in that house. You would see what a shrine I have made for you, utterly without any expectation that you would ever come to me in this lifetime."

In this lifetime. Rollo speaks with such extravagance, you can't possibly believe him. Yet, there is such genuine feeling in the man, such youthful energy, in contrast to his physical condition . . . (Does Rollo have Parkinson's disease? He makes no effort to hide the tremor in his left hand.)

You thank Rollo for his invitation but explain that you must return to your car, which has been hired to take you to the Buffalo airport. Yes, you did stay in a hotel, the previous night; but you are leaving now, for your home in another state.

"You have a 'home' elsewhere, to which you intend to return? Really?"—Rollo laughs, baring glistening teeth.

You find yourself laughing with him. Yes, really!—it does seem absurd, that you have a *home* not here in Yewville.

Uncanny, how familiar this dignified older man seems to you. The more you stare at him from this close perspective, the more he resembles the boy you'd known, when you and he were twelve, thirteen years old. As if you'd grown up together, not hundreds, or is it thousands?—of miles apart.

Indeed, Rollo is more attractive now, in some respects, than he'd been as a pudgy adolescent. He has dressed himself in a dapper tweed sport coat and a cream-colored shirt, open at the throat. On his wasted legs, trousers with a sharp crease. And on his feet limp as wooden blocks, black silk socks and polished black leather shoes.

So sorry. You explain to Rollo Kidd that you can't visit his house. With genuine regret, you just can't. Maybe another time . . .

Graciously you say farewell to the several "fans" who remain at the card table sipping punch from paper cups. One of them, who'd claimed to be your old friend Lizzie Heardon, glares at you with an expression of intense dislike. You are feeling magnanimous, however. Rollo Kidd's presence has suffused you with strength, even a sort of childish pride, and so you don't turn away from Marian Beattie as you would like to do; instead, you grit your teeth and thank the spiteful woman, *the woman you'd been meant to be*, for her hospitality in welcoming you to the library.

"In another thirty-six years I hope that I will be invited back again," you tell Miss Beattie, gaily.

You are leaving the library without a backward glance but—there comes Rollo Kidd wheeling himself after you. The man is not shy in pursuit but rather exhilarated, determined. As you descend the front steps he rolls himself down a parallel ramp, so swiftly that his thick graying white hair, a silky sort of hair, is blown in the wind.

"Please accept my invitation, my dear. You will be astonished to see my house—a shrine to *you*. I wasn't exaggerating! I promise I won't expect you to sign more than a few of your limited edition publications. These are kept 'under lock and key' in a specially designed bookcase with glass doors that lock . . ."

You see, at the curb, the stately black hired car awaiting you. Yet you linger, reluctant to be rude to Rollo Kidd. Your heart swells with the melancholy certainty that Rollo Kidd was meant to be your soul mate; yet, something went wrong in your early life, you'd missed each other. Even now you are thinking—*You can return. You can begin again. Here is the one person in the world who cherishes you.*

You are walking beside Rollo, who rolls himself companionably at your side. Astonishing how companionable the two of you are, how familiar with each other; that you loom above Rollo in his wheelchair feels familiar to you as well. You note with approval how Rollo is determined to ignore his infirmity. Indeed, his upper arms and shoulders, his back, have thickened with muscle, in the effort of rolling his non-motorized chair; the very slant of his head has been re-imagined by the man as, not a disability brought on by Parkinson's disease, but a sort of macho hyper-vigilance. This man is not meek, shy, *invalided*; he is aggressive, even belligerent. Here is a man not easily dissuaded. Here is a man who knows his own mind. He dares to take your hand that has drifted close to his, and will not readily surrender it.

You recall how as a boy, Rollo Kidd was admired by his teachers. He was invariably a class officer—eighth grade vice president, ninth grade president. Rollo was your (friendly) rival in English, science, math; Rollo received higher grades in math and science, but you excelled (usually) in English.

"At least stroll with me, my dear. Ridgewood Park is just a block away. And from the edge of the park, another five minutes to my house. From the front walk, I swear you can see bookshelves through the windows—you will see the spines of your own books, waiting for you. At all the windows! As if peering out at you. Wait and see— I've arranged it very cleverly—it will be quite a sight . . ."

Gently you tug at your hand, to be freed of Rollo's hand; but not assertively enough to induce Rollo to release it. And of course you would not jerk your hand away, that would be rude. You will walk with Rollo for a few minutes, into the park perhaps, but no farther; certainly not to Ridgemont Avenue. Your car is awaiting you at the curb in front of the library and you have every intention of returning to it.

"Only a little farther, my dear! You will not be disappointed, I promise."

Just the two of you. Rollo Kidd in his wheelchair, propelling himself along. You, on foot. Your (cool, slender) hand in Rollo's (hot, fleshy) hand.

It is a chill bright day. The sky overhead appears to be impacted with cloud, light comes from all sides, there are no shadows. In the distance, near-inaudible, a sound of thunder, or jet planes. Behind you and Rollo Kidd in his wheelchair, unobtrusively, out of the range of your vision the shiny black limousine follows slowly, keeping pace.

ACKNOWLEDGMENTS

My enormous gratitude and thanks to the editors of the magazines in which the stories in this collection originally appeared, including the *New Yorker* ("Sinners in the Hands of an Angry God," "Hospice/Honeymoon," "Where Are You?"); *Harper's* ("The Unexpected"); *Salmagundi* ("The Crack,"), *Lincoln Center Review* ("The (Other) You"); *Ellery Queen* ("The Women Friends"); *Idaho Review* ("The Bloody Head"); *Boulevard* ("Blue Guide"); *Conjunctions* ("Waiting for Kizer," "Nightgrief"); *Yale Review* ("Subaqueous"); *The Strand* ("Final Interview").

"Assassin" appeared in *Cutting Edge: New Crime and Mystery Stories by Women*, ed. Joyce Carol Oates (2019). "The Happy Place" appeared in the anthology *Speaking of Work: A Story of Love, Suspense and Paperclips*, ed. Bernard Schwartz (2017).

And deep gratitude as always to my editor and friend Daniel Halpern.